The Adventures Of Maddie And Liv: Joining G.U.A.R.D

Daniel J Hainey

Copyright © 2019 Daniel J Hainey
All rights reserved.
ISBN: 978-1-9160800-4-1

FIRST EDITION

All rights reserved.

www.green-cat.co

This book is sold subject to the conditions that shall not, by way of trade or otherwise, be lent, resold, hired out, or otherwise circulated without the publisher's prior consent in any form of binding other than that in which it is published and without a similar condition including this condition being imposed on the subsequent purchaser

CONTENTS

Chapter One	6
Chapter Two	43
Chapter Three	58
Chapter Four	126
Chapter Five	145
Chapter Six	163
Chapter Seven	172
Chapter Eight	186
Chapter Nine	201
Chapter Ten	223
Chapter Eleven	245
Chapter Twelve	252
Chapter Thirteen	271
Chapter Fourteen	285
Chapter Fifteen	311
Chapter Sixteen	325
Chapter Seventeen	339
Chapter Eighteen	358
Chapter Nineteen	371
Chapter Twenty	383
Chapter Twenty-One	398

DEDICATION

FOR GRANDAD

X

Chapter One:

The tranquil air of late spring was broken as Liv Winters stepped out of the school gates and yelled, "Freedom!"

She tugged at her tie, removing it from around her neck as she began to walk home. It was Friday, she was finally out of a sling from when she was shot in the shoulder, she was finished with exams; her sister Maddie still had three exams left and then she had three and a half months of summer holidays ahead of her. The icing on the cake for all of this for Liv was that it was her seventeenth birthday the next day. Without getting ahead of herself, Liv was beginning to think that life was starting to sort itself out.

She and Maddie had finally settled themselves nicely into a routine. They had a food shop delivered every other week, made sure they had a night off from their vigilante crime fighting once a week and made sure they got themselves into a routine of relaxation and pamper. On Fridays Maddie and her girlfriend Deanne went on a date night. Tonight, Maddie would go on her date and return Deanne home; her strict priest of a father not permitting her to stay round their house.

Since imprisoning their parents and all but toppling their criminal organisation, Liv and Maddie's life had become rather chaotic. A bounty had been placed on their heads by some of their parents' former business associates.

A hitwoman called Tanith decided to cash in on the

bounty. Changing her mind at the last second, she decided to shoot Liv in the shoulder as opposed to the head and helped them set up the other would-be assassins attempting to collect their blood.

In the process she made Liv develop strong feelings for her despite the age gap of four years. However, after she helped them dismantle a drugs ring a few months back she went radio silence, leaving Liv downhearted.

She didn't feel downhearted now, she smiled at the calmness of the afternoon and that the life of her and her sister was getting back on track and they were finally happy.

When Liv got to the front door of their house however, she noted that there was an unfamiliar car parked across the street, but presuming one of their neighbours had guests over she paid it no notice. She stopped to get her key out of her bag. When she retrieved her key, she looked up and her smiled vanished as she saw who the car belonged to as the man approached her.

She recognised the blonde hair and crisp expensive suit of Mr. Snyder, a lawyer who worked for the law firm her mother built and ran before she had been brought to justice.

"Afternoon, Olivia," he said warmly, extending his hand for her to shake.

"Afternoon," Liv said, cautiously shaking his hand to be polite and ignoring the fact he had called her Oliva instead of Liv.

"Is your sister with you?" he asked, his finger tapping the handle of his briefcase.

"Revision session for exams, then a date night," Liv said, resisting the temptation to look around comically, as it was clear that she was not standing there with her. "Why?"

"Her presence is needed at a board meeting to discuss some of the directions for the company to go. I also have some documentation for her. They require her signature," he finished uncomfortably.

"I will pass on the documentation and messages to her," Liv said shortly, putting her key into the door to unlock it.

"Certainly," he replied, handing the documentation from his briefcase to Liv.

"That is not the only reason as to why I am here," he said, pausing and lowering his voice. "Your father has requested you to visit him and your mother has requested to see Maddie. As it is your birthday tomorrow, Olivia, I presume that is the reason, they have been granted special visitation rights tomorrow and want to see you, perhaps even explain themselves."

"Thank you for being their messenger," Liv said, so defiantly that Mr. Snyder knew the conversation was over.

Liv threw the documentation onto the kitchen island before sinking down onto the floor and bursting into tears. Even from prison their parents still managed to interfere and ruin their lives. Anger burned like an inferno inside her. They had turned their parent's bedroom into a gym and removed all photos of them from the house. Removed all trace of them for their life and yet they still managed to affect them. From making her eighteen-year-old sister head of a law firm and now by requesting they visit them in prison tomorrow, on her birthday.

Whether she had cried for ten minutes or an hour Liv didn't know but she felt considerably better. Well enough in fact to begin making dinner. Wiping her eyes on her sleeve, she got up and began cooking. With Maddie going out for a meal, Liv decided to read the documents that Mr. Snyder had brought over; despite being a passionate reader, Liv could not get excited about the documents.

Whilst this was happening Maddie was at the restaurant, pulling out a chair for Deanne before taking her place at the table. They were sat in their favourite restaurant and for the first time that day they were beaming at each other.

A day of revision and the exam period in general was a stressful time for everyone taking exams but when

Maddie sat across from Deanne none of it mattered. They had a bottle of wine on the table, their favourite courses on the way. It was going to be an enjoyable night.

"Have you had the university talk with your dad yet?" Maddie asked her, stroking her hand as if it were the softest thing in the universe.

"I've been avoiding the talk. He knows I applied for Wimborne; however, he doesn't know about the unconditional offer from Airedale," Deanne laughed nervously.

"Probably smart, at eighteen you still have a curfew, you still can't tell him who you truly are. God knows how he is going to react when he finds that you're going to your dream university which is about four and a half hours away."

"He is going to have a heart attack," Deanne laughed, "I'm still unsure I want to go though, the freedom will be magical but it is such a distance for us to travel to see each other, we would struggle. It would be such a shame to move so far away from you," she ended sadly.

"You don't go till September, and you are going. This is your university and you're going," Maddie said cheerily.

Deanne was considerably happier knowing how much support she had from Maddie, knowing Maddie was by her side was always a nice feeling.

"I worry about you now," she laughed, "your nightly adventures scare me when I'm in the same city as you. The worry will be exponentially more when I'm seven or eight hours away."

"Well we aren't tonight or tomorrow, with it being Liv's birthday."

"The world's hardest person to buy for," Deanne laughed. "Have you actually gotten anything for her birthday?"

"Leather jacket, bath bombs, new perfume," Maddie shrugged, completely agreeing that she had no clue what to buy for her sister.

They talked and dined until it was time for Deanne to return home before her curfew, and the sadness of knowing the date was over and they would have to go back to hiding their relationship, overwhelmed them as it did every date night. So, Maddie had to walk home alone from Deanne's with nothing but her thoughts for company.

Liv was still uninterestingly reading the agenda for one of the meetings Maddie had to attend when her sister arrived home.

"What is all this?" she asked, as she saw Liv slide one of the pieces of paper away as entered the room.

"Documents for you to sign, agendas for meetings for you

to attend and a request," Liv said, trying to hide a yawn.

"A request?"

"Mr. Snyder brought it round. He had been contacted with a request for you to visit our father tomorrow and I visit our mother tomorrow. Different prisons, same time."

"No," Maddie said, after a short silence.

"That's what I said immediately," Liv said with a pause, "but, that's what worried me. Why would they wait till now to ask us, they have had visitation rights since they were imprisoned, so why now? I'm worried."

"Why now?" Maddie repeated. "I expected requests as soon as they were arrested, they didn't know the part in which we played so it would be natural for a parent to contact us, so why now?"

"Do we go? Definitively tell them to never contact us again? I mean, they reached out via the law firm which is making me suspicious."

"I don't want to. But I think we have to. The timing of it unsettles me. Not just because of your birthday tomorrow but remember that robbery three weeks back, it was rumoured that was a splinter group from the fallout of the Brigade of Karma; Now they don't have our parent's leadership, financial backing, or contacts it must be difficult to keep a criminal organisation that large afloat."

"I didn't even think about that," Liv said, her mouth slightly open.

"I still don't like it," Maddie grimaced. "If we go, we agree a time we are there for. Tell them straight up that they have that amount of time to talk and that this is the last that they will see of us, and we leave."

"Agreed."

"Now, enough about that trash, we have two nights off in a row. Let's have a relaxation, a bit of a pamper and be in such a good mood that it does not affect your birthday tomorrow."

Despite their best efforts however, they couldn't not let it affect them. Re-dying their hair, the facemasks, scented candles and nail polish only masked the subdued atmosphere and they went to bed sullen and annoyed that their parents had contacted them.

***

"So, we're agreed," Liv said, twirling around admiring the leather on the jacket that Maddie had gotten her. "We go in and say, 'you have seven and a half minutes', set the timer and when it beeps, we up and leave."

"Then, it's back here for some relaxation, you have your first driving lesson whilst I bake your cake and then we have an enjoyable night," Maddie finished, attempting to be as bright as possible.

At that moment a taxi pulled up outside for Liv, whilst Maddie would be driving her car to the prison her father was located in. She was not a confident driver by any stretch of the imagination but that meant that when she drove, she had little room in her mind for anything else. The last time she had seen her father they were engaged in a fist fight with him. A fight so brutal, he had re-opened a stab wound which had been stitched up, leaving Liv in agony, before he was finally defeated by them and was arrested and subsequently charged.

Both Darkwater Institute, where their father was being held, and Sky Vault Maximum Security where their mother was, were hours away in different directions. So, for Liv, this meant she spent the early hours of her birthday morning alone with nothing but music, in an attempt to block out her more intrusive thoughts as she sat in the back of the taxi, her head spinning.

Liv kept thinking the same thing; 'what could she possibly have to say to me?'. The same question was going through Maddie's head when pulled up in the car park.

Liv and Maddie arrived at almost the same time. Liv, hands shaking, got out of the taxi, hoping Maddie was just as nervous. She was. Nevertheless, they entered the prisons defiantly with their heads held high.

Liv sat down in front of the glass and glared at her

mother. Prison, however, did not suit Vala Winters. Slick suits, expensive make-up; all vanished. The smug sense of authority, superiority and power were gone. Instead a dishevelled, miserable shadow of Vala Winters sat on the other side of the glass.

"Hello, Vala," Liv said curtly, "You have seven and a half minutes before I walk out of here and you never see me again."

"Vala?" she asked. "Am I not still your mother? Hello, Mum?"

"It's debatable," Liv said, trying not to laugh at her comment.

"Firstly, happy birthday, my beautiful girl. I still remember your birth. That magical day has been in my memory a lot recently. My water broke in court. A double homicide."

"Even now, it's still all about you," Liv snorted. "Clock's ticking."

"I still love you as much as I did that day. Whoever caused our downfall deserves their due and they will have it. I cannot deny the crimes I was charged with, but I did it for

you two. We thought that you two would never have to work again, anything you needed - it would have been yours. It propelled our businesses and our income that changed your lives," she said, stopping for breath.

"'Cause a lawyer and a police chief couldn't have legitimately and legally looked after two children. Cut the fucking shit, Vala, why did you summon me here? Why did Henry summon Maddie on the same day? It isn't a coincident? The money has been seized so your goal failed."

"I wanted to see my daughter on her seventeenth birthday. I wasn't allowed visitation privileges for Madeline's eighteenth. I've had no contact with Henry since arrest."

"Well, you'll never hear from us again either," Liv finished, getting to her feet before saying finally, "have a good life in prison, Vala."

Maddie took longer than Liv did to pass through security when she arrived in Blackwater. She wore a fierce scowl as she walked to the glass indicated to her by the prison officer where her father was waiting for her.

"Hello, Madeline, my sweet Maddie."

Maddie showed him her phone as she started the timer.

"You have seven and half minutes before you never see me again. Start talking."

"You have no idea, do you? Why we started the BoK, my sister, your mother's father. They were murdered by government officials; it was then we said we would get our revenge on the government. Structured anarchy, working from the inside like a poison, to topple them. Creating a fire so vicious, no fireman could put out. Karma and chaos whilst in the process ensuring the best possible life for you and your sister."

"You're fucking insane," Maddie chuckled.

"Until you two ruined it all."

"What?" Maddie said, stunned, her stomach sinking.

"I finally figured it out, after months of nothing to think about. The two people who managed to defeat me in hand-to-hand combat. I trained you to take over from me and the two of you brought me down."

"You're insane. Get the prison doctor to look at you," Maddie laughed, a poker face firmly set in stone.

"Truly. Fucking. Batshit. Crazy. We were woken up by the doorbell to find police officers on our doorstep explaining everything to us and telling us you both were set to be imprisoned for life. Before that you were our heroes."

"It must -"

"Hero to zero, and that in fact is the amount of times you will see either of us again, no more visits. You're sick. You had an illness when you believed the BoK and your *philosophy,* but to think that we had a hand in it, is next level disgusting. Have a good life, Henry," Maddie stood up and, with her head held high, she walked out.

Maddie's hands began to shake as they gripped the steering wheel. Had she managed to convince him it wasn't them? If she hadn't, would there be consequences? It took a while for her to compose herself enough to be in a safe condition to drive.

The drive back did wonders for Maddie's nerves, the concentration needed for driving pushed her father's theory out of her mind. She arrived home to see Liv with a cup of tea waiting for her.

They began telling each other how the conversations went and what exactly their parents had said to them. Liv began.

"Vala did always have an over inflated ego," Maddie said, as Liv finished telling her about their conversation.

"Yeah," Liv sighed. "What did Henry say?"

"That we were the ones who brought him down."

"HE WHAT?!" Liv yelled, almost sending her cup of tea flying.

"I think it is okay," Maddie said reassuringly, "I played a good poker face and convinced him it was paranoia and that he was just insane. Spun a tale about how we only knew when the doorbell rang and the police told us everything. I think he believed it."

"Let's hope so."

"Enough talk of this," Maddie said with a false bravado, "it's your birthday and your driving instructor will be here in an hour. So I can get you out of the house."

"Rude. What are the girls doing tonight? We could invite them over for a bit of a party?"

"Come on, do you really want to spend your birthday with my friends? I know you've become part of the group but, you know?" Maddie asked cautiously.

"Not too fussed about that, you know how immature most of my school year are, that's why I didn't invite any of them, but the more the merrier."

"Well, if you're sure, I'll give some of them a ring and see what can happen, I'll go grab my phone," she said getting up and going into the kitchen.

"Shit!" Maddie muttered, as she picked up her phone. Maddie pretended to text them, knowing full well that they were already coming around and it had been planned for a couple of weeks. But then again Liv didn't need to know that.

"I've text them, but you need to get ready for your lesson, sooner you can get passed the better."

"Here, here!" Liv cheered, draining the remnants of her tea and checking the time on her watch. As she looked at it, she had a flashback to when she got the watch and the circumstances surrounding it.

On Christmas Eve, they were out on patrol when they came across a jewellery store in the midst of a robbery and, unbeknown to them, a hold-up. When they intervened, they saved both the shop the owner and the mayor. As a gracious reward the shop owner had presented them with the breath-taking watches; one of these the one currently on her wrist. It always made her smile to have a constant reminder of all the good they've done.

"Instructor's here," Maddie said, awaking Liv from her flashback. "Have fun, don't die."

Liv laughed as she put her new jacket on and headed towards the door, only stopping to give Maddie a tight hug, before dashing to the door.

As soon as the car drove off, Maddie went into maximum overdrive; the oven was on pre-heat, she blew up the balloons and began to crack eggs.

Deanne and Jessica arrived as Maddie was beginning to whisk the cake mix together.

"Mads, is this a blood stain on the island?" Jessica queried, as she sat at the island.

"Nail polish," she responded, quick as a flash. Not looking up from the mix, she was trying to remember if it was Liv's blood from when she was stabbed or shot, or if it were a mixture of both of their blood from when they'd entered after a brutal night; they'd lost so much it was hard to keep track of it at times.

"Oh, thank God! I was going to say…"

Maddie had just sat down after placing the cake in the oven before the doorbell rang again.

"I'll get it," Deanne said, placing a hand on her shoulder to prevent her from getting up again.

"It's the others," Deanne called from the door, letting the others in. They rallied together to put up the rest of the streamers and blow up the rest of the balloons.

"I can't believe that your parents are okay with this," Jessica said as Deanne and Maddie brought in the alcohol from Maddie's boot.

"Yeah, well they're on holiday so what they don't know can't hurt them," she laughed. It wasn't easy to keep so many secrets from her friends about her parents and their nightly activities, but it was even harder to keep making up excuses as to why they weren't around. Only Deanne knew the truth and that was sadly how it had to be kept.

The curtains were closed and the lights were off as Liv

entered.

Their yells of, "Surprise!" were met by Liv jumping into a fighting stance.

Once her shock subsided, they began to chat and get the party started.

The quadruple chocolate fudge cake that Maddie made was divine and they all thoroughly enjoyed it. The atmosphere and mood was light-hearted and the drinks flowed heavily and well into the night.

A few of the girls left just before midnight, Jessica got picked up just after one in the morning, and the last few left at half past two. Deanne had permission from her father to stay the night, which meant that she and Maddie went up to bed just after three in the morning with Liv following them to bed shortly after.

They all woke up late on Sunday morning. When they were finally all awake Deanne offered to cook for them all. She began making a full English fry up and soon the smell of sausages, eggs, bacon, hash browns and beans filled the kitchen.

Liv smiled as she watched Maddie and Deanne dance around the kitchen as they cooked, although Liv found their matching couples pyjamas cringy enough to make her feel a little queasy. Deanne's seasoning was absolute perfection as they began tucking into the mountain of breakfast in front of them. None of them really spoke too much until they had eaten their fill, but the light-hearted conversation was interrupted by the vibration of a phone coming from inside a kitchen drawer.

This phone wasn't one that many people knew about or had ever seen. This was the phone they used when they were on patrol, to contact the mayor, report crimes they had stopped to the police and listen to the police scanners.

"Text from the mayor," Maddie informed them.

"What is she saying?" they asked at the same time.

"Usual place, at three am, police chief coming as well."

"Intriguing," Deanne muttered.

Liv was especially interested in the fact the police chief was coming as well, and they spent a lot of the day trying to speculate as to what exactly it would be about.

It came as something of a blessing when they left the house that night. They wore bulletproof vests on top of long-sleeved skin-tight base layers that ran up to their necks, and thanks to Maddie's sewing skills they came to rest just under their noses; tracksuit bottoms tucked into their boots. They both carried bum bags with everything they needed whilst out.

Maddie wore a helmet for protection whereas Liv wore a pair of welding goggles; they didn't offer the same levels of protection as a helmet and were mainly for aesthetic when they sat on her head but when she put them over her eyes, they made her look intimidating. Both wore rather blood-stained but still functional knuckle dusters on both hands.

They patrolled the city for most of the night. One ear listening in to the police scanner for a sign of a crime, they eventually made their way to a dark secluded area of a multi-storey car park in which they held previous meetings with the mayor and Police Chief George Kyle, who was appointed chief after their father was arrested. They stood in the shadows and waited for the hour. As the clocks around the city chimed, the mayor and the police chief came into sight together.

"Thank you for agreeing to meet," The mayor said, making it clear they didn't have time for small talk.

"If you're contacting us instead of the other way around, then it's serious," Maddie said.

"Of the utmost importance, as you know, Willowdale City is being heavily invested in by governing bodies both in this country and from abroad. Millions upon millions are being pumped into the city for expansion and renovation work. New businesses, new opportunities, for thousands," the mayor said rapidly, the importance of the meeting being stressed in her voice.

"We cannot lose this opportunity," the Police chief interjected. "We're afraid that there may be a serial killer in the city, and we need your help catching them. Different cause of death, different victim types each time, all the victims from different backgrounds."

"What connects the deaths?" Liv asked.

"Biblical texts left at the scene, sometimes a piece of the bible left at the scene, other times a scripture reference carved into the skin of a victim."

"So, shut down every religious institution in town?" Liv joked; a joke that was not found funny by anyone other than Maddie.

"We will need everything you have on every single one of the murders, everything," Maddie demanded.

The police chief silently handed over a large file which Maddie put under her arm.

They began to turn and as they walked away, they heard the Mayor plead. "Stop this individual before they cost this city everything."

Instead of patrolling the city again they decided to head home to examine the file. They discussed the unexpectancy of the case as they walked home.

"This is going to be a pissing struggle, I guarantee there is nothing in this file to go on," Liv muttered pessimistically.

"Let's find out," Maddie yawned, dropping the file on the floor and lighting the lamps.

"He seems to strike on every other Tuesday," Liv muttered, scanning the document with the names of the victims and their times of death.

"And this is where you tell me he didn't kill last Tuesday, and we have about forty-eight hours before he kills again."

"Yeah, I wish I was taking the piss but no, we have forty-eight hours."

"Fucking brilliant, what's his hunting ground? Do you have a location map?"

"The west of the city."

"That's the best you've got?"

"That's the best we've been fucking given."

"Okay, tomorrow you're off school, start by re-visiting the crime scenes, in the light. Starting with the most recent and work the way back."

"Starting with Emily Beck; thirty-eight, married, no kids, retail worker in the centre of the city, never returned home from a night shift. Immigrated to the country five years ago."

"So, either a crime of opportunity, or the killer stalked and waited for the prime opportunity to strike, which would mean he knew her routine and waited for the perfect opportunity," Maddie pondered out loud.

"Can't be a crime of opportunity?" Liv sighed.

"What makes you think that?"

"Carving words or letters into skin takes time, so they would have known that they would not be discovered and did it where the bodies were found. Or they were taken to a secluded area and then brought to the place where they were eventually discovered."

"Fair point," Maddie pondered, "Anyway, let's get some sleep. You can investigate tomorrow when I am at school."

That is exactly what Liv did. When she walked into the city centre that morning, it was with a notepad and pen at the ready and she was ready to begin her investigation whist Maddie, frustrated and exhausted, went to school.

Although it was not uncommon due to the work happening all over the city, the first thing Liv made note of in her notepad was the location of the first crime scene; an alleyway a few streets over from a construction site.

"A woman walking to and from work would avoid walking

past a construction site due to a bunch of cat-calling fucks which is what ninety-nine percent of construction workers seems to do. A rejection or retaliation could have sent someone into a frenzy," she muttered, scribbling all of this down as an idea to discuss later.

Liv made notes of everything she could about a dead-end alleyway before moving onto the next crime scene. She walked for fifteen minutes before she reached the new location in a blur of déjà vu.

Liv had walked into another alleyway, this time connecting two streets together, near a construction site.

She looked at her notes again trying to decipher her own handwriting; *father of four, throat slit open. Worked as a pawn broker and money lender.*

This worried her. Serial killers are unlikely to change their victim type, and even more so to change how they kill their victims, yet this one was doing both, with the only things connecting them being a calling card left on the bodies and the locations they were being left. This meant that it was unlikely the killer was acting out a revenge fantasy, making them even more dangerous.

Liv let out an exasperated sigh when she reached the third crime scene as it was essentially identical to the others. The third crime scene was a biology teacher from one of the local schools. An occupation with little in common with the others. She noted everything she could about this particular alleyway, as if an alleyway could be much different and went to a local café to mull everything over in her mind and truly start the investigation.

Whilst Liv was working, Maddie was procrastinating. She sat with Deanne, Jessica and the rest of their friendship group.

"When the weather is this nice, I simply can't be motivated," Jessica moaned, looking lustfully out of the window at the sun.

"Same," Deanne said in agreement, playing with Maddie's hair as Maddie lay in her lap, her feet dangling off the edge of the sofa they were on.

"I'll ace it anyway," she yawned.

"Probably, that's the fucking annoying thing about it," Jessica muttered, rolling her eyes. "Still, don't know why you haven't applied to a single university, Mads?"

"Not really my thing," she said coolly. As she looked up into Deanne's face, Maddie thought honestly that had she not been a vigilante and not had to be there for Liv, she would have quite enjoyed university. However, her life didn't turn out that way. So, whilst her friends were planning to go off to university. Maddie had to make excuses as to why she wasn't.

Liv, whilst draining her fourth cup of tea of the morning,

almost sprayed the drink over her notepad and phone as she realised that she may have found the place to start.

Most of the city was under construction, and the bodies were all found by a construction site which was not surprising. What was surprising was that all of the locations of the crime scenes were near the same company. Through her research she had found that three major companies had eighty-eight percent of all construction work in the city, and these companies and their sub-contractors had come from all over the world in order to undertake this job.

One of these was the one she needed to investigate. She turned to a new page and wrote in the middle of it *'Jim Tallman Constructions'*. Opening a new internet tab on her phone, she began to investigate the worldwide conglomerate and the owner Jim Tallman, a man with a net worth so high, you wouldn't want to accuse him of harbouring and enabling a serial killer.

She emailed herself documents to print off about the construction company, before she wandered through the city to her favourite book store to see what they had in.

Considering the amount of deductive legwork she had done before lunchtime, she thought she deserved the treat.

By the time Maddie arrived home from school, Liv, after

losing an argument with the printer, had finally managed to print off articles from their website and newspaper articles about the company.

Liv discussed her thinking and findings over dinner, and it was a discussion that continued way into the night. When they were on patrol, they decided that it was a good lead to follow, although investigating an employee of a worldwide company with thousands upon thousands of employees would not be easy, it was as good a place to start.

They headed to the south west of the city, which was the area of the city with the most construction expanding and rejuvenation taking place and was therefore the best place to start their search.

"So, if he keeps to his pattern, he will kill tomorrow night. Our best guess is he is a member of a massive multi-national corporation, with shareholders across the world and one of their employees is a serial killer hiding amongst thousands in the city," Maddie summarised as they sat on the roof.

"Essentially, yeah."

"Okay, as you did the ground work, you take the lead."

"Let's start at the southernmost point of what his potential grounds would be and work in a clockwise motion, seeing if there are any alleyways that match possible dump/murder sites."

Despite there being little to nothing to go on, they patrolled. They patrolled the next night as well, being extra vigilant for anything out of the ordinary, but there wasn't. Until, the next morning when Maddie was in school, Liv received a text from the police chief saying that they needed to work harder and that another body had been found.

Liv, resisting the urge to tell him to 'fuck off' instead, ordered another cup of tea from the café she was sat in and formulated a plan. It was not the best plan they had ever had, but it was worth a shot.

She dialled the number that was on the construction company's website, when she finally got through to customer service Liv adopted a high and sickly-sweet voice that made her feel rather nauseous.

"Hi, my name is Annabeth and I have a complaint I would like to raise if possible. I was wondering if your crews rotated the jobs they were working on or stayed in the same location. I have been cat-called a lot recently, as have some of my employees, and they all have given similar descriptions of those who have been yelling abuse at us."

"I'm so sorry, Annabeth, we here at Jim Tallman Construction take these complaints very seriously."

"It has been quite distressing for some of our employees, including two girls on work experience from school. They came in very distressed about some of the comments made."

"We are so very sorry. Now, you said that these happened at different locations within the city."

"Yes, that is correct, we were unsure if it was the same team that had just moved onto different jobs or if everybody in the company acted that way."

"Well, it is certainly not company-wide, as for the moving of locations, some teams will, and some supervisors will change the locations. Could you perhaps give me the streets and times in which these actions occurred, I can have a look on our system."

"That would be excellent," Liv said, giving the locations of the sites near the murder locations and times.

She could hear the adviser typing rapidly on her keyboard, examining the claim. After about six or seven minutes of nothing but typing, the adviser on the phone said, "It may potentially be an isolated team that was at each of those

sites, the supervisor in question has a specialist three man-team who move with him."

"I see," Liv said slowly, her breath quickening. Heart racing, she tried to remain calm as she said, "I would never want to get anyone in trouble for the actions of a few, and would like to see if any of the girls in the office recognise the members, would it be possible for photos to be sent over, just so we are clear. I wouldn't want a member of the team to get a telling off when they were just working hard."

"Certainly, I will keep this in-house until you get back to us about this. As I say, we here at Jim Tallman Construction strive to be the best and this is certainly not the best. May I take an email address to send the files over too."

"Of course, thank you so much," Liv said handing over the email address she had just created under the name Annabeth.

The adviser gave them a unique reference number for this case and they ended the call.

Liv let out a sigh of relief. Shocked that the plan had potentially worked, she sat clutching her mug and waited for the email attachments.

"Sam Heenan, Jack Queen, Adam Piper," Liv whispered to herself, scribbling their names down in the notepad.

Liv left the café and headed home. As soon as she was home, she printed off the attachments from the adviser and spread them out across the kitchen table.

After about an hour she had conclusively ruled out Jack Queen. After doing a deep dive on all social media viewing more of his pictures, Jack Queen seemed to be quite scrawny with a technical and agricultural background.

He did not seem muscular enough to overpower and keep silent multiple victims. As someone who had been stabbed, she knew that to repeatedly stab someone takes a lot of muscles which Jack certainly didn't have.

That, left Sam Heenan and Adam Piper. Adam Piper had a criminal record dating back several years and was a divorcee. He seemed, based on social media at least, to have gotten his life back on track; living out of a local hotel, like most of the employees that have been brought into the city externally.

Sam Heenan was married to a primary school teacher, and a father of two. He travelled the world with Jim Tallman Construction in order to provide for his family. Heenan's social media was mostly bible scripture.

Stereotypes had taught Liv not to rule out that Heenan, despite how picture perfect his life seemed, could still be a serial killer, and to disregard his family man appearance.

Liv was excited to tell Maddie about this development and figure out how to progress from here.

Maddie, however, was not in a good mood when she

returned home. With an exam the next morning, Liv tentatively suggested that she invite Deanne round for a revision session and ice cream instead of going out on patrol that night. This made Maddie smile and was grateful for a reason to not go out that night. Thankfully Deanne's father consented, so Deanne arrived with tubs of ice cream and all of her revision notes.

The night for Liv was as enjoyable as it was stressful for Deanne and Maddie. Despite their confidence in the knowledge, the anxiety came in the examination process. The stress levels, and the process of just cramming the knowledge and regurgitating it in an exam, ~~gave~~ caused them stress and they were not handling it well. Liv suggested that Maddie and Deanne simply give up, stop worrying, as if they didn't know it by now then they wouldn't know it and just go to bed. They took Liv's advice and were in bed before eleven o'clock, leaving Liv to finish off the ice cream and unwind in the living room alone.

Liv wished them luck as they left the next morning. She wanted to make up for lost time, wanted to get visuals on either one of her suspects. Both were active on social media, and both being of the older generation had absolutely no knowledge of privacy settings, allowing Liv to see absolutely everything about their lives.

However, Liv needed more than their virtual lives, she needed to observe their mannerisms, their behaviour, see how they acted with other people and if either of them gave off any of the more characteristic tell-tale signs of being a psychopath or a serial killer.

With them being on the same specialist team, if she found one, she would hopefully find the other. Then again, anything could happen as she as of yet had no clue about what they actually did for Jim Tallman Construction.

After spending the whole morning walking around, she finally spotted Adam Piper just after midday, and spent the rest of the day sat in the café near the construction site, watching the workers, watching Adam, notepad out scribbling everything she could about his mannerisms.

Sam Heenan seemed more reserved, he laughed along with the others' jokes and was certainly in amongst the action, however he seemed to be the one who laughed along as opposed to the one causing everyone to laugh.

They both seemed remarkably friendly, quite hands-on with the other workers; they clapped them on the shoulders, gave out fist bumps and handshakes. Liv had to remind herself that the majority of high-profile serial killers are so successful because they blend in, they are friendly and trustworthy which is why they get away with it for so long.

She returned home after watching Sam Heenan and Adam Piper for hours, just in time for her driving lesson. That became her routine every day for the next week and a half. She watched Heenan and Piper like a hawk and as the night of the next murder approached, she was still none the wiser as to which one of them was more likely to commit murder.

"I have a plan for tomorrow," Liv said conversationally, over dinner on the Monday night.

"Let's hear it," Maddie said, looking up for her casserole.

"I'll watch Sam Heenan, follow him to where he is staying and watch him leave again. Both are heavily devoted to God, and as I am none the wiser as to which one is a serial killer, we will just have to stalk them tonight. I have been watching both of them and this is the only way."

"Why Heenan tonight then?"

"According to his social media, Adam Piper is going to a speed dating night at a hotel, three hours away. Now, that either means he is going to abduct and kill someone at speed dating, or he is a lonely divorcee and Heenan is going to commit bloody murder tonight."

"I suppose, we aren't even sure if this Tallman lead is actually the right one but how much choice do we have?"

"The mayor is texting me daily asking me for updates. If this is the right lead and we finish it tonight then good, if not we are fucked."

The next morning, Liv arrived bright and early at the café

near the construction site to watch Sam Heenan. Adam Piper, according to his social media, was having the day off work so he could prepare for his speed dating later tonight. She yawned and stretched as she loaded up a game on her phone, staring out of the window. She hated stakeouts and this was no different.

The only saving grace for Liv was that the barista who was making her tea was very cute, and when she asked Liv whether or not she wanted any sugar with her pot of tea, Liv couldn't help but joke that she was sweet enough, before accepting sugar as she died from embarrassment.

Liv kept a pad of paper and a pen as her cover for why she sat there for so long, pretending to be an artist and an author and that is why she was in the café for hours at a time; she just had to hope that nobody asked to see her art, as she could not draw to save her life.

It was mind-numbingly boring, especially as she couldn't see Heenan all the time and just had to watch people building. The monotony was broken a little after midday when Sam Heenan came into the café that Liv was sat in, to buy lunch and coffee for all of his workers, which wasn't something either he or Adam had done before.

"Bet, that was an expensive order," Liv said to the barista.

"Yeah, too right! Lunch and coffee for thirty people, tipped as well."

"Must be a good company to work for."

"Oh, I bet! I don't even get discount on a coffee or lunch, if I want a drink that I myself make," she joked.

Liv watched Sam Heenan as closely as possible until everyone began to finish for the day. She left the café in order to not lose sight of him. She followed him from a distance until he returned to the apartment block. With his family over on holiday, he had them now living with him until they returned home after their holiday; his family however seemed very happy with their holiday to Willowdale City and their children were overjoyed to see their father, according to social media.

Liv sat on a bench opposite the apartment block until sunset. At, half past nine she was joined by Maddie who handed over her gear. Liv changed and gave her normal clothes to Deanne who offered to drop them off at their house.

They both sat and watched the main entrance to the apartment complex. They waited to see if he ever left again that night. He did. At midnight, he left the complex and began walking toward the town centre.

They followed him as quietly as humanly possible. With no wind to drown out their footsteps, they followed him hoping that he would not turn around to see them, as with the way they were dressed they did look rather suspicious. He walked for over an hour, before all of a sudden, he stopped and sat down at a bus stop. He sat there and waited.

Maddie and Liv stopped as well. They snuck around and onto the roof opposite the bus stop. They watched him for any sign of movement, any glint of a knife or a gun in the moonlight or off a streetlight, anything that could be used as a weapon.

He sat for forty-five minutes before moving again. Following him, Maddie and Liv got off the roof and continued following him, ready to strike at any time. They could just about see him in the distance, however what they couldn't see without a night-vision scope was that Sam Heenan was also following someone.

Sam Heenan began to quicken his pace and they did as well. However, having to keep their distance so that they weren't discovered came at a major disadvantage, as before they realised what had happened, he had clamped his hand over the mouth of an individual and was dragging him into an alleyway before they could catch up.

When they caught up to the alley, they heard a gruff voice begin to speak. The voice was maniacal, his tone was excited as if this was something he was longing for all his life.

The voice that Liv now associated with Sam Heenan said, "Everyone who would not seek the lord, the God of Israel, was to be put to death, whether small or great, whether man or woman. The bible is clear that you are to die tonight."

They heard a muffled scream and knew that was their cue to turn into the alley and act. They saw the glint of what looked like a hammer being brought down and connecting with the man's kneecap, causing a sick, crunching sound.

Quick as a flash, they engaged. Heenan may have been bigger and stronger than both of them but that was no different to the majority of the people they stopped. Speed was greater than strength in their experience. Maddie threw a punch to the ribs as Liv hit him in the knee.

Heenan collapsed, dropping the hammer to the ground. Maddie kicked it aside, before kicking Heenan in the head. Liv threw a punch to his throat as Heenan began to curl into the foetal position to protect as much of himself as possible.

Just, as they went to deliver the final blow, they were dazzled by a blinding light from the roofs on either side of the alley. Spotlights and flashlights shone down on them as multiple voices shouted, "FREEZE!"

Chapter Two:

Maddie and Liv did not freeze, they ran. They sprinted, as fast as they had ever run before, in opposite directions. Liv ran back the way they had come with Maddie heading down the other way. They had discussed every possibility of occasion and possibilities of this situation and knew where to meet and after how long of hiding. They cut through alleyways and across traffic. Liv took the long route to the multi-storey they were to meet in whilst Maddie cut through a construction site.

They were heading to one of the multi-storey car parks and they knew it was on the opposite side of the city.

It took them over twenty-five minutes to reach the far corner on the fifth level of the car park. They arrived within minutes of each other, wheezing and clutching, stitches in their sides.

"Was that a fucking sting operation?" Liv gasped.

Maddie was about to answer when she raised a hand for silence, a split-second later Liv heard it too, footsteps coming from the upper level. They guessed it could have been ten pairs of feet.

They began to run towards the lower level but as they did, cars were flying up the ramp. They were caged.

"I guess we make a fucking stand," Liv snarled.

Maddie had her police baton in her hand, knuckle dusters as always on her fists. Liv pulled out her swiss army knife and flicked the blade open. If they were going down, they were going down fighting.

They stood back to back and readied themselves. They were beginning to see that they were heavily outnumbered, with at least twenty people walking towards them, guns drawn.

As soon as they surrounded them, they engaged. Maddie ferociously swung the baton to disarm their captors before striking them. She didn't care how clean the connection was as long as she heard a scream or grunt of pain, she then turned her attention to the next person.

Liv slashed up and down, left and right. Jabbing the blade in every direction, darting forward with thunderous punches towards whoever was in striking range. None of their assailants seemed overly keen to get stabbed; instead avoiding the knife which allowed them to be punched.

They put up a tremendous fight but it seemed that more people kept joining the fight after each person they knocked down. However, they were so outnumbered it began to take its toll and both Maddie and Liv knew the end was coming.

They were eventually subdued after a monstrous fight. Liv was knocked to the ground first, causing Maddie to change her position so she was stood over her little sister. She readied herself but the sheer number of attackers meant that she was eventually toppled as well. With them both on the ground they received sharp kicks and punches. As their balaclavas were pulled down they resorted to biting and kicking. They were eventually handcuffed, gagged, mesh bags put over their heads and thrust into the back of one of the cars.

Although they squirmed as the car began to drive, it was to no avail. The car kept driving, both girls in sensory overload, listening to every sound, trying to see through the mesh. Maddie suddenly remembered one of the Christmas presents they were given from their father, the last thing he had ever given them other than hatred. A pair of what he called 'universal' handcuff keys. He claimed they could unlock every handcuff type. In his paranoid mental state, it was in case they were kidnapped and held for ransom due to their jobs.

Well, they were kidnapped and now was as good a time as any to try it out, the issue was with reaching the key. After minutes of subtle stretching and reaching at her bum bag she faked a coughing fit so she could undo the zip. Her fingers rummaged until finally she found them. After struggling for a while, she managed to unlock her handcuffs. She put the key back in her bag and did it back up.

Maddie readied herself, slowed her breathing and waited

for the perfect opportunity. Then, without warning, she blindly lunged forward, throwing herself and punches toward the front of the car, elbows and fists went flying as the car swerved. Maddie reached for the steering wheel, still throwing punches and elbows attempting to get into the front seats, until with a heavy thud, Maddie was thrown back in her seat after being knocked out cold.

When Maddie awoke she found herself kneeling, and there was a cacophony of noise and commotion around them. She heard cars and people and they were coming from every direction.

Without warning, she had the bag ripped off her head. The early morning sunlight dazzled her eyes. She looked wildly around for Liv and saw the exact same thing happen to her. She noticed blood splatter onto the floor as Liv spat a mixture of saliva and blood at the feet of whoever was in front of them.

If Liv was annoyed and spitting at them before, it was nothing until she heard a very familiar voice shouting, "Carlson! WHAT, in God's fucking name do you think you're doing?!"

It was Tanith, the hit woman who had helped them so much, months ago. She was running over and was looking furious.

"They were engaged with the serial killer, we had to act," the bewildered man in a suit, with a bloodied lip and what looked like a broken nose said.

"Of course they were! You're an absolutely daft bastard," she screamed. "Why didn't you let them finish the job?"

"I chased that serial killer across Europe. I wasn't going to risk it."

"They're better than you! You unbelievable twat, I shot one of them for Christ sake, I've saved their lives."

"Someone please restrain Tanith before she breaks the rest of Carlson's face," a man said, walking over.

They saw him in full military uniform as he stopped in front of them. "I am Colonel Rathe; I am so sorry for what they've done to you. Ungag and release the handcuffs," he instructed.

As soon as the handcuffs were off, Maddie sprung to her feel and threw a powerful punch at Tanith, connecting with her jaw.

Col. Rathe burst out laughing. "Tanith, I see what you mean. I like them already! Come, girls, walk with me," he said, extending an arm.

They weren't sure they actually had a choice. So, they began to walk, Liv shooting a furious look at everyone she made eye contact.

"I am Colonel Rathe, a chief of G.U.A.R.D operations in

this area. We are a worldwide organisation working outside of the government control, with connections in every government on earth. G.U.A.R.D stands for Guidance, Unilateralism, Armour, Reconnaissance, Defence. We are the Elite. The best of the best."

"What does that have to do with us?" Maddie asked.

"We heard about vigilantes in Willowdale City, keeping crime down and toppling crime organisation; we were interested, we sent someone in undercover. Tanith was tasked with monitoring your activities, see your motives and see if you were a fit for G.U.A.R.D."

"Does that include shooting me in the fucking shoulder?" Liv asked, laughing sourly.

"No, she was never meant to actually meet you, when the hits came out on the two of you, then things changed. She was meant to take them out, not you. That's why she is here, she was benched for that. The grandmother's money that was discovered by the lawyers was actually from us, as an offering to help you out after losing your parents. But consider this the job interview process, become G.U.A.R.D agents."

"What is it that G.U.A.R.D agents actually do?" Maddie asked curiously.

"The things that need to be done; policy influencing, policing, unilateral war strategy, black ops missions, topple gangs, topple terrorist organisations. We have special operations groups, offices who deal with politics, environmental planning. We have fingers in many pies. Once your exams are over, we would like you to spend your summer going through basic training. After, that then you would return to Willowdale and just do what you do now. Only difference is that you would have the legal authority to do it. Liv can stay in school and you can vigilante at night. Then, if needed, you will meet up with your squad for necessary black ops missions. Your squad will be in basic training with you. Then once all is said and done you can just return to Willowdale."

"We would need time to discuss it," Maddie said, "I've, missed a day of school and have an exam tomorrow."

"I understand," he said, "although this is not to be discussed with Deanne." Maddie's eyes widened in shock at the information he seemed to know about their personal life.

"Excellent, I will have a driver take you back to Willowdale and give you some things to read over as you decide."

They walked back around to where they saw Tanith waiting, along with numerous other G.U.A.R.D members. He directed them to one of the nicer cars as opposed to a military jeep and then the Col. instructed all of their gear to be put in the boot and them driven back to their house.

They didn't say much in the car, Maddie felt a strong migraine and just needed to rest. They muttered if they had to speak but it was mainly them checking on each other, not wanting to discuss anything that the driver could overhear.

When they arrived home they didn't even make it to bed, instead they collapsed in the living room exhausted. They slept throughout the day and when they woke up the evening sun was shining through the curtains.

When Maddie checked her phone, it was to find a lot of texts from Deanne, Jess and the rest of her friendship group, all worried about her. She told them all she just needed to study at home before the exams to ease her mind.

As Maddie cooked, Liv read over the documents and they discussed G.U.A.R.D. They read every inch of the documents that Col. Rathe had given them. In the end they had a pro and con table in an attempt to weigh up the good from the bad.

"It's a job, that is one less thing for you to worry about. It will undoubtedly improve our fighting technique, and black ops clothing will make everything safer for us and hey, means we get paid for what we do," Liv reasoned.

"True, we stay in Willowdale, only called upon when we are needed," Maddie concurred.

"It'll stop them getting involved and interfering again," Liv laughed.

"Although, Heenan was still caught," Maddie reasoned.

"Though, everything Tanith said to me was a lie in order to manipulate me and get me compliant with her," Liv snarled.

"Well, she is no longer on missions, she is getting her payback for shooting you. Let's not forget if we do join G.U.A.R.D. you'll get the chance to punch Tanith," Maddie winked.

"Would you be able to lie to Deanne about what we were doing?"

This made Maddie look rather uncomfortable. "I wouldn't have a choice, but I could just be economical with the truth. That isn't lying, I would just say it is a government job?"

"Yeah, basic training over the summer holiday, before then we just continue doing the same thing together. Either way, you have an exam tomorrow, you need to do some revision and get ready for the exam," Liv said, in a tone that suggested so clearly that the exam should be her priority now.

"You sound decided?"

"Well, let's be fair," Liv said, beginning to laugh, "would not be the stupidest thing that we've ever done."

Maddie spent most of the night revising for the exam whilst Liv, after re-reading the files they had been given again until there was no new information, left Maddie to her revision and went off to bed.

Maddie was apprehensive when she set off to school the next morning, both about her exam but also the questioning about where she was the day before. Sure enough, from the moment she saw everyone they started asking her. Deanne was frantic but everyone else was just curious as to where she was.

"So, what actually happened?" Deanne asked her as soon as everyone else what out of earshot

"Job interview."

"Why didn't you tell me?" She demanded, pouting slightly.

"No point worrying you, and no point in telling you in case I didn't get it," Maddie said reasonably.

"What is it?"

"Just a government job?"

"That's all you're going to tell me?!"

"It's paper pushing, but it's paper that can be classified so it's all I'm really allowed to say."

"When will you hear back from them?"

"Soon, hopefully! It has a nice little pay cheque with it," she winked, "I'll be able to see you every other weekend."

"I like the sound of that!" Deanne laughed, reaching on her tiptoes in an attempt to give her a kiss before they got back to revising.

Four hours later, Maddie was free, her school days were over. She said as much as they left the exam hall, much to the annoyance of Jessica.

"Bath bombs and bottle of wine ahead," Maddie laughed, rubbing it in even further as Jessica scowled up at her.

Maddie practically skipped away from the exam hall. Knowing the others still had exams did not dampen her spirits and she would not let it dampen her post-exam celebrations. She had no thoughts in her mind about G.U.A.R.D or about her vigilante work, nothing but happiness about finishing school.

However, as she sat in the exam hall, in the back of her mind, the part of her mind not focusing on the essay in front of her, she had an epiphany about where everything had led to. It had led to G.U.A.R.D. Tonight, however, was a night for celebration.

They didn't need to discuss the future, it seemed clear as day in front of them, the path illuminated. They didn't

speak about it that night however, they left it till the morning. With sore heads they discussed the basic training.

"We're joining G.U.A.R.D. I'll make the arrangements whilst you're out with your friends today. We can discuss it all when you get back," Liv smiled.

With Maddie out of the house, Liv contacted the phone number Col. Rathe had given them and began the process over the phone with his secretary, who began making the necessary arrangements. The basic training was going to be about eight weeks. Liv shuddered with apprehension of this, Maddie and Deanne being separate for that amount of time was not an ideal situation.

Luckily, Liv had accidentally raised this to the secretary, who said this was something G.U.A.R.D dealt with all the time and had a few ideas. In the end they agreed that under the pretence of an anonymous gift to the priest of the city Deanne, her father and good for nothing brother would be sent on an all-expenses paid cruise. Liv knew that Deanne's father, who was in her mind at least a self-absorbed piece of shit, would not be suspicious and think that he is all too deserving and it was natural that he had finally been recognised.

When it was all said and done on the phone, they were to

set off for basic training at the beginning of next week. Liv told Maddie over dinner that night, where they were to go and what to pack.

The next morning, Maddie was surprised to find Deanne at her doorstep.

"Hey, sweet cheeks," she yawned, letting her into their house.

"Hey, is Liv up? We need to talk."

"Sure," Maddie said, puzzled, before screaming, "LIV!" at the top of her lungs.

Liv yawning, her hair all over the place, just waved at Deanne as she came downstairs.

They all went into the kitchen, and Deanne began to speak. "Dad got an anonymous donation in the mail today."

"A good donation or a bad one?" Maddie asked, concerned.

"Good. Like freakishly, amazingly good. A member of the church bought him a gift, obviously you knew how he took it, but they bought us an around the world cruise!!"

"That's amazing!" they both exclaimed, Liv playing a little dumb to what was going on.

"I know, we leave early hours of Monday morning! But I seized the opportunity and asked Dad if it was okay with you and *your parents* if I could stay until Sunday night! So, I thought I would come over and talk it over with you!"

"I'm not gonna say no," Liv laughed.

Maddie was overjoyed with this idea and Deanne rushed home to collect a few things.

"Do you reckon this is G.U.A.R.D?" Maddie asked her, "weight off my shoulders, but seems a little coincidental."

"Could be," Liv guessed, agreeing with her, "at least it would mean we would be away at the same time. You'll get some quality time after training before Deanne goes to university."

When Deanne returned, they could not continue to speak about G.U.A.R.D, but then again with Deanne there they had no reason. Liv couldn't help but smile as she watched Deanne and Maddie together. They danced around the kitchen with music blaring, and the way they sat together watching movies, it warmed her heart as much as she teased them that they were gross.

It continued this way until Sunday evening, with Deanne leaving the next morning for her cruise and Maddie and Liv, unbeknown to Deanne, leaving to join G.U.A.R.D the next morning as well.

As tears rolled from the eyes of Deanne and Maddie, Liv just rolled her eyes, needing them to get this over with so they could all go and pack.

Both Deanne and Maddie, having had their end of school party the night before, had done absolutely nothing that day, due to their hangovers. When Deanne eventually left, they began to pack. Passports and bag by the front door, they headed for an early night.

Chapter Three:

The driver pulled up at precisely four o'clock in the morning to take them to a private airfield. When the driver, who remained silent the whole time, pulled up, it was to find both Tanith and Carlson waiting for them.

"Welcome to day one in G.U.A.R.D," Tanith said brightly.

"Thanks," Maddie yawned, as Liv just scowled at her.

"You're going to meet your squad members here, you'll become J-Squadron," Carlson explained. "They're already in G.U.A.R.D but not a black ops group, so you'll fit right in, they've only just arrived."

They thanked Carlson, and under his instruction walked over to the cargo plane. They walked up the steps and the plane door slammed behind them.

Within seconds of the plane door slamming shut they were both grabbed in a tight hug.

"Hey, I'm Millie," a voice said from the middle of the hug.

When they were released, they looked down at who had hugged them. The girl was smaller than the two of them, muscular and smiley, her blonde hair tied back in a ponytail. Maddie and Liv introduced themselves to her and she took them further down the plane to introduce them to the others.

"This is my big brother, Pete," she said, indicating one of the men who got up to shake their hands. Maddie thought the only way to describe Pete was 'scary'. He was stocky and grizzled; his brown hair was styled similar to Liv's bright red hair, with one side heavily shaved and swept over to the other side.

"One of us is gonna have to change hairstyles," his face cracked into a smile as he looked at Liv.

She laughed nervously but didn't say anything.

"Hey, I'm Trent! Welcome to the squad," said the man opposite Millie and Pete. Liv looked at Trent and was surprised such a friendly voice came from the six-foot, eight-inch man-mountain with an impressive and impeccably groomed beard and moustache.

They took their seats and strapped themselves in, ready for take-off as they felt the plane taxi to the runway.

"Millie is our language expert, and resident hugger," Trent told them. "Only your age, Liv, and speaks seven languages; English, Japanese, Spanish, Arabic, Mandarin, sign and French," Trent recited.

"Impressive," Maddie said.

"Pete is our technical wizard; give him a laptop and he can topple a government, pilot, mechanic and inventor. All of our weaponry will be designed by Pete."

"Alright, you can get out of my arse now. I'm not that good," Pete laughed from his seat.

"You're the muscle," Maddie said to Trent, "we are underqualified."

Trent was about to reply but had to wait as the plane took off.

"Underqualified," Trent said, beginning to laugh. "You've toppled drug rings, crime organisations and are possibly some of the best hand-to-hand fighters."

"We've seen you fight, it's impressive. Very impressive," Pete said.

"How?"

"CCTV footage," Millie said simply.

"Tanith cramped your style and the changes she did to your fighting style ruined it," Pete said.

"Bitch!" Liv grunted.

"We're going to get on so well," Pete laughed.

"The change in fighting style was because the bitch shot me."

"They used to date," Trent explained.

"Did she use the 'married and killed her husband'

backstory?" Pete asked curiously.

"Yup!"

"yeah, I think that's a subtle dig at me," Pete said.

"Ah, fuck her."

"Go on then, Maddie, Liv. What's your vigilante story? What happened?"

So it began, knowing that the three around them were going to become like family and they needed to trust them, they told everything; how it started, the BoK, their parents. The hit that was placed on them, Tanith shooting Liv, the drug rings and Wrathhog drug, right up to Sam Heenan and G.U.A.R.D intervening.

"We heard about that. You injured a lot of G.U.A.R.D agents! It was impressive," Trent said happily.

"Well they stopped us from bringing down a serial killer, what can you expect?" Maddie said.

"Yeah, I made a stiff horny hangover after that, was an absolute rollercoaster," Liv added.

"Sorry?" Pete said, sitting up, "Horny hangover? Bourbon, Sambuca, Jäger, spiced rum, peach schnapps, amaretto, topped up with Coke?"

"Lemonade?"

"So, she steals my drink and changes the mixer?! Cheeky bitch!" Pete said incredulously.

"In that case, I love and thank you for inventing the drink," Liv said to him.

"We've told our backstory, who is next?" Maddie said.

"Broken home, joined the Army as an escape and then got recruited into G.U.A.R.D after three years," Trent said briskly, "was approached about having my own special operations squad, i.e. everyone here. So now I'm leader and given how young you guys are, I'm now also a part time babysitter."

"Very funny, Trent," Millie said, rolling her eyes.

"Seventeen, seventeen, eighteen," Trent said, laughing. "Hell, even Pete is twenty-one, I'm babysitting all of you!"

"Oi, pipe down, dickhead, you're only three years older than me."

"We must be the youngest squadron?" Liv asked.

"Obviously, hence why we are J-Squadron. J as in Juliet, for the phonetic alphabet."

"Yeah, we're Juliets, which is cool!" Millie said enthusiastically. "Least we aren't like the uniforms or something like that."

"No, we're J-Squadron," Trent said, rolling his eyes.

"Our parents work for G.U.A.R.D.," Millie explained, "they work at G.U.A.R.D. headquarters."

"So, we are the accidents and you're in by design," Maddie laughed.

"You're gonna be hated by the instructors, I literally cannot wait," Pete said.

"Why?"

"Because you're incredible fighters, like different forms of martial arts mixed with a scrappy brawler. Teaching Millie will be easy as they can mould her to their fighting style, you on the other hand are already established hand-to-hand fighters that are gonna need to be improved and not changed; but they cannot mould you, like a teacher who encounters a child who can already think for themselves, you're gonna piss them right off!" he said, a delightful smile across his face.

A little while later, Millie decided that as a bonding experience it would be a good idea to have a game of Monopoly, as she had packed the slightly battered board.

They set up the board and after a lighthearted argument about whether or you could buy on the first trip round the board and whether you could collect in jail, the answer to both was finally agreed that the answer was no.

Pete and Trent, albeit reluctant, eventually agreed to play. Liv was privately thrilled that Millie had suggested this game as it allowed her to feel relaxed, and worked as she intended as a team building experience; as when you're going to be on a plane with people that you don't really know for fifteen hours, you need an icebreaking game of Monopoly.

Maddie decided to stab Liv in back and make a deal with Trent, so Liv and Millie joined forces; meaning that after only three hours Pete sold out and was out of the game. The game lasted for another two hours until Trent's poor decision making meant that he and Maddie lost by him rolling a one when he had to roll anything but.

After that, Millie and Maddie started having a discussion about past and present relationships, both chatting rather animatedly, whilst Pete sat with Liv and Trent as they began to talk more in depth.

"Is she gonna be able to cope this summer away from her girlfriend?" Trent asked Liv, as they watched Maddie and Mille chat.

"I think she will be. They can still text and facetime," Liv replied hopefully, "if not then she's just gonna be dead upset."

"Are they dead in love?" Pete asked.

"Oh yeah! Big time!" Liv grimaced and pretended to throw up.

Liv's actions caused Pete and Trent to laugh.

"How long were you and Tanith together then?" Liv asked Pete.

"About a year, then I found her in bed with someone, so packed my stuff and left. Haven't thought about her for a year until she got embroiled in your mess."

"That's a funny way to say 'shooting me'," Liv said, tugging at the necklace on her neck, pulling it outside of her t-shirt so they could see the bullet which was cleaned and placed on the chain the night Tanith shot her.

"Yeah, she got into so much shit for that," Trent laughed, "when we heard the vigilantes had a bounty put on their heads, we sent her in to attempt to take down the bounty hunters. Next thing G.U.A.R.D. heard she had shot one of the vigilantes and there was a dead cop. She was benched shortly after her last mission with you two. Now she is a pencil pusher."

"Good!" Liv said, rubbing her shoulder absentmindedly.

"So, what happened the night you took down your parents? Like what happened after?" Pete said curiously.

"We went home, got into PJs and waited for the police to

come round and explain to us what had happened. After that Maddie turned eighteen and became my legal guardian; she became the adult and we just kept doing what we do."

"Very mature of both of you," Trent said, impressed, "not many people of any age could go through what you've been through! G.U.A.R.D. have got two winners here. We have two winners."

"Yeah, no rules, nothing. Just us and what we do," Liv shrugged.

"Well, now you're a Juliet, you're gonna have to follow Trent's rules now!" Millie said, laughing.

"No," Trent and Pete groaned.

"What?!" Millie said innocently.

"Don't try to make *Juliets* a thing," Pete said disapprovingly.

"Because J-Squadron is so much cooler," Millie argued.

"Personally, I think It has a nice ring to it," Maddie said, watching Pete for his reaction.

Pete put his head in his hands and sighed deeply, before getting out his headphones, yawning heavily and stretching out as much as possible.

Despite the hours that Monopoly had killed there was still a long way to go before they landed. Trent yawned heavily soon followed by Pete, attempting to catch some sleep, leaving the girls as tired as they were to continue to talk.

Stretching legs and trying to get comfy was easier said than done on a cargo plane which was not built for the comfort of the passengers.

Mille walked over to Trent and moved his tablet off his lap, so that she could lie down and use his lap as a pillow.

"Good idea," Liv said, doing the same thing to the other side of his lap.

As Maddie laughed, Pete removed his headphones to say, "Don't even think of it!"

Laughing, Maddie just sat down, putting her own headphones on as they all took some downtime.

Hours later, whilst they were all awake Liv started to ask questions about what would happen when they landed.

"So, who takes basic training?"

"Choovio 'the wise' and his daughter Tula. Native American family. Choovio has taken basic training for forty years. He isn't one to mess with," Trent said, hiding a yawn.

They were all very grateful when the plane landed. Bodies aching, cramping and hungry, they put on sunglasses and stepped out of the plane into what turned out to be a hot Texan desert sun. As they walked off the runway with their bags on their shoulders, they saw to figures waiting for them.

As they stood in front of them, Liv, Maddie and Trent all had to look up into Choovio's face. Liv would have guessed that he stood at over seven feet tall. He was extraordinarily muscular for a man in his sixties. He stood wearing camouflage trousers and a tight black t-shirt. His facial expression was unfathomable.

He stood looking at them in silence for a few minutes before he let out a harsh laugh, turning away and walking off.

"That means he likes you," a woman said, stepping forward. She looked exactly like her father and they knew this must have been Tula. They were both dressed the same way, although Tula wore a friendlier expression.

She indicated that they should follow them. They followed her to the medical centre.

She introduced them to a doctor called Lyam Lanthier, a doctor from Quebec and she let him take over.

"Okay, everyone. Into your underwear, for height measurements, damage discussion and for documentation," he instructed to J-Squadron before turning and saying to Tula, "Which ones are the vigilantes?"

"Red and Blue."

"Wait, are we stripping like here?" Maddie and Millie asked together.

"Obviously," Lyam said, not looking up from his notes.

Rather awkwardly, they all got unchanged and had their height measured.

"Sorry, Liv, is that a bullet?" Millie said, looking at her necklace, having not seen it on the plane and then noticing her bullet wounds and stab wound.

"Yeah, it's the one the doc dug out of my shoulder," Liv said lightly, as if this was a normal thing for a seventeen-year-old to say. "I don't know where the other bullet went, that one only nicked me and left a bit of a flesh wound. The scar is still very visible."

"Jesus, girl," Trent laughed.

"Maddie is the lucky one, no stab wounds, no bullet wounds."

Millie, after being reprimanded for laughing, was finally measured at five foot four inches, and was dismissed by Dr. Lanthier.

"Titch!" Pete shot at her, after he was measured at five foot six inches.

"You're both titches!" Maddie said, when she was measure at six foot three inches.

"Yeah, it's true," Liv agreed, sticking her tongue out as Dr. Lanthier measured her at six foot one.

"Shut up, I own all of you!" Trent said, as the doctor noted down his six foot six inches of what was probably all muscle.

"Tula, I'll get these measurements and exact feet sizes, chest sizes over to the barracks clothing. Get everything made up for them, they'll have them as soon as possible."

"Thank you, Doctor," Tula said, as she waited on them to get changed.

Trent's stomach let out an almighty grumble that caused Millie to jump and Liv to laugh. Tula gratefully announced that they were about to head to the mess hall and get some breakfast.

They plated their food and sat down together. Liv, Maddie and Trent were shocked and surprised at just how fast Millie ate her food; by the time everyone else had taken a few bites of their food, Millie had shovelled her food into her mouth at lightning speed with one arm wrapped around her plate as if she was shielding it.

"Jesus Christ, Millie, did you actually eat any of that or did you just inhale it?" Trent asked, his jaw dropping dramatically.

Millie laughed, "I learnt at a young age, eat fast and protect your plate otherwise some prick would come over and just take your food before you could eat it," she explained, glaring daggers at Pete.

"I was a hungry and growing lad," Pete said, unabashed.

When they had all eaten, Tula came over and told them it was time for a basic fitness assessment, so her and Choovio could see their levels before training fully started tomorrow.

Yawning and stretching, they were taken to one of the gyms on base and put through their paces.

Not that Tula and Choovio showed it, but Liv and Maddie were sure they were impressed by their cardio abilities. They were outstripping Trent, Millie and Pete.

"How are you two so unphased?" Millie asked, panting as Choovio raised their altitude and speed for them.

"We ran around a city every night for months, our cardio levels improved over time and practice," Maddie said proudly.

"Not bad," Choovio said in a deep, low voice.

Liv and Maddie smiled at each other as they continued to run. They ran for another fifteen minutes before they eventually stopped and moved onto weight training, seeing what exactly they could and couldn't lift with strength assertation.

Trent and Pete, being the most muscular, were in their element here.

Everybody was sweaty and exhausted after Tula and Choovio put them through their paces. They stood in the middle of the gym in front of Tula and Choovio.

"None of you can fight," Choovio said. "How bad you are is up to us to find out."

"Tag teaming is pathetic," Tula said, looking and Maddie and Liv.

"Let's see how you can get on in one-on-one fighting. We will do offensive then do defensive."

"Liv," Choovio said, beckoning her forward.

"You're on the offensive, try to take my father down like you would a robber, only instead of breaking bones or unconscious, try submitting or pinning the shoulders."

Everyone gave them some space and watched carefully.

Choovio stood with his hands by his sides as Liv walked towards him. As she got close, she threw a cautionary right hand which he blocked. With a flurry of fists, which he blocked, Liv smiled, just waiting. She threw a high fist before going for a leg sweep. She put her leg in one of his, causing him to interlock his leg. She threw a punch into his gut and put all of her weight onto Choovio's knee pushing it back, the way it definitely shouldn't bend. Using her weight for leverage she slammed him forward, landing on her back. Liv sprang across onto his back, wrapping one of his arms around his own neck and back. She wrapped one leg around his neck as she placed one knee on his upper back, wrenching the torque on his shoulder, waiting to see if he turned blue which he certainly was. With his other hand he tapped a few times on the ground and Liv released the arm lock and released her leg from around his neck.

As he got to his feet he grunted, "Basic. Millie."

Liv growled as Millie stepped forward. Millie took a very different approach. Whilst Liv measured the strength of her opposition, Millie ran full speed at Choovio, kneed him in the gut; before he could react, she lifted as much as she could before attempting to drop him on his back.

He dropped to his knee but even then, Millie was only slightly bigger than him. He grabbed her head and, flipping her over he pinned her shoulders for three seconds and then got up and moved away.

"Poor. Pete," he said, looking unimpressed.

Pete snarled as he walked forward.

As they watched Pete and Choovio, Liv whispered that this was 'fucking bullshit' to Millie who simply nodded in agreement. As Pete attempted to wrap the ankle around his arm, he attempted to snap it until he tapped again.

"Pathetic. Trent," Choovio grunted.

"I loosened him up for you," Millie said to him bitterly.

"Of course, you did, sis," Pete said, giving her shoulder a squeeze.

After Liv and Pete had both aimed for the leg, Trent did the same. Using his size and power he lifted and dropped him onto the floor, before jumping onto his leg and simply placing a foot on his throat.

"Maddie," Choovio said, as Trent helped him up.

Maddie decided to take what could only be called a brave approach, hitting a running drop kick on Choovio before he was fully ready. She wrapped her body around his arm, wrenching it, before he picked her up using his entire body, dropping her to the floor and pinning the shoulders.

"All of you, terrible. We have a lot of work to do," he said, as he dismissed Maddie.

Liv snarled so audibly that Choovio looked at her.

"You disagree?" he asked her.

Before Trent could cautiously advise Liv to keep her mouth shut, she said, "Yeah, when we fight it is with one aim, you knock them down and they stay down. We don't go for arm bars or ankle locks or sleeper holds. That's why some of us lost. We break or we KO. What we do - you snap or you make them nap, no need to make them tap."

"You wear knuckledusters. I've seen the footage."

"That's only to even the odds, they carry guns and knives," she snarled.

"Try and KO me," he said calmly.

However, as she took a step forward, so did Trent and he put a hand on her shoulder, squeezing it as he said, "If you've seen the footage then you will have seen what Maddie and Liv did to G.U.A.R.D. agents.

Agents that you trained. Add to her arsenal but don't dismiss it and KO'ing her would not help anyone."

Choovio glared at him, before snorting. As he turned to leave he said to Tula, "At least the leader has a brain."

He walked out, leaving Tula in front of them, "I'm to take you to where you're going to be staying," she explained.

They followed her, Trent whispering encouragement to

Liv who was still seething, trying to ensure that she did not fully blow up.

Liv nodded at his words but did not calm down. Her thoughts were too furious for her to notice where they were walking. Maddie and Millie chatted light-heartedly.

"So, we aren't staying in barracks then?" Trent said to Tula.

"No."

"That is a house," Millie said, causing Liv to snap out of her bad mood.

"We thought a house would be better for team building and morale; eat together, work together, live together."

"Is there a shop on the base?" Millie asked Tula.

"Map of the base is in the kitchen," she said, before bidding them a good day.

They entered the house and all quietly sat down to rest. Given the fact that the fridge was completely empty, it was with great effort that Liv and Millie went to the local shop on base to get as much food as the shop had and that they could carry.

The two girls walked through the base keeping their eyes averted but chatted merrily. Millie spoke about what she knew about G.U.A.R.D. having grown up with connections and knowledge of the organisation. Liv admitted that seeing G.U.A.R.D. agents in their normal lives was intimidating, as opposed to seeing them in uniform.

Mille had to remind Liv that she was more dangerous than most of them and was dressed in sweatpants and a crop top and not crime fighting gear. Millie also had to remind Liv that there was more to G.U.A.R.D. than just black ops, and a lot of G.U.A.R.D. agents were 'political nerds and science geeks'.

This actually calmed Liv down a lot and as she let out a sigh of relief she asked, "Do you always know the right thing to say?"

"Not to brag, but yeah, essentially that is my thing!" Millie laughed.

"I'm still annoyed that they refused to sell us booze, we will need to send one of the boys to buy it."

"Outrageous, that being underage means that they won't sell us alcohol?! I am shocked and outraged."

When they returned home, they all knew that in an attempt to defeat jetlag they would need to go to bed at a reasonable time. So they all fought and argued about what to watch on the TV that was in the house, in order to keep them awake till a reasonable time where they could all go off to sleep before a gruelling day tomorrow.

***

They showered, got into their gym kits and met Choovio and Tula at seven-thirty that morning.

Choovio took them to an empty area of an aircraft hangar where there was nothing around them but a single steel ladder.

"This," he said in his gruff voice, looking at all of them as if they had each done him an awful personal disservice, "is a trust exercise; you must be as one, have each other's back. Constantly. Always."

One by one they were instructed to climb the ladder, put on a blindfold at the top of the ladder and fall backwards into the arms of the rest of J-Squadron waiting below.

Every single one of them hesitated at the top of the ladder except for Liv, who often used her body as a weapon and was just glad that someone would be there to catch her. Pete took the longest pause, but finally fell and was caught by the rest of the group.

Choovio then ordered them to go again, and then again, and again, and again every time one of them hesitated, the whole group had to go again until they had each been three times and not hesitated.

Choovio was, as to be expected, unimpressed, and directed them towards the next task. Tula paired Trent with Millie, Pete with Liv, and Maddie would be working with her. Trent's words yesterday about adding to the skills they already had, may have sunk in with Choovio and Tula, as they began working on mixed martial arts to add and enhance, to close combat fighting techniques as opposed to the brawler fist fighting style of Liv and Maddie.

When in their pairs, they watched Tula who, with Maddie, went through a demonstration and then they copied taking it in turns. All of them being fairly proficient in some martial arts, took to it quickly.

She put them through holds, submissions, throws and taught them how to tweak the moves so they could be used to either tap an opponent out or snap their limbs.

Although, the conditions did not make it any easier, she put them through all of this under the gruelling sun; refusing them water breaks until Millie was close to passing out and Trent was retching in the sand, close to throwing up.

Regardless of how Pete felt he was not letting it show. Sweat running off his brow, he tore off his t-shirt, using it to towel some of his sweat and then put it through the loop on his belt, sipping his water sparingly.

Seeing this, Tula took his t-shirt from his belt loop and threw it into his face, before saying, "If you want to tan and be topless do it by the pool in your house, put your top back on now."

When Tula turned her back, Pete rolled his eyes at Liv, making her giggle.

"That is another reason for you to keep your top on," Tula said, turning back around, misinterpreting the giggling at Pete's physique for his eye roll.

"In Pete's defence I will eye up everyone in J-Squad, blood sister excluded, so I can say that everyone is yummy," Liv smirked, winking at Millie who snorted whilst drinking water and began to choke. Trent sprayed water down his front, laughing.

"Enough of the cheek," Tula snapped, "now, all of you go home, shower, change and meet me at the range."

As they walked, and they were out of earshot of Tula and Choovio, Trent clapped Millie and Liv on the shoulders as he congratulated all of them on how well they had done this morning, as praise and positive reinforcement was not something that Choovio and Tula seemed capable of giving.

In a positive mood, they later set off for the gun range, in fresh gear and suitably re-hydrated.

"This part is surely gonna be a breeze for you, isn't it?" Maddie asked Trent, thinking about his past in the military.

"I was never the best shot, but better than most," he shrugged modestly.

"That reminds me," Pete said, beginning to laugh, "did Tanith, show you those bedazzled guns?"

"Oh yeah, with the fake jewels."

"Oh, no they were actually real, but they were stolen from an African warlord that was stopped from carrying out a genocide, but it is actually tragic that she carried diamond encrusted pistols."

As they walked, Trent began to double check that Liv, Millie and Maddie had eaten enough and they were suitably hydrated. Once they insisted that they were fine, he allowed them to walk to the gun range.

That afternoon was spent assembling and disassembling various firearms. Once they got good with one weapon, they were then instructed to do it blindfolded.

Once the weapons were assembled, it was then shooting practice. This was taken by Tula, unaccompanied by her father which meant it could only be described as a rather enjoyable afternoon.

It became clear to Maddie and Liv that this would be the area that they would need to work hardest, so that they would be on the same levels as the rest of J-Squadron.

"Millie and Liv, stay behind. The rest of you can head back to your house," Tula instructed at the end of the training.

"Why?" Millie and Pete said automatically, Pete glaring at Tula suspiciously.

"It's nothing bad," she said exasperatedly, "I just need to discuss finalising their driving lessons and their licenses. Once you have your full licenses, then as a team you can take motorbike, truck, lorry and tank tests."

"Okay," Trent said, taking Maddie and Pete outside after pushing Millie towards Tula, as they were all rather suspicious of Tula at this stage. Pete, for all his silent and gruff exterior, was very unwilling to leave Millie alone with Tula.

"I'll be giving both of you driving lessons this evening, we have an onsite qualified driving instructor who will be allowing you to take your tests."

"So, by the end of this we will have licences and will be able to buy any vehicle we wish?" Liv asked, her eyes lighting up.

"Yes, hypothetically...Why?" Tula said.

"I can buy a Harley!" Liv said, a grin spreading over her face.

"I mean, yes, but we would also prefer you to have a car as well, for safety reasons. I'll see you in two hours' time."

They returned home and Liv, Maddie and Millie were all in for a treat, as they were all about to experience the wonder that was Trent's cooking. Whilst he worked his magic in the kitchen, the others decided to take advantage of the summer sun and decided to lounge out the back.

Whilst they were out there, they discovered that underneath the patio there was a pool. Fully heated outdoor pool.

"How the piss did we not realise there was a pool?" Pete asked, as he dipped a toe in to test the water.

"Get ya bikinis on, Pete, tea is gonna be hours," Trent said, coming out.

"Hours?!" Maddie groaned.

"Slow cooked chilli has to be slow cooked; it'll be done for when these two come back from their driving lessons, but I've made a platter of sandwiches for now," he said.

With them all in their swimming gear, they had an enjoyable game of water football and water American football in the pool. Begrudgingly Millie and Liv got out of the pool, showered and changed before heading off to meet Tula, and to their dismay, Choovio, for their driving lessons.

Liv was paired with Choovio, and Millie was paired with

Tula. Choovio's instructions consisted of mostly grunts and three-word sentences. Nevertheless, after a productive driving lesson they returned to a mountain of chilli and rice, all beautifully prepared by Trent. After an hour, they returned to the poolside and with Millie connecting her phone up to a set of speakers and they had an enjoyable night.

"I don't know if it is the absence of parents for so long," Maddie began, before Liv finished her sentence.

"But this might actually work out as a new family," Liv finished, smiling at her.

They all headed to bed relatively early, knowing that tomorrow would be another demanding day.

However, if they thought the day before was brutal, they were incorrect. Under the sun, they were pushed ~~them~~ to their limits and beyond; no rest, and if they fell down, they were told to get back up again. Choovio was yelling at them, and in their exhausted state, Millie was close to tears.

Taking a 10 minute break, Trent told them that he suspected that the aim was to push them to their limits so they could see where their limits were, and also so that it would create unity between them, as much as he didn't approve of their methods.

Nonetheless, they had to deal with it. However, spite was

an excellent motivator and motivation was exactly what they needed. Despite it being Maddie and Liv's weakest area, they were improving as quickly as they could, something they were finding difficult with Choovio's unrelenting criticism every time they fired their weapons.

It was with no surprise that when they got home morale was low and Trent knew he had his work cut out for him to raise everyone's confidence. He tried his best to raise their self-esteem before Liv and Millie had their driving lessons. He understood that no matter how bad the day was, if they went to bed happy then they would be okay for the next day. He wasn't entirely sure that he would succeed in this task, but nonetheless as the leader of J-Squadron and dad of the group it was a responsibility that fell on his shoulder.

Full stomachs helped massively in making them all feel better as did him power-bombing Pete off the poolside into the pool. He also made Millie the DJ and instructed her to put music on before they left for their driving lesson, and when they all went to bed that night, Trent thought that he may have succeeded in his task somewhat before it all started again tomorrow.

The next day was just as tough as the previous two, with the only upside being that when it came to the gun range portion of the day there was a noticeable improvement on the part of Maddie and Liv. Instead of going straight to the pool after they finished for the day Pete napped on the sofa, exhaustion finally getting the best of him.

"Everyone who is awake get in, Trent get driving, you loser," Millie said to them, flinging the car keys at Trent.

"Why? Where are we going?" he groaned.

"Town."

"It is a thirty-minute drive."

He grumbled and groaned but reluctantly got into the driver's seat.

"I have decided," Millie said, "that all we have is Monopoly, which is time consuming, or a pool, which is energy consuming. So, we are going to buy a games console with a load of single and multiplayer games."

"Good idea," Maddie said from the front seat, plugging her phone into the aux cord, "I forgot to pack my knitting needles and wool from home, so I need to pick them up as well."

"You knit?" Millie asked her, surprised.

"Yeah I started doing it as it was something for my hands to do to keep me busy and focused when I wasn't on patrol."

"I like it," Trent said approvingly,

Maddie and Millie then proceeded to irritate Trent by playing a sing-along playlist at high volume for the proceeding drive.

For Trent it was then a blessed release when they pulled up at the shop.

They had an enjoyable time going through the giant store, picking out games and a console.

They were doing the software update on the game when Pete awoke and noticed that they had left and come back in the time in which he was asleep; he was happy with the idea, until he found out that it was Millie's idea, he then decided to call it dumb.

This became their routine over the next couple of days with the driving lessons becoming shorter as Millie and Maddie improved.

The MMA training also became shorter as Tula became impressed with them, and Choovio grunted less and less.

Tactical weapons training became their main focus after they were satisfied with the hand-to-hand combat nature of the training. They started as they normally did, building the weapons fully, loading them and then walking over to the targets, placing the weapon down then returning to the table to build the next one.

"You actually look competent," Tula mused as she

watched over them.

"A very gracious comment," Trent muttered.

"On Monday, however, training begins. You will be putting it all into practice, going against G.U.A.R.D. agents in different training exercises, using high powered paintball guns. They'll feel like being shot."

"I doubt that," Liv blurted out before she could stop herself.

"Yes, Liv," Tula said, through gritted teeth. "You've been shot, we get it."

None of the others could resist smirking at quite how annoyed Tula and Choovio were looking.

"So, rest up this weekend, or it'll only be worse for you. Dismissed," she finished, through gritted teeth.

"She hates that you've been shot," Trent laughed, clapping her shoulder. He inadvertently clapped her on the shoulder that she got shot in, causing her to elbow him in the gut.

"Have either of them been on missions?" Maddie asked the group.

"Choovio has, I know that much," Pete shrugged.

"Rumour has it, he retired when a mission went south

and he missed Tula's sixth birthday," Millie added.

"He refused for Tula to join any special forces or combat squad, so she became an instructor. Most don't like her but her methods are affective," Pete finished.

"So, pool party?" Millie enquired.

They all consented and Millie, Liv and Maddie instructed Trent to go and buy some alcohol for them.

"Fine, but Tula will literally disembowel us if we are hungover on Monday."

"Two-day hangovers aren't a thing," Millie laughed.

"Wait till you're my age," he muttered.

"She will be waiting till she is the legal age, before she ever drinks," Pete said, pushing Millie.

As Millie began to protest, calling him an over-bearing brother and every swear word she could think off, Pete just casually winked at them.

"As Liv's guardian I give her permission to drink, but as Pete is looking after you, Millie, you have to respect his wishes," Maddie said, in a motherly and worried voice.

"As the leader of J-Squadron, I cannot condone you drinking," Trent said, sternly.

Millie let out an irate scream and stomped her feet, angry at all of them until Liv picked her up and put her over her shoulder. Millie protested all the way home until they all burst out laughing at how annoyed she was. Pete doubled over, clutching a stitch in his side.

The evening sun, a BBQ and music all whilst poolside was exactly what they needed after what was a long and brutal week. Millie and Liv threw an American football to each other as they stood at the either end of the pool. Maddie helped Trent with the BBQ whenever he needed it and mostly sat with her knitting needles in her hands drumming along to the music and ever so occasionally knitting a crop top. It struck Maddie how strange it was that although they had only been together a short space of time, just how close they were to each other.

"Mads," Pete called, from one of the chairs by the pool, "Deanne is calling you," holding up her phone.

She yelled gleefully and ran over to take the phone call.

"It's quite sweet," Millie shouted, "how cute they are together."

"Yeah," Liv said, "I remember the time we beat the crap out of her brother," she laughed.

"You did what now?" Pete said getting off the chair and walking over to her. Trent also came over to listen to this story.

"We've told this story, haven't we?"

"No! But now you have to," Millie said, coming around so they could hear the story.

Liv regaled them with the story about how and why she and Maddie, with Deanne and Robyn in tow, went around to Deanne's house, beat up her brother and the ensuing argument between them, their parents and Deanne's father.

"I approve," Pete said, when Liv finished the story.

"Metal as fuck," Trent said, smiling.

"What's everyone laughing at?" Maddie said, coming back outside and sitting by the pool edge.

"Liv was just telling us about you two beating the crap out of Deanne's big brother," Trent said, pushing her into the pool.

After spluttering and inhaling a lot of pool water she said, "That seems as if it were a lifetime ago."

"If someone had told you then, that you would be here now, you probably would have told them they were insane," Trent added.

"How is her cruise going?" Millie said, seemingly interested in how it was going, as opposed to just the story.

Millie and Maddie chatted whilst Pete took over Millie's role with the American Football until Trent said everything was cooked.

As they all sat down and began tucking into the mountain of food, Trent raised a potentially problematic question. "Where did you tell Deanne that you were?"

"Government job had sent me to the U.S. for seminars and training, just landed and how boring it was going to be," Maddie shrugged.

"It is only stretching the truth I suppose, are you okay with that though?"

"Not a lot that I can do about it really."

Looking at Maddie sat next to him and seeing the sadness in her eyes, Trent gave her a squeezing hug.

"Liv, come try this drink," Pete shouted from the kitchen.

"What is it?" Liv replied cautiously.

"Miss Lynch's Bexploding Drink Of Fire."

"What is in a Miss Lynch's Bexploding Drink Of Fire?"

"Tequila, rum, a lot of fire whiskey, ginger ale or cola. Served with a cinnamon stick."

Liv took one of the glasses Pete offered and raising her

eyebrow took a sip.

"Not too bad actually! I was sceptical but no, it is quite nice!"

Pete smiled proudly as they clinked glasses.

After they had eaten as much as they could and the swimming costumes and shorts felt particularly tight, they retreated inside for an evening on the consoles. This continued for the rest of the weekend, their muscles aching too much for them to actually do anything else over the course of the weekend.

Muscles tender and yawning widely, they met Tula at five o'clock on Monday morning, ready for whatever she was going to throw at them.

They assembled their weapons and waited for Tula to speak.

"In the top of that building," she said, pointing in the distance where there was an eleven-storey building, "is a teddy bear called Abbey. Abbey is being held hostage, she is cute and adorable and needs rescuing. Enter, engage, save the bear and get to the extraction point. When you hear the air horn, you're free to begin."

As she walked away, Trent beckoned them into a huddle.

"We go in compact and fast. Millie and Pete go in low,

Maddie and Liv you go high and you all follow my lead. We most certainly will be outnumbered, so gotta be quick, play dirty if we have to, double shoot and don't take unnecessary risks."

"Why did you look at me when you said don't take unnecessary risks?" Liv scowled pettily.

"Let's do this, J-Squadron," Trent said.

"Go Juliets," Millie said.

"Go Juliets," Maddie and Liv said together as Trent and Pete rolled their eyes.

When the airhorn sounded Trent said simply, "It's time."

They ran together, and got to the front door of the building.

Trent signalled for Maddie to pick the lock, which she did, and they entered the building as a team. They cleared the first floor with no sign of anyone. They entered the stairwell to the second floor. On the second floor they were immediately called into action as one of the balaclava-wearing assailants was hit four times in the chest by Trent, Millie, Maddie and Liv.

Pete hung back before they covered him going forward. As he moved forward, he shot someone who jumped out at him once in the chest and then again in the throat.

There were three assailants on the third floor, four on the fourth floor, five on the fifth floor.

Whether this was to lull them into a false sense of security by making it predictable, they didn't know. But as they proceeded it made Liv nervous, her finger shook on the trigger expecting all hell to break lose.

Hell did indeed break lose on the seventh floor as they quickly got pinned down by a shower of paint bullets.

Liv signalled for them to cover her with heavy fire, as she ran sliding feet first into the legs of one of the gunmen. As they fell, she fired three shots into them before throwing the butt of her gun into the ribs of another, as Trent shot them three times in the head.

They regrouped and on Trent's signal they re-joined the firefight and swiftly moved upwards.

Out of breath and paint guns reloaded, they were ready to enter the eleventh floor. Cursing all office buildings, they readied themselves for Trent's signal.

They entered the floor and began searching for Abbey the bear; they saw her in the last office, with multiple blind spots between them and their target.

They waited like it was a game of chicken; the Juliets and the instructors waiting to see who would make the first move, who would go on to offence and who would go on the counter-attack. Liv and Maddie were ready to attack first, but Trent kept them in their positions, forbidding them from doing it.

The instructors made the first move. A figure resembling Choovio turned the corner and began opening fire in an attempt to make them draw back in retreat or to just keep them where they were. As he opened fire, Tula and one other person began creeping forward, attempting to get a shot away.

Maddie snuck around one of the part-partitions, and as Tula turned the corner to see if anyone had done exactly that, Maddie connected with Tula's jaw as she swung a vicious roundhouse kick. Tula staggered just enough to fire seven shots into Tula's torso.

Trent managed to shoot the unknown assailant, and they congregated on Choovio's location.

Upon seeing them he moved back into the office where Abbey the bear was seated. He picked up the bear and held it in front of him as a human shield. After a brief non-verbal discussion Trent, Maddie, Millie and Pete moved forward.

"Shoot me, I shoot the bear," he breathed.

"I don't think so," Liv said from above. As Choovio looked up, Liv fired four shots into his head from the ceiling panel that she had quietly just removed. The initial surprise caused Choovio to change his stance, giving Trent the opportunity to shoot him in both kneecaps.

As Choovio released the bear having to now pretend to be dead, Trent secured the hostage and Liv awkwardly jumped down from the ceiling.

"If you're gonna do it, *Die hard* it!" She said, smugly high-fiving Millie.

"Didn't expect you to get this far, congratulations," Tula said through a clenched jaw, "but fuck me, Maddie, I think you broke my jaw!"

"You said to be realistic in our approach," Maddie shrugged, shooting a wink at Trent when nobody was looking.

"The shot to the knee?" Choovio ask Trent, rubbing his knee tenderly.

"Just to be safe."

"Liv, that was impressive, I didn't see you go into the ceiling and I didn't even hear you remove the panel above me," Choovio said, turning his attention to her.

"Don't feel bad, we use the shadows to our advantage, thinking outside the box. It is kinda our thing," Liv said, as she walked round to where Trent was stood next to Abbey they bear.

"Phase one complete," Choovio scowled. "Now, escape with the hostage alive. On the airhorn."

"Well done, Juliets!" Millie said enthusiastically. "Same again."

"J-Squadron," Choovio and Tula snarled together.

When they were alone in the office, Trent began giving his orders. "I will take the hostage. Maddie and Millie, Millie from behind, Maddie from in front. Liv and Pete, you lead and we follow in a one-one-one-two formation."

"Agreed."

"Let's do this, Juliets - I mean J-Squadron."

"OH MY GOD?!?! IT'S OFFICAL! OUR LEADER SAID IT!" Millie squealed.

"Focus. On. The. Task. At. Hand," Trent said, rolling his eyes at Pete.

The airhorn sounded and they were off again.

Going downstairs was considerably easier than going up. They had the advantage, in terms of seeing and hearing people entering the building, to stop them from leaving with Abbey the bear still alive.

By the time they had reached the third floor they had neutralised twelve people. They opened the door to the stairwell only to have paint fly past them in multiple colours, indicating multiple shooters.

"Back up," Pete mouthed to Liv.

As more and more people began charging up the stairwell, paint ammunition low, they began racking their brains for ideas.

"Flip and dick with a two-man follow up?" Liv asked Trent.

"I don't know what that is, but sure, we need something," he responded.

Maddie ran to the door and got down on all fours. Liv then proceeded to run at full speed, using Maddie's back as a springboard. She jumped, flying over the banister onto the crowd of people who were about to come up the stairs.

As Liv landed on all of them, Pete and Maddie came rushing down, firing shots into every single one of them as Liv's momentum carried her painfully down the stairs, she readjusted and began firing.

They made it into the clear and, sprinting back in the original formation, they made it into the extraction zone. Where they started that morning; Abbey the bear without any pain on her, meaning that for the purposes of the exercise she was very much alive.

They sat on the asphalt and waited for Choovio and Tula

to come over to them.

"You successfully completed the mission," Choovio said, looking down at all of those who were sat there. "Despite that bollocks you pulled in the stairwell, Liv. Trent, disappointed you allowed it, you should have thought of something else."

"Oh, fuck off," Liv snarled. "In a real situation a grenade would have cleared the stairwell, so failing that, we improvised and changed the rules so BACK. THE. FUCK. UP."

"Excuse me?"

"You heard my very valid point," Liv responded, getting to her feet.

Choovio walked forward, looking furious. He kept walking past where Pete and Millie were sat as if he was about to get in Liv's face but instead was met by Trent who sprang to his feet and got in between them, his face inches away from Choovio's.

"Specify the rules or we will make our own. Two tasks, two completed tasks. Now back up and stop being bitter that we've won. If you have an issue with my team, then you come to me and it is my responsibility to deal with it. Until then you stop being a bullying twat."

"Or what? I will teach in any way I see fit. Don't let your

ego get the better of you, I could snap the two of you so bad you would wish you were in a coma."

"Fucking try it," Liv snarled from behind Trent, Pete now physically restraining her from launching herself from around Trent at Choovio. "Nothing but a washed-up prick."

Choovio pushed Trent out of the way as Liv shook off Pete's grip, before a punch was thrown. However, Maddie and Millie had gotten in between them and Tula had broken it apart.

"ENOUGH!" she bellowed. "WE ARE DOING THAT EXERCISE AGAIN."

"Why?" Millie groaned.

"Maddie and Liv's stairwell action counts as a fail, use your actual weapons as weapons and you won't have to resort to using your body as a weapon."

"Our bodies are weapons. I thought that was the whole part of MMA training, constant hand-to-hand combat," Maddie growled.

"Well they have to be weapons because they are shit shields," Liv added, Millie and Trent still with precautionary hands on Liv to stop her jumping at them.

"Listen for the air horn. We won't tell you where the bear is," Tula said, snatching Abbey off the floor and marching towards the building.

"Take a seat," Trent ordered them, handing out bottles of water from the cooler, before he got an extra bottle and poured it over Liv's head. "We all need to cool off. They are trying to get under our skin and break us, we will not let that happen. We cannot let that happen."

"Here, here," Pete said, splashing water over his face.

They had a breather as Trent tried to get them to see sense.

"What is the plan for this engagement?" Millie asked him.

"Don't fix what isn't broken, but be warned they will do everything and anything to ensure we fail."

They reloaded and grabbed as much ammunition as they could and waited for the air horn. When it sounded, they entered the building, however as they entered the first floor, they found thirty people waiting for them, and as a result they got pepper sprayed in paint.

"That was payback for winning," Tula said.

When they got to their feet, she ordered them back outside.

"Arseholes," Pete muttered, as he attempted to wipe paint off himself.

Their next exercise, which turned to be another hostage exercise but in pairs instead of as a team, they all rotated who they worked with.

As Trent and Liv completed the final rotation, they collapsed in the extraction zone as Maddie and Millie handed them water, discussing how desperate they all were for sleep, when Tula informed them that they would have a night mission that night.

Trent shipped them all off to bed for naps before they were made to get up again.

When their alarms went off later that night, nobody was in much of a mood to get dressed again and nobody was talkative as they walked to meet Tula.

Liv and Maddie were used to working at night and without light found it strange to actually have the technology such as night-vision goggles. However, when using the equipment, they found it a lot easier than just squinting into the darkness.

Tula finally released them to bed at four o'clock in the morning and just before they were out of earshot, she told them that they were to meet again in just three hours.

When they met three hours later their bodies were practically screaming for more sleep, and Millie was close to literally screaming when Tula and Choovio announced they were about to put them through a ruthless physical workout.

It took ten minutes for Millie to drop to a knee and wheeze, "I can't."

"Excuse me?" Choovio said, walking towards her.

"My body is exhausted, I am exhausted. I need a rest; do you know how many miles we covered yesterday?"

"We are all exhausted," Trent said.

"Back off," Pete growled as Choovio was still walking towards Millie.

"Okay," Choovio said, looking at them all, "knowing your limits is important, go and rest, we will see you tomorrow."

Completely stunned, they left the gym before they could change their mind and they headed home for a much-needed sleep. Trent woke up at six o'clock that evening, made dinner for them all and then went back to bed.

Maddie woke up shortly after. Whilst she was eating, she made a mental note of asking Trent to write down some of his recipes, but needed to go back to bed before she made anything herself. Millie, woke up due to an exhaustion-related nightmare, only to go in with Liv to calm down and fall back asleep.

"I don't know how we will manage months more of this," Millie yawned, as they got dressed the next morning ready for more tactical training.

Before the tactical training, Pete had to drop off some blueprint for weapons at the armoury on base.

"Why did you need to drop off so many, weren't they all identical?" Liv asked him.

He laughed. "Each member of J-Squad will carry between eight and twelve of those identical rods on all missions. Those black metal, twelve-inch rods are our most valuable weapons, inside them will have battle axes, knives, Bo Staffs, grappling hooks, first aid equipment, nunchakus. You can never rely on ammunition and guns alone. Whatever happens we need to be prepared, and we are prepared together."

"Together," Trent repeated simply, clapping Pete on the shoulder, "we move, we rest, we cope as a unit."

"Damn right we will," Maddie said.

"Because that is what Juliets do," Liv said.

Whatever they were expecting Tula to say they were doing that morning, when she said the words 'sky diving' they were convinced they had misheard her.

She taught them how to pack a parachute, and they practised how to land safely before they got into sky diving gear and she directed them towards a plane.

"Unfortunately, Pete, you will be jumping and not flying today," Tula laughed.

Maddie and Liv were comforted by the fact that nobody else seemed especially thrilled with the idea of sky diving by themselves and they weren't alone in feeling queasy.

They boarded the plane and, knees trembling, they mentally readied themselves for their first jump. Trent gripped Millie's shoulder and Maddie's leg as they trembled on either side of him. Liv, disregarding everything, stood up and began to pace as much as she could. Not knowing what to do, she punched Pete in the arm and he responded with a playful punch back, although out of all of them he seemed least fazed.

When they were signalled by the G.U.A.R.D. agent that it was time to jump, they joined Liv who was already on her feet, set the calculation for the jump and waited.

Millie's trembling hand took Liv's as Pete clasped her other hand. They braced themselves for what they were about to do.

They followed Trent and took the plunge.

Adrenaline and exhilaration took over, any pre-emptive emotions that they felt before left them faster than how they felt they were currently plummeting.

Thanks to G.U.A.R.D. technology, all they needed to do was keep an eye on their watches and wait for it to tell them when to pull their parachutes. Remembering to take wind speed and direction into consideration, they pulled their chutes and landed safely in the drop zone.

When they finally hit the ground, they did nothing but begin to laugh. What they were worried about they could not remember.

It took them a while to get to their feet. They removed their parachutes and began waiting for their next instructions.

"Now you've successfully landed, time to unsuccessfully land. Landing safely means that you're detectable by radar. On the next jump you will have to leave it as late as possible to jump so that you are not detectable by our equipment."

"Just no pleasing some people," Millie laughed.

"Were you expecting anything less at this point?" Trent asked, eyebrow raised.

"True," they all agreed.

"Up and at 'em, Juli- J-Squad," Trent said.

"He was about to say it," Maddie whispered to Liv and Millie.

As they sat in the plane again Trent began discussing the plan, and it was a plan that made Maddie, Millie and Liv a lot calmer. "Everyone pull up on my signal, if it's too high then I get a bollocking, if it is too low, then again it is my fault. Follow my lead."

They followed his lead and jumped. There was no fear in this jump, a fear in landing certainly but no hesitation in leaping from the plane. This landing was a lot rougher due to the less time but they all landed safely.

Safe enough, and apparently well enough, as Tula put her hands together enough times for it to potentially constitute clapping. "Impressive work, Trent."

"Are we jumping again?" Millie said excitedly.

"No, you're heading to the gun range. You have two hours of shooting practice then all but Liv and Millie are free to go."

"What have we done?" Liv questioned suspiciously.

"Nothing, but you're taking your driving tests in the morning and your motorbike tests tomorrow afternoon."

By sunset the next day both Liv and Millie clutched their new driving licenses, very proud of themselves.

"Time to buy a Harley, time to buy a Harley, time to buy a Harley, time to buy a Harley," Liv chanted around the kitchen as she helped Trent with his cooking.

"G.U.A.R.D. rules dictate that you have to have a car as well," he reminded her.

"I know, I know," Liv huffed.

"Make sure she buys a helmet and some protective gear," Maddie shouted in from outside.

"Don't worry," he called back.

"Don't you walk to school?" Millie asked Liv as she entered the kitchen.

"Yeah, so?"

"So, why would you need a bike? You and Maddie go most places in the car together, don't you?"

"Yeah, but it is a Harley?!" Liv said, as if this was the most obvious thing in the world. "Also, as I won't be walking with Maddie, then I might as well ride it to school."

"I'm with Liv on this one, I'll come with you. We can buy them together." Trent smiled, "I've always wanted one, now is the perfect time to do so."

On their next free day, Trent and Liv set up a playlist and with a bag full of sweets in the cup holder between them, they set off on what was a four-hour drive to an exclusive Harley Davidson dealership.

When they got there the pair fell in love with every single

bike they looked at. They walked round the showroom, trying to find the perfect match; the perfect motorbike. After a painstaking decision, Trent finally fell in love with a *Fatboy* whilst Liv eventually found love with a *Custom Sportster*.

With the decision made on which model they wanted, they then sat down with the sales adviser, Phoebe, who talked them through specifics and rather rudely questioned whether or not it was wise for Liv to get her bike made with the top and most powerful specifications. Both of them spent far longer ensuring they were as perfect as possible right down to the colour than they would have admitted, but they finally had their babies exactly how they wanted them, order placed on the system.

Bank accounts were drained, but they were ecstatic over their purchases and the bikes to be delivered just in time for them to return home from training.

With the basics now all but covered, repetition was how they spent their days. They completed an exercise and they re-did the exercise. They completed team exercises so they were made to do individual exercises. Liv got in serious trouble with Tula and Choovio when she stole

Abbey the hostage bear in an effort to help Millie, whose exhaustion-induced nightmares were not stopping even after they began building up cardio from storming mock-ups of airports, office buildings, embassies and hotels.

They meticulously ran through every potential scenario that they may come across. Something that Maddie and Liv were accustomed to, having done the same thing before they decided to take up being vigilantes full time.

The more they repeated exercises and the more their non-verbal communication skills improved, they did not need to communicate out loud with hand movements and funny looking dances; all they needed to run through all plans and engagement exercises as well as team and tag moves to take down groups of assailants.

"I don't normally give compliments," Tula said after a gruelling hand-to-hand combat sessions.

"We've noticed," Millie muttered to Maddie.

"However," she said, with something that could be considered a smile, "by the end of this, you may be the greatest team I have ever trained, and that is saying something."

"Is that a compliment or an ego boost?" Pete asked sceptically.

"Now, anyone have a fear of drowning?" she asked,

ignoring his comments.

"It is up there with a jar full of maggots being taped to my face and the jar headed up so the only way the maggots can escape is by eating through my face," Pete shrugged.

As everyone began to laugh and Maddie looked rather ill, Tula sighed deeply before saying, "We are scuba diving today."

They all thoroughly enjoyed scuba diving and it truly made them realised that they were being trained for every situation; being made to ignore the cold and the warm, being trained on how to survive in every situation.

They sat at home, still damp after scuba diving and Maddie noticed something most suspicious. Pete was sat away from the others, his head lolling onto a pencil and a pad that sat in front of him.

"What is Pete doing with a pad and a pencil?" Maddie asked Millie.

She quietened everyone and gathered them round.

She put on impression of a nature documentary narrator; "Here we see the artistic Pete, the creative and in touch with his earth. I don't think I've seen him pick up his pencil and pad since he used to partake in the devil's lettuce. The *mamajuana*. He is never normally this comfortable drawing with people around."

"Eve's special flower, a kiwi earring," Trent laughed, "It has been months."

"I didn't realise he used to use it," Maddie and Liv said together.

"Yeah, he uses it occasionally, it's harmless but just relaxes him; allows him to partake in the things he doesn't normally do."

"Because he was bullied?" Maddie asked, remembering a past conversation with Pete.

They crept together towards his sun lounger and began to look at his drawing, but as they got closer, he awoke from his doze and pulled the pad closer to himself.

"You not gonna show us what you're drawing?" Maddie asked.

"I'm happy to see you drawing again," Millie said to him.

"Yeah, I wanted to get back into drawing," he shrugged.

"So, let's see," Liv asked.

"When it is finished," he smiled at them before ushering them away.

"Alright, here, you dicks!" he said, handing them his notepad.

"Finished?"

"Obviously."

When they gathered around the pad, they smiled at the drawing.

"It's a Juliet," he said nervously, as they looked at his drawing of a tall and muscular woman, with rosy cheeks, her long black hair swept behind a bloodied long sword which she held in one hand, allowing the blade to run behind her neck with her arm hooked over and resting on the other end of it. She had a strong, stocky build and a black dress, with a ribbon on either side of her middle reading *The Juliets*.

"I guess we are officially the Juliets," Trent smiled.

"Eh, every time the girls said Juliets it really pissed off Choovio and Tula," he laughed.

"You know what this means now," Millie said seriously. When none of them replied, she smiled and said, "The Juliets needs tattoos of THE Juliet."

"Suppose it would be cool," Maddie said, looking at the drawing, "To mark the end of training."

"And then we could get tattoos after every mission across the world to go with it," Liv added, thinking out loud.

"Well, I do know someone who could do this for us," Trent said with a secretive wink.

"Would this person by any chance work in the on-base tattoo parlour *Inklined*, would they?" Pete said to him.

"Yes," Trent said, causing all of them to roll their eyes at him.

As they went for a group fist bump before picking teams for a game of water American football, Liv pointed out that when they all put their hands in the circle together how great it would look if they all got the tattoo on the left forearm. Even though she, Maddie and Trent were all left-handed, the visual of them all on their left forearms was a good one that they all seemingly agreed on.

"What will your parents say?" Maddie asked Millie.

"They're letting me do this, aren't they?" she responded, laughing.

"Getting it done before we leave would be so cute," Maddie said.

Liv and Millie noticed the first genuine beaming smile from Pete. Millie, later that night, confessed how much she believed it meant to Pete for him to open up his artistic side and for it to be truly accepted, accepted for his love of art and computers, rather than shunted for it.

Using this information, they gently and subtly began to nurture this side of Pete to make him more comfortable about his art, and soon they were discovering a whole different side to Pete that he had clearly buried deep until he was comfortable enough to share it.

Millie confessed to Trent, who obviously knew about this side to him, that she was surprised he showed it so quickly, thinking it would take a year or longer for them to know he was drawing again let alone them actually seeing his artwork.

Before they could get Pete's artwork tattooed upon themselves however, they had a long way to go in terms of their training. Neither Choovio or Tula were relenting and them actually passing out of training was not something that was guaranteed, as they constantly reminded J-Squadron.

Their bodies constantly aching with only weekends to recover became their natural state, however it did not make the simplest acts like holding a rifle any easier.

Trent also scheduled Maddie and Liv a separate appointment than the others with the base tailor. They all had a meeting in order to get kitted out with black ops, stealth gear fitted with everything they would need for weaponry and bulletproof instalments.

Maddie and Liv met with the tailor again and he kitted them out in a Kevlar mesh from under the nose to their

boots. He also built the suit with areas for Pete's designed weapons, night-vision goggles as well as a grappling hook, and everything all built into a lightweight suit as opposed to them wearing tracksuit bottoms, carrying bum bags full of all their gear. This would improve their night jobs once they were back in Willowdale City.

Pete's weapons were incredibly well designed. They had

Viking Seax, O Tanto, Katanas, lightweight longswords as well as Bagh Nakhs. Bo Staffs and grappling hooks were fitted with them, they tested their new special operation suits and fitted them with their guns and ammunition.

In their new suits they were set what Choovio called a *four-stage challenge*. Liv and Trent would rescue a hostage from an office building, whilst Maddie, Millie and Pete would rescue a hostage from a hospital. They would then move as a team to a mock-up of a hotel, to take out the leader of the group organising kidnapping of hostages, before finally being pinned back in a condition requiring them to get to a helicopter being guarded and unable to take off.

They readied themselves as Choovio called this the ultimate test, before reminding Liv that as they were going up against G.U.A.R.D. agents not actual hostage takers, that she should act accordingly. So, the use of the knives and acts of defenestration were out of the question. He also reminded them about the weaponry they carried was to get used to the weight of them and not to use on people who were actually trying to murder them as if it were a real situation.

"Let's go," Trent said, as they all threw their firsts in the middle as an act of support.

"GO JULIETS!" Millie cried.

"GO JULIETS!" they all shouted back.

This naturally led to a shouting Choovio berate them about using that and how they were to be known as J-Squadron only. However, they went their separate ways and waited for the signal.

Liv liked being paired with Trent, he knew her worth and truly how good she was, whether it was utilising a flip and dick or hoisting her into a roof panel so she could sneak up upon someone. He knew that they could take those risks together and it would work out okay. The ability to take risks and get engaged in the hand-to-hand combat aspect of it is where Maddie and Liv thrived, and Trent knew how to bring out the best in them doing that.

They entered the office together. Trent and Liv jogged together and as they didn't know what floor the hostage would be on or how many people would be there to stop them, they took precautions. They used the partitions to their advantage, tripping them over to use as shields and generally caused havoc to the office to protect themselves and expose the enemy.

Whilst Liv and Trent went through the office, the others, cursing the luck of Trent and Liv, made their way through the hospital, covering operating theatres and mannequins posing as civilians in hospital beds.

Trent and Liv had to go to the seventh floor until they could extract their hostage from the building.

However Maddie, Millie and Pete had to go to the

furthest side of the sixth floor of the hospital to retrieve their hostage.

They met back up outside and made their way together towards the hotel. When they entered the hotel, Trent made the decision that they would cover the floors separately and reconvene if one team found the hostage. He sent Maddie, Millie and Liv together covering the odd numbers whilst he and Pete covered the even numbers.

Maddie, Millie and Liv worked quickly and efficiently, Maddie and Liv rotating in the opening of the doors whilst Millie went in attempting to search for the hostage.

"Ninth floor, my location, high number of enemies, could be hostage," Millie said over the communication system.

"Could be a diversion, Pete is on his way. I am continuing," Trent replied.

Pete got there to help with the impending onslaught of enemies. However, he was barely there five minutes when they got their first glimpse of the hostage, they called Trent to help in the rescue.

Once they retrieved the hostage, Trent could finally allow his team to do what they did best, with a mile stretch between them and the helicopter that they needed to get to.

They could spread out and cover ground quickly, Maddie

and Liv taking to the roofs and the skies when they could. Millie and Pete covered the rear, raining paint upon anyone they came across, then managing to scramble onto the aircraft, with paint bullets being sprayed in their direction, they closed the door. Pete was unsure whether or not he was meant to take off or not.

They received Choovio's voice over the plane's intercom to let them know they could leave the aircraft again.

As they did, sweat pouring off their foreheads, they all collapsed on the ground, with Trent stood behind his team looking immensely proud of all of them all.

"Congratulations!" Choovio said, coming over to them, four paint bullets on his chest and one on his genitals.

"For what?" Millie said from the floor, attempting to not laugh at the fact one of them had shot him in the genitals.

"You're done," Choovio said, his manner and tone completely different to how it was before the exercise started. "You pass. There are few things more that we can teach. You have combatted the extreme summer heat, us being dickheads, and every single thing that we could have thrown at you, and have risen to the occasion amazingly. You're technical experts, have learnt all manner of skills, such as sky diving and scuba diving to a satisfactory ability and you have all improved massively in hand-to-hand combat."

"We are two weeks early?" Trent said, unsure what Choovio was getting at.

"Yes... I suppose you are, a bit more of bomb disposal but you're finished," Tula said, smiling.

"It is Wednesday now, you fly home a week from Monday, enjoy your time off, J- Squadron," Choovio said. shaking their hands individually.

"Shower, and we will meet you in town for a celebratory dinner," Tula said, dismissing them.

As Choovio and Tula walked away, they all enveloped in a group hug.

They could have been stood in the sweaty hug for one minute or ten, before Trent said, "I am so proud of all of you."

As they released the hug, Pete let out an almighty yawn. They began walking home to shower before driving to meet Choovio and Tula for a meal.

When they arrived in the bar and grill, they saw a completely different side of Choovio and Tula than they had seen day in and day out, both of them being friendly and talkative towards the whole group.

They arrived home late, and got up the next morning even later, not doing anything other than laying by the pool and eating Trent's phenomenal cooking.

It was exactly what they needed after a brutally exhausting summer.

They were tanned and recovering nicely from the gruelling training they had been through; their muscles had grown considerably since they started and it was something that made Millie very happy.

Before they realised, they had to pack everything they needed to and were ready to get tattooed as a team.

"This is so exciting," Millie said, as they walked towards the parlour.

"I know," Liv said giddily.

"Pete gets the first tattoo as it is his design," Trent smiled.

"Damn straight," Pete chuckled.

As they walked in they saw that the artist, Steve, had

brought in his business associate, Tony, as it was the entire group getting the same tattoo on the same day at the same time.

Pete and Millie went first as the others watched Pete's creation come to life. When Pete and Millie had their tattoos finished, they were replaced in the chair shortly after by Maddie and Liv.

Maddie and Liv were bombarding Steve and Tony with all

sorts of questions about the tattoo business and what exactly they do in their jobs and the creative aspect of it.

Liv kept getting told off by Steve as she could just not stay still, her legs wiggling and bouncing in the chair, but they both finally had Pete's design imprinted on them. They all sat around having a drink with Tony, as Trent finally had the design tattooed on him left forearm.

After it was done, they put their arms forward for a group photo of them all together, tattoos in shot. The Juliets with their Juliets tattooed upon them. Liv beamed at the photo once it was sent to her, to see her new family smiling together filled her with a happiness that she had not experienced in such a long time.

What a summer full of photos meant to her was more than anyone else could have known. Liv suspected that Maddie felt the same, but to see all of the photos on her phone, and the memories associated to those pictures, made her smile as they relaxed on their last night in the desert heat before they headed home.

"These photos are gonna get me through going back to school in September," Millie said, as they boarded the plane ready to fly back home.

"I know!" Liv groaned. "I've been thinking that all morning, how are we gonna do it?"

"At least you two are still gonna kick all the names and

take all the asses being vigilantes," Millie reasoned. "You got that adrenaline pumping until we get called on a mission."

"The upgrades from G.U.A.R.D. are gonna make it a lot easier," Maddie added.

"How much gear are you *borrowing?*" Pete joked.

"Nah, I made them make double the tactical gear so they can have one set locked up waiting for G.U.A.R.D. missions and one set for their vigilante work," Trent said, winking at Liv.

"And if you need us crime fighting, give us a ring," Millie said, hugging Maddie as they strapped themselves in ready for take-off.

Just like their flight to begin their training, they began the flight on the way home from training with a game of Monopoly. However, this game was a lot more vicious and cut-throat than the game they played on the way to training, now they were more comfortable in each other's presence; Millie coming out as the eventually winner.

When they landed, they bid each other farewell and all went on their separate ways for now.

As Maddie drove, she looked at her hand and arm as it gripped the steering wheel and said to Liv, "I think now we are away from the others, it has only just hit me how truly different our lives are now as opposed to when we got on that plane."

"Yeah, I completely agree," Liv said, "to return home to our house after everything we've been through, it has truly changed us."

"Exactly! Although I don't have school to go back to, unlike you," Maddie smirked.

"Oh, don't remind me," she groaned.

"I am only messing, being a senior is way more relaxed. You're going to be fine."

"Yeah, but can I really be bothered to do it?" Liv pointed out.

"Based on Tula, it could be a mission every couple of months so you're gonna have to ride your Harley to school like a badass and deal with it."

"I cannot wait for my baby to arrive," Liv said.

"Same."

"You didn't buy a Harley?"

"I meant Deanne; you utter knob!" Maddie said, rolling her eyes.

Chapter Four:

When they arrived home, they deemed it wise to go to bed and attempt to combat jet lag. Before they eventually fell asleep, Liv contacted the mayor to let her know that they were back in the city and Maddie contacted Deanne for a catch-up before she arrived home. She was happy to hear that Deanne's brother had fallen ill towards the end of the cruise and had to stay in his cabin for some of the trip.

The next morning, Liv relayed the information that the mayor had requested to meet them next time they were on patrol, as a catch-up was needed.

They moved the numbers of the mayor and the police chief into a new phone which Pete had upgraded to the next level for them. It allowed them to disable security cameras, alarms, listen to police scanners and listen to calls into the police.

That night they changed into their new stealth gear, full of weapons and items to assist their crime fighting. The darkest of black allowed them to blend in faultlessly to the night around them, their boots were streamlined and soundless with steel-capped boots for if they needed a kick to hurt. As they hit the familiar path towards the multi-storey car park they waited for the mayor and the police chief, after a summer of not knowing what went on in Willowdale City.

When they arrived, they found the mayor and the police chief waiting for them.

"So, what is this meeting about?" Maddie asked the mayor from the shadows.

She jumped about a foot in the air and span around clutching her heart. "You've gotten stealthier... You utter bastards!"

"You've gotten new gear," Police Chief Kyle grunted.

"We've been upgraded," Liv shrugged.

"Well, I am glad you're back," the mayor said, "you caught the serial killer then vanished."

"Well, shit happens," Maddie said, "What is this meeting about?"

"We are in desperate need of help. There is a cop killer on the loose, and a serial killing gang murdering families too. The media are looking into the cop killings and every move is being scrutinised."

"I will take the cop killer," Maddie said.

"I will take the killings," Liv said. "Any connections between the families?"

"None that we could find."

"Essentially, we are up shit creek with a paddle made of shit," Chief Kyle growled. "The cop killer is making us look weak."

"How many cops have been killed?"

"Four. Nine-millimetre shell casings placed at the scene, first cop was killed with one bullet, second cop was killed with two bullets, third cop with three bullets, four bullets in the fourth cop. We DO NOT want a fifth dead cop with five bullets in."

"We will need all of the police files at our house, in the meantime make sure all patrolling officers check in every fifteen minutes, if they're on patrol alone make them wear body cameras," Maddie instructed.

"How do you know if the family murders are connected? Liv asked. "Is it just the fact families are being murdered, because that happens all the time?"

"Rhinic cigarettes were found at each crime scene, none of the parents smoked and it's too coincidental."

"We will have a look into everything, keep us updated," Maddie said, turning to leave.

"Thank you," they both responded.

"We leave the city for two minutes and everything goes to fucking shit," Liv muttered.

"Agreed," Maddie said, as they walked across town.

As they stood on the rooftop, their phone went off.

"What is going on?" Maddie enquired.

"One of the jewellery shops has had its cameras disabled, ten minutes away."

"Let's get this party started."

It only took them five minutes to reach the jewellery store. Once there, they were taken back by the level of sophistication of the heist that they were about to interrupt. Two men guarded the door, which had been removed from its hinges and placed next to the getaway car.

Maddie crept forward, blending into the night. She slashed the front tyres and for good measure, slashed the brake pipes. Whilst she was doing this, Liv took out the guards and laid them silently on the ground.

Four men were inside the shop, their backs to the doors, stashing the contents of the glass cabinets into duffle bags. They couldn't spot any visible weapons other than the ones the door guards were holding and some knives that hung on their thighs.

"Should you really be doing that?" Liv asked.

Startled, they turned and attempted to run, unsheathing

the knives as they did.

It was child's play taking them down, Maddie implementing a leg sweep and a stiff elbow to the face with Liv just opting for a throw a lot of punches until they stopped moving.

With the robbers tied up and unconscious, they contact the police and left the scene, it wasn't the quiet return to Willowdale that they wanted but they didn't expect anything else. They decided to call it a day and head back home as the effects of the jet lag still lingered on their bodies.

When they returned home, it was to find that the mayor had followed their instructions and they had police files sat waiting for them.

They didn't touch the files till after breakfast the next morning. They were so invested in the files which were being spread out that they did not hear the doorbell, until it went for the fourth time.

Liv and Maddie went to answer the door to see someone in a Harley Davidson jacket at the door with papers to sign and a motorbike to deliver.

Liv and Maddie stood looking at the motorbike as Liv's fingers trembled holding the keys.

"She is beautiful," Maddie admitted.

"I need to shower, I need her," Liv said, turning back inside to do exactly that.

Liv had to endure Maddie making sure her helmet was safely adjusted, but she put on her jacket, embossed with the logo, sunglasses, and with a euphoric feeling she kicked the bike into life and began to drive.

It was hours before she returned home to find Maddie where she left her, pouring over the files.

Liv conceding that she should probably do some work as well and joined Maddie on the living room floor.

As Liv worked, she became more and more confused by the case she had been given by the mayor. Two families were wealthy, one of the families was middle class and one was a close-knit working-class family; none of the children seemingly had any interaction with each other, based on schooling and social media profiles. None of the parents seemingly had any crossover, occupationally or otherwise.

There was no discernible reaction as to why these families had been targeted or why they were killed in the manner that they were. The only thing Liv could deduce with any certainty was that it most certainly a group acting as a unit to carry out these murders.

It plagued her for four days. Whenever she got frustrated, Liv took out her Harley for a ride and drove until she either had a breakthrough or was no longer frustrated. Maddie also dragged her shopping when she got frustrated, in the hope that something came to them whilst in a shop.

Maddie, however, was having more of a theoretical success as with targeting police officers, albeit random police officers, indicated someone with a vendetta against law enforcement. So she began looking into recently released convicts, which was a painstakingly slow task as the digital police files in which she was attempting to 'borrow' from police headquarters were encrypted.

After a week of absolutely nothing other than roadblocks and dead ends, with Maddie becoming stressed at Liv and vice versa, Liv decided that she would video call Millie for a rant about the case.

Millie seemed rather interested in the murders and began asking questions.

"Do they have mutual friends?"

"No."

"Do they go to the same schools?"

"No."

"Do they, either for school or outside of school, play the same sports."

"Nope."

"Any connection between the schools?"

"No, private and public schools. One academic, one specialising in art and drama."

"Shit, do they share a bus company perhaps, you know that drops the kids off?"

"No, I checked that, for one of the families the eldest drove the family in, one family walked in but no shared bus company."

Together for any hope of an idea, they sat there on every school website attempting to see any link, following Liv's belief that the children were what connected these murders.

"I've got it," Millie said, after twenty minutes of searching. "Go to the code and conducts section of the website."

"I'm there."

"All uniforms must follow the specifications below, blah blah blah, all uniform and sport accessories must be purchased from -"

"Berenato Uniforms," they said together.

"You absolutely beautiful genius," Liv sighed. "Let's have a look on the uniform company's website, see what we can see."

"There is a branch in Willowdale, although that isn't overly surprising."

"They seemingly employ students during the summer holidays as well as their permanent staff. Smart plan, university students and school kids are off all summer."

"They would have access to addresses and phone numbers if they store accounts."

"I might have to go in undercover, see if I can get the names of the employees," Liv muttered.

"Did you borrow any G.U.A.R.D. tech before you left?"

"Only what we would use out on patrol or on missions, why?"

"Disk data getter 900 - I don't know the actual name for it, but all you need to do is connect it to any till or computer and it will download all information on the server that they are on."

"I'll need to order one, see if they can get it me ASAP. I don't want them killing again if this is the route we need to go down," Liv said.

"Let me know if you need anything else," Millie said to her, before they moved on from work and just began talking.

The disk arrived the next day, so Liv mounted her Harley and left to buy uniform from the shop.

She picked a uniform and went to the counter to purchase a tie. She chatted to the friendly sales adviser around her age called Francesca, as she put the tie through the till. Liv slipped the disk drive out of her pocket and, under the impression of attempting to see how much the gum shields behind the till costed, she surreptitiously placed the drive on the till.

Cleverly designed with a smiley face, Liv watched it as she purchased her tie and talked to Francesca. When Liv refused to give an address, she asked 'why exactly she needed to give one?'.

"It's for the stupid kids who lose things on the first day. Parents can come up, give their address and we can see what sizes of everything they bought, so they can just pick them up again instead of bringing the kid with them and having to try everything on again to get the correct size," Francesca explained.

"Oh, that won't be necessary, my sister just likes to doodle on her ties, so I picked one up for her whilst I am in the area," Liv laughed, "but thank you, Francesca."

Liv left shortly after, leaving the disk in place to continue collecting data. When she got home, she opened her laptop and as she began to see the data collected, she contacted Millie.

"They have five part-time staff working there. Customers give their address and the shop can see what sizes of everything they bought so they can just pick them up again instead of bringing the kid with them and having to try everything on again if they lose everything."

"Or to help the staff murder people."

"So, the five part-time staff there," Liv read from her laptop, "are Francesca Oak, Carrie McIntosh, Bryan Daniels, Alex Rae, Hunter Niven."

"Who the piss names their child Hunter?!"

"I know, it is not great," Liv laughed, miming vomiting.

"I am trying to find them on social media," Millie said, typing ferociously. "Mind, if I get Pete on this, see if he can bypass some security features if we get into their social media accounts, see exactly what is going on?"

"Let's hope we find something," Liv laughed, giving the go ahead.

Millie disconnected the call, hoping to get back to her in a while.

Liv let out a sigh of relief as she took a gulp of tea, hoping beyond hope that she was on the right path before another family was killed that summer. She went to consult with Maddie and see how she was getting on.

"You and Millie have made more progress than I have," she huffed.

Maddie then began running through how little progress she had made and how she may need to enlist the help of Pete, to investigate all the recent releases of criminals and any family members who may have grievances against the police officers in the town.

"Take the night off," Liv advised her, after Maddie repeated a sentence for the third time.

"Why?"

"You're distracted by the fact that you're going to see Deanne."

"How can you tell?"

"You've repeated that last sentence three times, and you're holding your notes upside down," Liv sighed, "anyway I have plans, so you and Deanne have the house to yourselves."

"You have plans? You?"

"Yeah."

"You?"

"I'm going for a drink."

"Have fun?" Maddie said, stretching.

"Have you told her about your tattoo?" Liv said, nodding at her left forearm.

"Yeah, I have! I told Deanne that me and you saw the image in an art gallery and then decided to get it tattooed together," Maddie shrugged.

When the time came Liv slipped out of the house, moments before she saw the exuberant Deanne with gifts in hand practically skipping up the drive, towards the front door.

Liv walked into town, instead of driving either the car or her motorbike. She had music on and just walked until her feet led her to a suitable bar. Her thoughts were that of her happiness, and how happy she was for Maddie to finally be reunited with Deanne.

Liv was reluctant for her mind to wander about being a senior in school, Deanne going off to university and Maddie being the one in limbo, not in school, not in university, just waiting for G.U.A.R.D. to call on the two of them.

Liv also thought about how new people would be joining as seniors and how it may be a silver lining to be a senior as she would finally have someone to talk to who she didn't despise. However, her thoughts about school stopped when she entered a bar, threw her leather jacket over the high chair at the bar and ordered a drink.

It wasn't until the bartender, Shayna, had placed a bar mat down in front of Liv that she realised, she had walked into a bar with the worst name in history. As she looked at a bar mat emblazoned with the name *The Terrible Dragonfruit.* Ignoring the name, she accepted her whiskey and coke.

Despite the terrible name, the whiskey was not terrible and neither was the conversation, as Shayna chatted to her about all manner of things. Liv used the pre-determined cover story of what she did as a job, as saying she was seventeen would have gotten her kicked out of the bar.

When she was on her seventh whiskey and coke, Liv noticed that Shayna had written her number on the bar mat with a kiss, as she bid Liv farewell, finishing her shift for the night.

"You not gonna come this side of the bar and join me for a drink?" Liv asked, shocked.

"Can't, I'm afraid," Shayna said apologetically, but nodding towards the bar mat making sure Liv saw what Shayna had done.

Liv, however, did not stay much longer as Mike, who had

taken over from Shayna, was far less welcoming and much more of a creep, despite the wedding band she could clearly see on his finger. Draining her whiskey and pocketing the beer mat with Shayna's number on, she began walking home.

When she arrived home, it was to find that Deanne and Maddie, in the midst of cooking and baking, had broken down into a food fight with a Victoria sponge and a quadruple chocolate velvet cake.

"You two are utter children!" she exclaimed, after seeing them covered in flour and chocolate, although Liv paid for her insult by having a wooden spoon thrown at her.

"I'll be upstairs should you need me," she yelled from the hall.

Liv didn't see Deanne or her sister until she had already began cooking brunch, after working on her case for a few hours. They were halfway through bunch when Pete messaged her saying that they needed to talk.

Liv excused herself from the table and went to talk to Pete, leaving Deanne and Maddie to continue eating

When Liv re-entered the room, she inadvertently lowered the tone considerably. "Maddie, I'm afraid you may need to rearrange your plans for tonight."

"Why?" Maddie and Deanne said together.

"My informant," Liv said subtly, shooting Maddie a meaningful look, "has indicated we are needed on the streets tonight for some erm, murder prevention."

"What time?"

"We need to leave," Liv said, stretching the truth slightly, "at eleven, to prepare suitably."

Maddie looked a little put out but eventually accepted. Liv prepared the file ready to hand in, with evidence for when they had taken down her family murders.

As they sat on a roof, Liv began to explain.

"This is all down to rudeness, literally. I have all of their texts here; they targeted the families based on which ones were rude to them whilst they were getting their children fitted and kitted with school uniform and sports gear. That is why I had such a hard time finding a link, throughout the summer they had all been to the same school uniform shop and were just rude people."

"That is what drove them to kill?" Maddie asked, shocked.

"It is probably the rush of breaking and entering as well. But it is how they choose their victims."

"Madness," Maddie muttered.

"Parents give their addresses willingly, but in the hands of people like this, it is so simple. No crossover between the families, just happened to be rude pricks at some point between May and now."

"Pete get you into social media?"

"Yeah, hid between a firewall in Beijing, Odense and Djibouti. Given me everything we need and also given us a steam connection mirrored on our phone so we can see if they get any more messages."

"When is everything meant to be going down."

"Three o'clock tomorrow morning. The Stanway family, three children, Elly, Becky and Chloe, two golden children and Elly is the trouble child apparently."

"One trouble child is enough to justify five murders?"

"Apparently so, now let's go. We need to wait for them to congregate and then do what we need to do and call Mr. Police Chief Kyle."

They ran across the city to a housing estate and waited in the children's park, which was the predetermined location for them to meet that night. They arrived and began to wait, Liv re-reading all the evidence in front of her and keeping an eye out for any new messages to be sent between the group.

As the time crept closer to three o'clock, they started to see figures congregate in the darkness. They held their breath as one by one the group began to meet.

As the group stood clustered under the playset, Maddie and Liv began to creep closer, eager to overhear any snippet of conversation.

They got to a distance that was near enough for them to overhear the conversation, but no so close that they might spook the group.

Recapping their plan and who was going to take which role was not the smartest thing they could have done out loud, but nonetheless it helped reconfirm the concrete evidence that these were the teens they were looking for.

On Liv's signal, Maddie began to creep around to the other side of them and waited for the perfect time to engage.

When Liv gave the signal, they engaged. Liv took a run at them, and by sliding managed to take two of them to the ground, before she flipped from her back to a standing position, ready to fight.

Maddie, however, decided to take the stealth action to get close and used her considerable power to her advantage, simply lifting two of them out of thin air and as if their heads were coconuts, she used one of them to headbutt the other, causing both of them to be in considerable pain.

As Maddie's two crumpled, they both ensured that all of the teenagers were considerably beaten, as they used zip ties to bind their arms and ankles before they contacted Police Chief Kyle notifying him of the location of the family murders. One of them may have been inadvertently knocked unconscious but neither of them mattered too much. They left the file of indisputable evidence with them and retreated into the shadows as they waited for the police to turn up and pick up the group.

Deanne was delighted to see them return safe and without injury when they did eventually arrive home, and was ready to make hot chocolates for all of them to help them settle and unwind after the night that they had been through. With hot chocolates made, Liv decided she would stay sat downstairs with Maddie and Deane as opposed to going straight up to her room like she had the night before.

It was a surprisingly enjoyable way to spend the predawn hours; all of them talking, Maddie and Deanne cuddling by the fire, as they discussed everything until Deanne, almost dropping her hot chocolate as she nodded off, led to the agreement that they should probably go to bed.

Chapter Five:

That was how the dwindling time of the summer was spent, and before long Liv, in a foul and disgruntled mood, was putting her leather jacket on over her uniform and Maddie was reminding her for the seventeenth time that morning that she must not forget her motorcycle helmet before she left for school that morning.

"This is going to fucking suuuuuuck," Liv groaned to herself, as she put her bag over both of her shoulders, put on her sunglasses and kicked her motorbike into life to head off to school.

Her journey passed those being dropped off by parents, those who walked and the few now fellow seniors who drove. Her arrival seemed to cause quite the stir, as people watched her park, remove her helmet and put it under her arm, and with leather jacket and sunglasses on walk to the seniors only area, which she was now a part of, her keys dangling off her pinkie finger.

She opened the door and looked around for the best desk before striding to the far side, dumping her helmet on a desk near the window. Pulling out her chair, she used it to get up on the windowsill, behind her, took off her leather bag and put that next to her helmet, looking around the room.

Liv took her time, removing her sunglasses and tucking them into the top of her shirt.

As she looked around the room she made awkward eye contact with Robyn, who was sat with some friends on the opposite side of the room. Liv quickly began looking for some unfamiliar faces.

There were no unfamiliar faces until the room had filled up and the first introductory lesson was going to begin. They were introduced to four new students. Alexa, Brent, Nikki and Mikey.

Alexa, Nikki and Mikey put their stuff down only a few desks away from Liv whereas Brent timidly shuffled towards the corner where Robyn sat with her friends.

"Was that your motorbike? It is really cool," Alexa said, smiling at Liv.

"Thanks," Liv said cheerfully, getting off the windowsill after a spotting the teachers walking round handing out their new timetables.

"I wouldn't get too friendly with Olivia, Alexa. She is nothing but trouble. Trouble who needs to remove her leather jacket," said Mr. Powers, who had just walked over to hand Liv her timetable.

"Oh, so witty, *Sir,* you must have spent all summer coming up with that insult, calling me trouble! But it is not surprising those who uphold the patriarchy will always attempt to belittle those who work to smash it," Liv retorted.

Mr. Powers was one of the few adults and the only teacher in which Liv had any respect for. Mr. Powers was also one of the few adults alive who knew about Liv's vigilante activities, having procured body armour for them when they were in desperate need for it.

"Why are you trouble?" Alexa smirked, as the three of them picked desks slightly closer to her.

"Is that silly haircut not enough evidence?" he said, having disapproved of how severe Liv had shaved the side of her head and the vibrant nature of the red it was dyed.

Liv scowled at him, swishing her hair before beginning to consult her timetable. She was pleased to see that with a free first period she was finally able to enjoy the other seniors only area and have a well needed cup of tea.

When she sat down in the seniors only area, she stretched out, let out a sigh and began to enjoy the freedom until lessons took it away from her.

As she had done for most of her school life, and anytime she was forced to wear a shirt, Liv began to roll up her sleeves as far as her muscles would allow her to.

Liv smiled at her tattoo, as it reminded her of summer and the rest of the Juliets. She laughed at the thought of Millie starting today as well, however as she thought about texting Millie she was joined by Alexa and Mikey, both looking rather nervous asking if they could join her.

As Liv greeted them, she surreptitiously rolled down her left sleeve, leaving her right one up.

"Is that a tattoo?" Mikey said, pointing at the black dress and aspects of red blood still visible through her white shirt.

"Yeah," Liv said, stifling a sigh and rolling her sleeve back up to where it was, now the secret was out and showing them the art.

"That's so cool! When did you get it done?" Mikey asked, impressed with Liv's daring of getting a tattoo at seventeen.

"This summer, me and my sister got matching ones."

"Awesome! I like it," Alexa said, smiling at her. "But what will the teachers say, aren't they meant to be really strict here?"

"I'll have my sleeve rolled down or a bandage over it when I'm not in here," Liv shrugged. "And yeah, they can be fairly strict. Today was the first time I have ever heard Mr. Powers tell a joke, and they're strict in lessons but my hair the way it is, and my sister's blue, they kinda let slide."

Alexa and Mikey spent most of that free period quizzing Liv about her timetable and experience at the school, which was awkward given that as Liv was normally so sleep-deprived that a lot of things just passed her by without her actually realising.

"I'm what some people call an oblivious, bisexual mess, who most people don't like. I have been here years and still don't know most people's names. I do my own thing."

"So not the person to get the gossip off then," Mikey laughed.

"Sadly not, some people date then sometimes it ends badly, would be my guess, but I'm excited to find out with you."

This continued, until Liv and Alexa had to say goodbye to Mikey and head to their second period English.

As they waited outside, they were soon joined by Robyn and a few of her friends, who were all chatting happily until they saw Liv and Alexa, and then fell silent and walked into the classroom ahead of them.

"What was that about?" Alexa whispered.

"Long story."

Mrs. Noah had devised a seating plan for them in this class. Thankfully Alexa was placed next to Liv. Unfortunately, Robyn was placed on Liv's right side.

Liv was sure she could see Robyn looking at her left arm curiously, attempting to see what was under her sleeve, however she could not be sure as Mrs. Noah had just began explaining about how they would be covering the Romanticism movement.

"Do you have a problem with that, Olivia?" Mrs. Noah snapped, as Liv let out an audible groan.

"No but Liv does, the coursework guidelines state that there would be four different aspect to do the project on," she retorted.

"That is true. However, I have made the decision that everyone will be doing the Romanticism movement."

Mrs. Noah became increasingly frustrated as the entire class let out a groan at the fact that they were not being allowed to create a question for their coursework.

After flying into a rage, she eventually lamented, allowing them to choose their own question but strongly advising their question be on the Romanticism movement.

"Wow, Liv, I can't believe you got her to change her mind," Alexa said, as they left the class.

"Well, there is no fucking way I am studying poetry. If it isn't a book or play, I am not interested."

As Robyn and her friends walked past, Alexa prompted Liv to tell her the story about why Robyn and her friends seemingly disliked her.

Liv explained the story for the most part, leaving out the sections about crime fighting and how it was her eventually stabbing which led to them not being on speaking terms.

"But why do her friends hate you?"

"Robyn was new last year, and we became friends in the first couple of days when," she nodded backwards to Mrs. Noah's room, "kicked me out of class and Robyn decided to join. Then when we stopped speaking, she found them. So, I guess it's my fault they didn't become friends till the latter half of the year."

"Hardly your fault then?"

"Exactly, but I am beyond caring at this point," she shrugged, "but, don't let it cloud your judgement of her or them, I'm sure they're probably quite nice."

As they walked back to drop their things off at their desks, it struck Liv at just how exhausting school was. There were cliques, there were people swapping gossip stories and rumours from over the summer holiday and Liv was blissfully unaware of everything.

The different voices from every direction, and kids running around and shouting sent her senses into overdrive. She tapped her fingers rapidly on her leg trying to focus on one constant.

"You look agitated?" Mike observed.

"Nah, just done with life," she laughed, fingers tapping and legs shaking.

Mikey following Liv's eyes around the room said, "So what is everyone's deal? What are the inside jokes and gossip of the year?"

"I wouldn't know to be honest, I hung around with my sister and her friends in the year above. They were older and more mature and some of these were very childish last year. However, when you find out the gossip, be sure to tell me."

"Tell us some gossip about you then," Alexa laughed.

Liv paused and said, "Two truths and a lie, I have a fake ID, a tattoo and am a disaster."

"I'm guessing that is three truths?"

"Yeah, see you're good at this! You'll know all the gossip in no time."

The noise and the amount of people kept Liv on tenterhooks for the rest of the day, and given how she spent her summer and her nightly activity, she felt off balance and naked without walking around with weapons everywhere, causing her to physically trip over due to feeling off balance.

When the final bell rang, Liv put her leather jacket back on and walked to her motorbike. As she got on the seat, she wished that when she arrived home there would either be a message from G.U.A.R.D. with a mission or that Maddie was able to have a breakthrough in her cop killer case.

But no, when she arrived it was to see Maddie frustration-knitting, as that day she had not been able to find a breakthrough, so in order to release some of the pent-up frustration that they had they hit the streets that night.

"So, go through the circumstances again," Liv said.

"All the police that have been murdered were killed whilst on patrol, none of them responded to the same type of call and then over the police radio there are reports of shots fired and a dead police officer."

"Have any of the cops worked on the same cases together?"

"I have asked for complete, remote access to the police files but Chief Kyle has said no," Maddie sighed.

"So, we have fuck all then?"

"No, we have Pete working on it from his end. We also have Trent coming down to help me with the paperwork, when Pete gets into the police servers and gives us everything."

"Excellent," Liv said.

Their discussion, however, was cut short as they received a notification on their phone that there were two bank robberies happening simultaneously in polar opposite directions of the city.

"Ready?" Maddie asked.

"Ready!" Liv said.

They hugged tightly and headed off in different directions. Before, they never would have gone separately, but they were better trained now than ever before and they were confident enough in each other's ability to get the job done, quickly and safely.

Maddie ran as fast as she could, and as she got to the bank she saw that an SUV had been driven through the door of the bank, sending shards of glass everywhere. Sliding one of her knives out, she slashed the tyres on the SUV under the presumption that it might also be the getaway vehicle.

She saw just inside the bank that the ATMs had been smashed open and money being hastily stashed into bags, whilst some of the men inside had moved round to where cashiers would sit to empty money from there.

However, with the alarm and the ATMs making an ear-splitting cacophony of noise, it was the perfect cover for none of the four men inside to hear her coming. She snuck behind one of the men and secured a sleeper hold on his neck, lifting him off the ground so that all of her muscle and weight was on his neck; he soon went limp.

As she dropped him to the ground, she knew her element of surprise was about to disappear so she needed to seize it now. She ran and swung her elbow into the second of the men who was emptying the ATM of money.

As he crumpled, she kicked him for good measure before laying in a few punches.

As one of the three left standing reached for a pistol on his side, Maddie was just too quick for him, kicking his arm and using her knife cut at the holster causing it to fall to the ground, before Maddie moved close with the strikes.

She used the man's body as a shield as another assailant began charging at her with a knife drawn, not wanting to injure his co-robber too badly he limited his slashes, meaning that Maddie could use the shield to knock him down.

She jumped onto the man, throwing punches at every part of him, sure she had dealt enough damage to keep him down temporarily.

As the final man approached her, knife drawn, she realised he had her cornered due to how the bank was built. However, it didn't faze her as she remembered her training. She let him approach, him slashing the air with the knife until he was close enough for her to lunge. Grabbing his arm and twisting it up and round towards his shoulder blade and applying pressure she heard his cries of pain. She applied enough pressure on the shoulder before implementing a leg sweep and kneeing him in the head.

She began using zip ties on all of the robbers and proceeded to exit the bank.

Liv dealt with her bank robbery in a very different way, when she arrived at her bank and saw an SUV had been driven through the bank doors.

Knowing the sound of the alarm would cover the sound of her footsteps, she ran into the building as fast as she could and, seeing one of the men by the ATM, she jumped and connected both her feet to the side of his head. He crumpled and Liv followed through, using her momentum she threw a punch into the jaw of a second goon.

The three others in the bank span round and one of them threw a knife towards her, she dodged and allowed the three men to attempt to corner her.

She used the space and the number to her advantage; she dropped to one knee so she could punch one of the men hard in his kneecap, forcing it back. She jumped back to her feet and hit a high kick to another man's jaw. They staggered and Liv hoisted one of them up high and threw him across the room. She kept throwing the men until she was in a position where kicks and punches were enough to ensure everyone was unconscious or in too much pain to actually escape.

Liv made her exit and went to meet up with Maddie, rubbing her knuckles but happy with the night's work.

They continued their discussion on the cop killing case as if two simultaneous bank robberies had not interrupted them, right up until Maddie ordered Liv to go to bed as she had to be in school in a few hours' time.

It took Liv three attempts to leave the house, as she forgot her bike helmet and then realised she had forgotten her keys. However, she made it to school in time.

She threw her helmet down and let out a yawn as they were given their morning brief by one of the teachers.

"You look exhausted," Alexa said, as she and Mikey walked over to her.

"Yeah, I didn't sleep much," Liv shrugged, taking off her sunglasses to do her hair in the lens.

As her and Mikey were about to walk to Mr. Powers'

history lesson, they had to remind her that she was still wearing her leather jacket. But they eventually got her to the lesson in one piece.

Liv drank as much caffeine as was humanly possible that morning in order to function like a human and interact with Alexa and Mikey, as they actually seemed interested in being her friend.

They sat in the seniors area at lunch, Liv now caffeinated enough to begin pacing and tapping her leg and fingers like she normally did.

"Do you need to work out to calm down?" Mikey asked her, as he watched her leg bounce.

"I am too tired to work out, I'll do it when I'm at home."

"Do you work out every day?"

"Obviously!" Liv said, tapping her six pack. "Although I don't tend to wear crop tops."

They managed to keep the conversation going and Alexa and Mikey managed to keep her awake until the end of the day.

When Liv arrived home, it was to find another Harley Davidson parked in the drive; Trent's Harley Davidson.

He greeted her with a bear hug as soon as she entered the kitchen and they sat down with a cup of tea to discuss the two major problems they faced.

"Problem one," Maddie said, "is Pete has worked his magic, however it means we have so many things to work though, it is a staggering amount."

"And they second problem?" Liv yawned.

"Deanne is coming around as she is going to university soon, and we need a good cover for Trent being round."

"You gonna be coming on patrol with us?" Liv asked him.

"Obviously, I didn't come all this way to just do paperwork. Tactical gear is upstairs."

"Excellent."

"OI!" Maddie interjected. "Deanne can't stay the night so patrol can happen but what is Trent's cover?"

As Deanne was walking up the drive, they swiftly decided that Trent was a barrister from a café that Liv had started seeing.

They had to come up with a lot of the background information on the spot as they got talking to Deanne, however Trent and Liv managed to find an excuse to leave them to it and went to the gym to work out together.

They sat in what used to be their parent's bedroom, which they turned into the gym, beginning to file through the police database and looking at the police officers who were killed.

They worked on the case, until Maddie and Deanne called them down for food. They made small talk over food, Trent and Liv beginning to run out of things to discuss about their non-existent relationship.

Deanne returned home and finally Maddie could join Trent and Liv with the case they were working on.

They made little progress by the time they went on patrol.

"No wonder you two have such good cardio," Trent wheezed, "doing this every night."

As they patrolled, they had a strong sense of Groundhog Day as at the same time as the night before two banks on the opposite sides of each other were being robbed."

"Guest's choice, who you want to go with?" Maddie asked Trent.

"I wanna see how Liv rocks and rolls," he said.

Maddie headed north as Liv and Trent headed south.

When they arrived at the bank, Liv was shocked at the symmetry of the robbery from last night, with a SUV driven through the doors of a bank.

"What's the plan?" Trent asked her.

"Just follow my lead," Liv whispered.

He followed her as she ran at full speed into the bank, using all her speed to swing a fist at one of the men, knocking him out in one.

Using the momentum of the swing she went onto her heels and span, allowing the motion to turn her back and elbow another of the robbers in the temple.

Trent just went with the flow and engaged two of the others, firing fists at every inch of them until they collapsed onto the ground.

With four down, the two of them converged on the last remaining thief. He put up a fight, but it was futile and he was tied up with other waiting for the police to arrive.

Trent followed Liv as they ran through back alleys and across the city to one of the multi-storeys.

"How do you know she will meet us here?"

"We have everything planned for if anything kicks off or goes wrong anywhere in the city. we have rendezvous points across the city. This is the agreed car park from where we were when we got those alarms."

"I'm impressed."

"So, you should be," Maddie panted, arriving behind them, sweat and a small cut under her hair causing a horrible mixture between blue and red.

"Hey! You're bleeding as well, high five," Liv said brightly, high-fiving her sister.

Trent raised his eyebrow and both of them laughed as they began to patch up their cuts.

As they patrolled, it made such a difference to have Trent with them as it was added energy, and was so invigorating that when they eventually arrived home, they were tired but in relatively happy moods. Trent set himself a bed in the living room and they all bid each other good night.

Chapter Six:

When Liv awoke ready for school a few hours later, she was tired and jumpy. In order to ease her nerves, Trent's suggested that Liv conceal her Bo Staff on her as she had in training in order to maintain a sense of work life balance.

Liv felt a lot less nervous when she got off her bike than she did the previous days, although as she had received texts from Maddie's friends asking about her *boyfriend*, she was sincerely looking forward to the day when she and Trent could stop *dating*.

As she entered the seniors area, Trent and Maddie were finally able to set out the police files and get to work to find the connection between the murders.

They worked feverously, Maddie wanting to get the case wrapped up so she and Deanne could spend some quality last days together before she went to university.

"I've found it," Trent said, almost spitting his tea over the paper he was holding.

"Oh, fuck off!" Maddie sighed, reading it.

"What?"

"Fucking lawyers. I. HATE. LAWYERS, I. FUCKING. HATE. LAWYERS."

"I remember why, but look here, over a seven-year period all of the murdered police officers have gone up against the same defence attorney. However, more recently it has been the police officer cases won."

"Let's investigate them then, every police officer that was killed had won at least one case against this lawyer."

When Liv arrived home, it was to find them still pouring over everything they could find on the lawyer.

"Who is this?" Liv said, picking up his photo.

"William Pager," Trent yawned. "Lawyer who has lost cases to each of the police officers this year. His private social media is all anti-police sentiment."

"We have anti-police sentiments, they are useless. Is there any non-circumstantial evidence?"

"If you wanna join, we need help finding them?"

"He looks like a cock," Liv said, setting her stuff down and sitting next to her sister to help see if William Pager was a wasted day or a breakthrough at last.

As night approached Liv, who was scanning lists of records, found something that would give them something to physically do. "It says here that William Pager lost a case. Yesterday! This could mean he is going to attempt to kill tonight."

"How are we only making this connection now?" Liv asked.

"He is seemingly working on 'three strikes and they're out…. of life' basis, each time he wins the score resets," Trent read from a folder.

"So, all three of the strikes match up with the third case loss?"

"Yeah."

"Why now?"

"He got mugged in December. I have the report here, there were no witnesses, didn't give a good enough description so nothing happened with the case."

"So," Maddie said, getting to her feet, "Trent and I will watch Pager, Liv you're going to watch Allana Hill, the officer who just won a domestic abuse case in court against Pager."

"Understood," they said together, and when night fell that is exactly what they did.

Liv sat contently at a bus stop near Allana Hill's house, whilst Maddie and Trent waited for Pager to leave his house. They did not know when he would strike or even if it would be tonight but given the rage escalations after each kill, they assumed it must be. Their suspicions proved to be right for the most part when he left his house at three o'clock that morning in camouflage gear and began to drive.

Maddie and Trent couldn't do much other than follow on foot which was difficult to say the least. They followed him the best they could for half an hour before Trent managed to put a remote tracking beacon on Pager's car as he continued his late-night travel.

It was another hour before he was seemingly going in the direction of Allana Hill's house. Maddie and Trent notified Liv who was hidden in a bush, stretching out to avoid getting serious cramp.

It was nearing five o'clock in the morning when Maddie and Trent met up with Liv to monitor Pager. They saw him park relatively close to them, meaning that he was a ten-minute walk to Allana Hill's house.

They watched him get out of his car and they closed in on his position.

He walked towards Allana Hill's house and as he walked, they saw him pull a hunting rifle.

They were not going to allow him any closer to Hill's house, especially with her children at home.

Not wanting to get shot they moved cautiously, with the sun rising they had lost the elements that the night provided them.

Without the knife, they had to use their speed. Liv loved using her speed. She ran as fast as she could from behind and, leaping on both of her feet, connected with the back of his head. As he fell forward Maddie and Trent joined the action. As Maddie and Liv went on the offensive, Trent disarmed the dazed Pager, taking the hunting rifle off his shoulder as Liv and Maddie did the damage. Pager pulled out a knife and began slashing and punching, but the numbers advantage worked in their favour and they soon subdued him.

Trent patted Pager down in an attempt to see if he was carrying any other weapons. He was, he had a pistol on his waist and a pistol on his ankle.

With it being early in the morning as opposed to late at night, once they subdued William Pager they had to move quickly.

The police were called, the evidence was left with him and Maddie, Liv and Trent headed home as fast they could as to not be noticed by any early morning commuters.

Sweaty, cold and in Liv's case stiff from being sat on a bench for most of the night, they settled in the living room. Instead of heading to bed they threw off the unnecessary tactical gear, opened the alcohol cabinet and toasted to a job well done.

The mayor and Police Chief Kyle both messaged them, thanking them for the capture of William Pager and to see if they could get a written confession out of him that day to cement the case against him.

As they sat, Trent started to become increasingly worried about the cut and bruising around Liv's eye, which was swelling at an alarming rate and the cut wouldn't stop bleeding. However, Liv had to stop his worrying so she could shower and get ready for school.

Exhausted, exhilarated and still slightly bleeding Liv set off on a walk to school.

When she arrived at school, she began counterbalancing the exhaustion and alcohol with caffeine before her lessons started, although this did come with its complications, mainly with everyone asking her what happened to her face.

It was only when Liv saw her reflection in a spoon, she realised it was quite badly bruised.

However, the students who had been at the school for long enough knew not to ask the Winters sisters why they had cuts and bruises, as they were often covered in them and Liv just kept saying it was a boxing or kick boxing or MMA injury and not to be concerned.

However, Alexa and Mikey were new to the school and hadn't seen Liv wearing a battle wound before and were alarmed at the sight of her. It took a while and a lot of energy that she did not have for her to calm the two of them down.

"Why did you not take a sick day?" Alexa asked, standing on her tiptoes attempting to see the cut above Liv's eye.

"I don't have a concussion or anything, it is literally just a cut," she yawned.

Liv yawned her way through the next week with nothing of note happening on the vigilante front.

Liv was sat in her Monday morning Mrs. Noah's English lesson when there was a knock at the door.

"Mrs. Noah, I am sorry for the interruption. I need a word with Olivia. She will need to bring her things with her." Liv, who was daydreaming, looked round at the sound of 'Olivia' to see one of the school administrators.

"Why?" Mrs. Noah asked suspiciously, not wanting to let her leave.

The administrator looked at her nervously before saying, "It is her Aunt Francesca."

It took Liv a few seconds to realise that she didn't actually have an Aunt Francesca and that she should not be worried.

Liv followed the administrator to one of the offices and

was handed a phone.

"Wheels up, Liv, check your phone for the location to meet us. Maddie has your tactical gear packed."

Liv discussed things over with the administrator who insisted she had a glass of water before setting off.

Liv checked her phone as she sat on her bike and began driving to the location that Trent had sent, an airstrip an hour and a half away, that Liv previously believed had been closed.

When she arrived, it was to see Trent and Maddie waiting for her, Pete and Millie.

"We have a mission?" she asked tentatively.

"We HAVE a mission," Maddie said, brimming with excitement.

They changed, but not into tactical gear like they were expecting; instead, under Trent's instruction into pyjamas, as apparently it was going to be a long flight.

Pete and Millie turned up shortly thereafter. Millie, already in her pyjamas, hugged everyone as they readied themselves for Trent's brief.

"This," he said holding up a photo, "is Hirota Yoshikazu, an industrial tycoon who has recently started expanding his wealth by providing safehouses, new identities, drug routes, brothel location, and drug dens to gangs and terrorist groups."

"And what are we going to do with Hirota Yoshikazu?" Millie asked.

"The original plan was a simple extraction. However, things have gotten a lot more complicated. He was recently discovered to be selling to rival gangs. Those Japanese gangs are really, really not happy."

"So, we're keeping him alive?" Pete asked.

"Yes, G.U.A.R.D. want him in custody by Friday, he is going to be extorted for every inch of his assets and they are going to keep him alive for as long as it is convenient to do so. He was abducted from Kyoto, but sources say he has been moved to Niigata. COVERT mission. The rest we can discuss on the plane."

Chapter Seven:

Millie had come packed with handheld games consoles for the flight, but Trent had made a wise suggestion for them to all be in their pyjamas as it was a lot comfier than flying in normal clothes; and when they landed, they could not be seen around Niigata in tactical gear.

As Liv and Millie sat together, Liv looked over at Millie's game to see and although she thought they were playing the same game it looked very different.

"I'm playing the Japanese version of the game," she explained, "I'm a bit rusty on my Japanese and as the games are Japanese it is the perfect time."

"Thought I was playing it wrong," Liv sighed, relieved.

Pete rolled his eyes, but he and Maddie continued their in-depth discussion.

"How has Maddie been coping with Deanne going to university?" Millie asked Liv in a hush.

"With Trent at home with us, quite well. Deanne being all nervous and not really knowing anyone closely yet means that they have been messaging a lot. With a cop killer and things like that to cope with, she has actually been coping better than I would have expected."

"Good, as long as she is happy."

Liv didn't reply instantly, her fingers flying over her phone screen, before she finally said, "Sorry I was having to reassure Alexa and Mikey that my imaginary aunt is okay."

"Alexa and Mikey?" Trent said, peering over the top of his book.

"Yeah, because you interrupted a lesson which I was in with a family emergency, she told Mikey and now they are both messaging me."

"They seem to be very interested in you since they started."

"What are you on about?"

"Do they fancy you?"

"How. The. Piss. Am I meant to know this?" Liv said, rolling her eyes and going back to her game.

They did not relent about either of the two having a crush on her until they began drifting off to sleep, as Trent wanted to ensure they were all fully rested by the time they landed in Niigata.

As, they landed, it was not Trent but Millie who took the lead. Being fluent in Japanese she was the one to get directions and information from the locals. She acted under the presupposition that they were tourists looking to explore other areas of Japan before moving onto the larger city.

She was animatedly talking to an elderly gentleman for fifteen minutes when she returned to the group.

"What did that man say?" Trent asked, as she returned to the group.

"He just insulted my accent, then propositioned me," Millie sighed.

Millie took them to a bar to discuss things through and change the plan. Over their drinks they discussed how Millie was the translator for Trent, who was a businessman looking to make a deal with Hirota Yoshikazu who was nowhere to be found and missed their meeting.

Millie relayed the information to nobody in particular, in a raised voice so that most of the people around could hear, the others sat there blissfully unaware of anything that was being said by anyone.

They spent much of that day and the next using both the tourist strategy and the business strategy until they decided to stop in a local restaurant whilst Millie was making phone calls to local businesses. Pete began using his laptop in an attempt to hack into security cameras around the city, searching for Yoshikazu's face. But with such a densely populated city it was proving difficult.

A guy tapped Millie on the shoulder after her phone call and they began talking in hushed voices.

"Wow," she said to them in English, explaining to them all that the man worked in a local hotel and said that they should go there for their business meeting.

So, following the tip, Pete began running facial recognition around the hotel the man mentioned. It was a few hours before they saw that he was indeed taken to the hotel under force days before.

They split up; Pete, Maddie and Liv to their hotel to change into tactical gear, whilst Mille and Trent went to the hotel to see if they could meet Hirota Yoshikazu. They arrived and explained to the receptionist that they had a meeting with a resident of the hotel.

However, armed security that were not part of the hotel met them and told them that the hotel was limited on space due to a bug infestation caused by a mouldy dry wall, much to the suspicion of Trent and Millie.

Pete however did not need suspicion, following Millie's conversation he was able to use everything they had learnt and all of G.U.A.R.D. intelligence to pinpoint every move that Hirota Yoshikazu made, from arriving in Niigata to when he entered the hotel under armed security.

He downloaded the schematics for the hotel and they began getting ready. They weaponised every inch of their bodies and began preparing themselves for an assault on the hotel.

As they prepared, Pete dedicated all of his being and fibre attempting to access the hotel security, but he couldn't.

"We don't need hotel security footage," Maddie said.

"Of course, we do," Pete dismissed, close to crushing his mouse in his hand.

"Pete, I wanna make you wet," Liv said, everybody looking around at her. "Every hotel has regulations about smoking in rooms and general fire safety about sprinkler systems."

"Go on, this sounds interesting," Trent said slowly.

"So, we cause pandemonium, set off the sprinkler system and cause a full evacuation of the hotel?" Maddie finished.

"Hold up," Millie said, jumping up, grabbing the schematics Pete had borrowed and looking at them. "These are different to the floor plan of the hotel we saw earlier, none of these walls are dry walls."

"So?" Maddie asked.

"When we went to the hotel, they had no vacancies due to the fourteenth floor being infested, so as a result they had to close off the six floors above and the floor below it," she said, scanning the documents.

"So, we think the fourteenth?" Maddie said.

None of them could reply however, as Trent began quietening them as his brain raced at what seemed to be a thousand miles an hour.

"The way I see it," he said slowly, "we have a few options. Option A; we go in all guns blazing and find him. Option B; Sprinkler system. Option C; we could pump knock-out gas into the entire building."

"I have another option. Option D;" Millie said, thinking. "We could tell them that we are coming."

"What in the fuck now?" Pete and Maddie said together.

"Tell them that we are here for Hirota, and that if they do not release Hirota, we will pump gas into the building killing them, but we are willing to negotiate if they release him."

"What happens if they say no?"

"We do it?" she suggested.

"Or," Maddie said, "We ring them. Set off the sprinklers, then say that they need to release Hirota, but whilst having the conversation attack them from both the roof and from below, using a fire exit?"

"Millie, turn around," Pete said.

"Why?"

"Your face annoys me."

"What?"

"Do it, Millie, he might be onto something," Trent said, causing Millie to angrily turn around.

Pete sat there looking at his laptop screen, without moving for forty-five minutes before he finally spoke.

"I know how to do it. The building opposite has a roof we can gain access to. One team enters from the roof, the other team can use the food delivery entrance underground, set off the sprinklers on floor seventeen and eleven after barring the rooftop, forcing them downwards if anyone is on the upper floors."

"Will it draw them out?" Maddie asked.

"It would if we set off the sprinklers with an actual fire as opposed to just setting off the sprinklers?" Millie reasoned.

"No, we are not setting off an actual fire," Trent sighed. "Teams are as followed: Liv, Millie, Pete. Maddie and me, we will attack from above, you guys from below. Pete, find a way to set off the sprinklers within the hotel and let's go."

They moved to the hotel, swiftly and silently. When they got close to the hotel they embraced and split up.

Trent and Maddie manoeuvred up a fire escape whilst, thanks to Pete's computer work, Pete, Millie and Liv entered silently into the underground level and moved swiftly and silently through the hotel.

When they reached the seventeenth and the eleventh, they activated the pandemonium that was the sprinkler system. Immediately, from all around, they heard screams of panic, confusion and bedlam erupt around them.

Then, activating their night vision goggles, Pete killed the power to the hotel.

As doors flung open, they began to move through the floors. They didn't get far before people started shooting.

These, Millie theorised, were the bad guys. Trent and Maddie also theorised the same thing, as they were caught with bullets being fired at them from unknown individuals.

They returned fire and moved through the halls, approaching the fourteenth floor. As they fought their way through the masses of people, both fleeing the hotel and those who were getting increasingly soaked through but staying put in the hotel, Pete though this was where it would be appropriate to send a message demanding the release of Hirota.

Millie also put forward a similar message. Once they reached the thirteenth floor however, Pete left the building, leaving the two teams of two converging on the fourteenth floor.

Pete leaving, however, did not act as a hinderance. Pete, leaving meant that Liv no longer had to control her impulse control and using the various knives, daggers, flash bang grenades and bullets, she hacked, slashed, blinded and shot her way through hired Japanese hitmen, until Trent smashed through the window in the hotel room that had Hirota Yoshikazu hostage.

Liv, after being slammed against the wall, released her Bo Staff. She twirled it through her fingers before smacking it against his head and limbs, spinning it to keep a distance between her and the attacker.

The onslaught from the Juliets, and the pandemonium of the no power and sprinkler system pushed Hirota Yoshikazu, and those who were holding him hostage, out into the hallway.

"Liv, do not shoot the person we are meant to be fucking rescuing," Trent screamed, as one of the men fighting for escape doubled over, clutching his arm.

With most of the men subdued due to various injuries Trent, picking Hirota Yoshikazu up in a fireman's lift, ran with the others towards the closest exit.

As they ran, one of the hostage-takers fired a shot that entered into the sole of Yoshikazu's foot, causing him to yell in pain.

Trent threw him into the boot of an SUV, which Pete had stolen from someone they did not know. With Yoshikazu in the boot and everyone bundled into the car, Pete began to drive at high speed throughout traffic and away from the hotel.

"Put on your fucking seatbelts!" Pete screamed from the driver's seat.

"We know you don't have a fucking seatbelt," Millie shouted to Hirota, as he screamed in the boot, being tossed around like a ragdoll as Pete drove through the streets, back alleys and pavements with no concern for anyone else; let alone someone they had just abducted from the hands of an angry Japanese gang in order to save him from a different Japanese gang or two diametrically opposed terrorist groups.

"Why the fuck did you never have to take a driving test?" Liv screamed, as the force of a turn threw Millie into her lap.

"Evade the fucking cops and get us out of here," Millie squealed, attempting to get off Liv's lap.

"Pete, pull over," Liv said.

"Why?"

"Fucking do it!"

Pete managed to find a safe space to for Liv to get off and she ran into oncoming traffic, stole a car and began to drive it. As she and Pete drove together, Liv veered off to the right as Pete carried on straight.

This had the desired affect she was hoping for and the pursuing cars split, following both of them. She drove as fast as she could in the opposite direction attempting to escape and evade the police and whoever else was chasing her.

Pete's evasion took seven hours and a whole tank of fuel before there was nobody around them. They dumped Hirota Yoshikazu at an airstrip ready for collection and went back to their hotel. It was at the hotel where they met back up with Liv, who managed to evade everyone in half the time and make it back to where they were staying.

When they woke up, bloodied, injured and exhausted, Millie dragged them all out of bed before they were due to fly back.

"Where are we going?" Trent groaned.

"You'll see," Millie said.

Millie avoided all of their questions for an hour and a half, until they arrived at a place with a flashing sign サンシャインパラダイスホテルタ トゥーパーラー, which Millie informed them was a translation of Sunshine

Paradise Hotel Tattoo Parlour.

"A tattoo parlour?" Pete sighed exasperatedly.

"Yes, we got a tattoo to commemorate passing out of training. It is only fair for our first mission we get a tattoo for celebration."

"Are we getting a gunshot to celebrate Liv shooting the victim?" Pete said.

"Are we gonna get a fire with a child crying to symbolise you attempting to drive?" Liv retorted.

"No, we are in Japan, you animals," Millie said, aghast, "we are getting five traditional Japanese cherry blossoms in a traditional Japanese style."

"Five. For the five of us," Maddie said, smiling.

"Exactly! Let's go."

They entered the tattoo parlour, and Millie conveyed what exactly they wanted, and Hakuryū Sakiko drew them a design of a branch of cherry blossoms in bloom, and some that weren't on a backdrop of a Japanese red sun.

She and her assistant, Enomoto Takara, sat Millie and Liv down first and began. As the tattooists worked, Millie answered their questions and translated to the others that they were concerned about the cuts, bruises and general looks of all of them.

After they were all tattooed, they paid and thanked the two before heading to the airstrip ready for their flight home.

Like their Juliet tattoos, they all got their Japanese tattoos in identical placement at the top of their left arms.

They were exhausted as they collapsed on the plane; in pyjamas they slept for the entire flight, exhausted from infiltrating a hotel, and a car chase involving the police, a terrorist organisation and a Japanese street gang.

However, they could not sleep away the bruises, cuts and swelling that they were all having to deal with. To make matters worse, Liv had missed a week of school and could not think about a suitable excuse as to why she was so beat up.

When they landed, Maddie and Pete, who were deep in conversation, made it their job to check in all their equipment as the others gave their debrief to G.U.A.R.D. headquarters about the mission, now that G.U.A.R.D. had Hirota Yoshikazu in custody and in interrogation.

G.U.A.R.D. informed Liv that they had already contacted the school explaining her time away from school, but they informed her she would still need to go to school tomorrow.

Still tired, but pleased with their whistle stop tour of Japan, they departed the airstrip in opposite directions.

Liv and Maddie, both exhausted, managed to get home safely before falling asleep in the living room together.

Chapter Eight:

When her alarm went off the next morning, it was greeted by disgruntled swearing from Liv, however she got changed and went to school.

Her arrival caused more of a stir that morning than it usually did. The seniors gawped at her as she held her helmet under her arm.

"Fucking hell, Liv!?!" Mikey asked her as she got to her desk.

"You should see the other guys," she shrugged.

Everyone questioned her about the scrapes on her knuckles, and cuts and bruises all over her. Teachers did not rise above Liv's physical change, and like her fellow students questioned Liv about what was happening.

The teachers also provided Liv with some unfortunate news that parents evening was fast approaching, and the headmaster had instructed that no matter personal circumstance every student must have at least one parent or guardian attend to discuss future career prospects. However, with nobody in the school knowing that Maddie was actually Liv's guardian this put her in an awkward predicament.

Mrs. Noah, however, was of no help to Liv when she brought up the excuse that she was always using, that her parents were on a cruise.

"How the stuck-up bitch expects them to attend is beyond me," she whispered to Alexa mid-way through their English class.

"Olivia would you like to repeat that," she snapped.

Before Liv could repeat the statement however, both Alexa from her left and Robyn from her right instinctively raised their hands over Liv's mouth to stop her, as both of them knew full well that she would have repeated the sentence loudly enough for everyone to hear.

After the English class, Liv had a free period. She went to Mr. Powers' classroom, as he was the only teacher who knew about their vigilante activities, and knocked on his class door. When given the all clear she entered the classroom.

As she entered the classroom with an essay for him to mark and a discussion with him to parents evening however, he spluttered and almost swore in front of his class of eleven-year olds.

He excused himself from the class after accepting her essay and they stood by his door, with a few nosy pre-teens watching them curiously through the door window.

"What's wrong?" he asked her.

"Nothing is wrong."

"There obviously is, you were polite when you walked in, apologised for disturbing the class, now as much as I appreciate you bringing me essays, it is not your love of history that brought you to my classroom."

"You're aware of my extra-curricular activities?"

"I am."

"And you're aware of the criminal organisation known as the BoK?"

"I am, their leaders were taken down and the group split into smaller groups."

"Our parents were those leaders," she sighed bluntly. He stammered and stuttered until Liv cut him off. "Mrs. Noah is being a stubborn bitch about parents evening, and I have no parents, so I would very much appreciate help on this."

"So, your parents aren't on a cruise then?"

"No, that is me being creative."

"Well that explains your tattoo, Madeline was always awful at being your moral compass and impulse control.

Although she was always ninety percent of your impulse control."

"Parents. Evening," Liv prompted, getting the discussion

back on track.

He sighed deeply before saying, "Leave it with me, I will see what I can do."

"Thank you," Liv said gratefully.

"Wow, you must be stressed," he said, performing something at looked like a smile with his facial muscles.

Liv was on tenterhooks, not having the energy to get angry or stressed and was relieved when Maddie took her on a stroll through town on Saturday morning.

However, Maddie directed them past their favourite shops directed her out of the city centre to a used car dealership.

"What in piss are we doing here?" Liv said as the entered.

"I was talking to Pete. He said the anxiousness is down to what we do, school, work-out, vigilante fight. We need a proper release."

"And we are here because...?"

"You love your bike, so we are going to find a bike that does not work and a completely run-down car. We fix them, do the leather, do everything and have pet projects."

They walked round the car shop until the owner put them

in contact with the owner of scrap metal dealership who would have exactly what they were looking for, once they explained the situation and what they were looking for.

They met with the owner, a sleezy, oily man who nonetheless gave them exactly what they needed; a broken, rusted motorbike with torn leather that wouldn't run and a broken, old, American muscle car.

They paid for them to be delivered to their house and returned home. The more Maddie spoke about the idea, the more Liv realised how good an idea it was, as it was clear Maddie was very deeply missing Deanne.

"You realise we know literally nothing about fixing cars and motorbikes," Liv laughed, "other than a few lessons in training."

Since having the realisation about Maddie and how she must be feeling, Liv made an active effort to ensure that Maddie did not feel any essence of loneliness, texting her more times during the day.

That night, they got back into the routine of doing their vigilante work. After the Japan mission, they had needed to rest and recuperate before they beat the streets of Willowdale.

It was an uneventful night until three o'clock that morning, when they noticed that an electronics store was receiving an unusually high level of activity, considering it was closed and wasn't meant to open until nine o'clock in the morning.

However, when they got closer they found an unusually organised heist taking place. Maddie presumed that given how many low-time crooks they had caught that the criminals must be getting smarter in the hope that the mysterious vigilantes that guarded Willowdale would not notice the crime in progress.

A driver sat with the engine on waiting for the off, with five men standing guard and only one-man loading electronics into the boot of the car.

"This is odd, it is normally everybody in, grab what you can and get out," Maddie whispered to Liv.

"I know, this makes it interesting. We need to start by taking out the driver, and then the guards at the door."

"I'll take out the driver, you get onto the roof of the shop. On the signal, try to take out as many guards as possible, when the car is totalled, I'll help you inside."

They moved into position. Weapons drawn, they waited; Liv on the roof and Maddie across the street from the car.

Maddie gave the signal as she shot out the tyres on the car and ran towards the driver's side door as quietly as she could, until she jumped, kicking out the window and dragged the driver out of the car. Running their back along the shards of glass she had just caused, she jumped up and removed the keys to the car. With the car key in between her already weaponised knuckles, she turned and threw a punch into the gut and face of the driver.

The guards were startled by the sound of smashing glass. As they turned around, Liv leapt off the roof using four of them to cushion her. They crumpled, and she stood, seax in one hand and her Bo Staff in the other. She used the blade as a deterrent for the fifth man to keep his distance and also to even the odds, as the four she had just jumped were stirring and attempting to get back to their feet.

Knife slashes and punches were thrown by everyone, Maddie and Liv needing to use their speed to counterbalance the numbers disadvantage that they were at. Using the electronic shop to their advantage, they drove the men back into the shop, limiting the space to fight in, and after a lengthier fight than they were used to with the scourge of Willowdale's underworld they left, victorious.

"One thing I've noticed," Liv said, spitting blood into a drain on the pavement, "is quite how often we have a split or busted lip."

"It is inconvenient for sure," Maddie agreed, copying her actions and wiping some blood from her nose.

"I don't think it has ever fully healed or not been split

since we started this shit."

"Hold up," Maddie sighed in an exasperated tone, "take ten, it's Deanne. She is ringing me."

Liv walked till she was almost out of earshot and waited for Maddie, who from what she could hear sounded as if she was dealing with a toddler as opposed to her girlfriend, which raised Liv's curiosity as to what exactly was going on.

When the call was over Maddie walked towards Liv, rolling her eyes as she did.

"Drunk Deanne?" Liv queried.

"Drunk Deanne," Maddie said miserably. "She is going hell to leather just because she can."

"It'll settle down, it's the party weeks at university. Once she starts lectures proper and gets settled in, then she will only be out like four times a week but will be more mature in her drinking." She ended this by giving her sister a slightly bloody kiss on the cheek.

"I know, I know, I miss her and just wish she was in control. It is fucking with my head. Now she is away from her father she is going crazy. Sure, she would drink when she was with us but never like this, and now with no father for, like, three months, she is just completely out of control with it."

Liv looked at her, the dark night hiding the concern in her eyes. "Come on, let's head home."

"This early?"

"Your heart isn't in it and my head is pounding."

"Thanks," Maddie said gratefully.

When they arrived home, Liv moaned a sigh of relief. Putting an ice cube on her lip and a few ice cubes in a glass for her and a glass for Maddie, she filled them with the whiskey they had brought back from Japan and they slumped in the living room, attempting to unwind.

Maddie left Liv after one drink to go to bed, Leaving Liv nursing her lip to drink alone downstairs.

Two days later the scrap dealership they visited dropped off the car and the motorbike so that in their spare time they could set about restoring them.

Not having a clue how to restore them however, they started with the upholstery, ordering in rolls of leather, carpet for the car and everything they would need to start the restoration process. Luckily they could order all of this from G.U.A.R.D. rather than having to find a shop in Willowdale.

Over the next few days they were interrupted whilst working at night by Deanne calling Maddie on an increasingly frequent basis.

Two weeks after the first time Deanne called, she called again, this time was when they were sat in the kitchen. Liv just home from school was sat doing her homework with a cup of tea. Maddie excused herself from the kitchen to take the call.

Liv didn't notice Maddie return to the kitchen until she heard the clatter of Maddie's phone as it hit the floor.

Startled, she looked up, to see Maddie looking as white as a snow, colour draining from her face as her hands shook as she sank down onto the floor.

Liv cautiously sat down next to her, alarmed at what she was seeing from Maddie.

"What happened?" she whispered.

Maddie didn't say anything from fear of throwing up.

She sat with the emptiness inside of her swallowing her like an abyss, the pain she was feeling far worse than any physical pain she had been through before.

They both sat on the floor, Maddie trembling, just looking at her hands as if she was wishing that the world would swallow her up and so she could feel the blissfulness of not feeling anything ever again.

The paradox between feeling so much and feeling so empty was agonising torture. Liv putting her arm around her, just looked at her, shocked.

"Another girl," Maddie croaked, her voice hollow as if her soul would slip from her mouth if she spoke again or opened her mouth too wide.

Liv kept one arm around Maddie's neck, and using her other arm scooped her up into a carrying position. She carried Maddie up to bed, lit her scented candle, put on her fairy lights and made sure she was wrapped up in her covers.

Liv sent a message to Trent, Millie and Pete explaining what had happened, put on her bike helmet and jacket and left the garage on her Harley.

She drove as fast as she could. Once she got on the motorway and on the country roads, she disregarded all speed limits as she set off for Airedale University.

She completed the four-and-a-half-hour drive in three-and-a-quarter-hours. She made good time and finally found Deanne's halls of residence.

Leaving her helmet on her bike, she ruffled up her hair and waited by the door. The door needed an ID card to open. This was something she did not have.

However, with the lighter she carried being flicked and played with, it was the perfect excuse ready in waiting as someone came out for a smoke. She lent them her lighter, explaining that she was keeping someone company and had come out for a cigarette, forgetting to pick up their

ID.

They let her in, and she cautiously went to the fourth floor and picked the lock to room twenty-four.

As she opened the door, it was to find an empty room. She entered and locked the door. Whilst in Deanne's room, Liv logged onto the guest Wi-Fi and sat in Deanne's desk chair waiting for her. Seeing a photo frame with a picture of her and Maddie in it enraged Liv, as did seeing the various gifts Maddie had given Deanne in their relationship around the room.

After an hour of Liv being sat in Deanne's room, the lock clicked as if a key was being inserted and Liv waited expectantly for the door to open. As it opened, Deanne froze in the doorway and an unknown girl behind her let out a stifled scream.

Deanne spluttered words and began to shake as Liv got out of the chair.

"It's a nice room," Liv said, smiling widely at Deanne, her voice so sweet it was dangerous. "Little reminder," she continued, towering over Deanne. "It took me less than three minutes to get into your building and into your room. So, I am warning you. Your bridges in Willowdale are burnt. You will never contact, harm or speak to my sister again."

"Liv, I am sorry," she whimpered, "I- I ..."

"Over the fuckin' phone, Deanne? That is how you end it? Disgraceful. You're on thin fucking ice."

As Liv walked past the two of them to leave, she noticed Deanne scanning Liv's body for weapons and Liv made it known she had her favourite seax on her.

As Liv walked past them, she heard the girl start to berate Deanne for not telling her that she had a girlfriend, or that she had just broken up with her. As she was putting on her motorbike helmet, Liv saw the girl running out of the block. She smiled softly to herself as she began to drive back to Willowdale.

It was late at night when she returned home. When she did, it was to notice a familiar Harley Davidson parked out front and a car she did not recognise.

When she entered the house, it was to see the Juliets reunited in the living room.

"Where have you been?" Trent asked, as they all looked around at her.

"I had someone to speak to," she shrugged, kissing her sister and sitting next to Pete.

"I'm not great with emotions and how to deal with them," he muttered to her.

"You don't say," Liv said sarcastically.

"That announcement has me shooketh," Millie said.

"Did you really just drive all the way to Airedale University?" Trent asked.

They all looked up at her as she smiled sweetly at them.

"Is she…" Trent asked.

"Obviously, I didn't commit murder."

"I wasn't worried you had, until now."

"Wait, did you log on to the internet whilst you were there?" Pete said.

"Yeah, why?"

"Give me your phone," he requested, getting his laptop.

Trent, Millie and Liv attempted to console and make Maddie smile, when this didn't really work, they just decided to get quite drunk. Although Pete was on his laptop, he got drunk with them.

"Also," Millie laughed, "Liv, What the actual fuck?"

"What?!" Liv said, confused.

"We went into your room, books, neat, tidy. FAIRY LIGHTS?! SO, I repeat, WHAT THE FUCK!"

Everyone laughed, including Maddie, which was nice to

see.

"What were you expecting from my room?"

"Bloody bandages from every night where your fists are bandaged. Swords everywhere, maybe someone's thumb on the floor," Millie suggested.

"Not fairy lights," Pete added honestly.

"Maddie has scented candles," Liv replied.

"Yeah, we expected that but not the piles of clothes on the floor! As your stressed grown-up, I am disappointed," Trent smirked, as he stood behind Maddie before engulfing her in a hug causing a bleak, teary-eyed smile.

Trent kissed her on the top of her head and would not release the hug. Maddie was glad he was not releasing the hug as she liked the smell of his beard oil.

When Maddie was asleep, and had been so for twenty minutes, it was only then that Trent release the hug. It was also when Pete confessed to them what he had done.

"It was easy once I was in, I located her laptop and devices on the network and downloaded a virus on the devices putting them to factory settings, so she has lost everything on them, including all of her university work."

Trent laughed as he picked Maddie up as if she were a child and took her to bed.

Chapter Nine:

Liv and Millie who were the first to wake the next morning. They sat in the kitchen making a cup of tea. When the doorbell rang it started the entire house.

By the time they got to the door, Trent, Pete and Maddie were all downstairs. When the door opened, Deanne was stood there.

"You shouldn't be here, Deanne," Liv growled.

"Maddie won't answer my texts, and when I was doing work my laptop crashed and there was nothing on it."

Deanne barged her way into the house and froze instantly when she saw Millie, Trent and Pete all stood there. This scene looked a lot more intimidating by the fact that neither Trent nor Pete had t shirts on, and they were stood either side of Maddie.

"You shouldn't be here, leave now," Liv repeated, stepping in front of Deanne.

"No, I need to speak to Maddie."

"Listen to Liv," Millie said.

"Who are all of you, why are you doing this?"

"Family," Trent said simply.

"I tried to warn you, Deanne. Now go," Liv reiterated.

"No," she fired back.

"Leave," Maddie said from in between Pete and Trent, "you lost your privilege to speak to me, to walk into this house, when you cheated on me."

"Listen," Deanne began, but was cut off by Millie who walked very calmly and stood as close as she could to Deanne. She grabbed the front of her, lifting her up off the ground and placing her outside on the doormat.

As Deanne screamed, Pete instinctively moved forward in case Deanne attempted to do anything to Millie.

"ENOUGH!" Maddie bellowed over all of them, so loudly it caused Trent to jump and everyone to spin around. "You have twelve minutes. Millie, start a timer and everyone go into the living room."

Eleven minutes and thirty seconds later, the Juliets left the living room and waited for Deanne and Maddie to leave the kitchen.

Deanne left in silence and Maddie, turning around, let out a deep sigh and said, "Let's work out then go out for lunch."

Nobody said anything during the workout or over lunch, it was clear that they were not to bring anything up.

The only thing that was said was Maddie asking Pete about the virus that he put on Deanne's computer to which Pete confessed to, citing he wasn't good at emotions but was good at revenge, so he did the first thing that came to mind that would give Maddie some vindication to know that he had caused Deanne everything she would have worked for since she started university.

After a filling lunch they returned home, Maddie now questioning how long they were going to stay in Willowdale for, but Millie simply told her that they would stay for as long as she wanted them to.

Trent excused himself from the group to take a phone call, as Pete examined the battered and broken car and motorbike that Liv and Maddie were planning on restoring. Looking at the engines, he began giving them some pointers on what exactly they would need to do.

"Maddie, you know you asked how long we would stay?" Trent asked, coming back into the room from his call.

"Yeah."

"Until the job is done. That was G.U.A.R.D., Willowdale is on amber alert and as we are already in the city, it is our job."

Stunned, everyone in the room looked at him.

"What do G.U.A.R.D. think is going to happen?" Liv asked him.

"With the expansion of Willowdale and the current political climate, the government is moving printing plates and the machines that are used to print money out of cities to the countryside."

"But printing plates aren't in Willowdale?" Liv asked, confused.

"I know that, however, with a port, airport, airstrips and train stations all in Willowdale the two sides of the note plates will have to be split up and sent differently, all with an armed escort."

"I'm sensing a 'however'," Pete said.

"However, with a storm looking like it is going to hit Willowdale in the next twenty-four hours, they are keeping the prints in Willowdale Central Bank in the vault until the storm subsides, which could be a week."

"That means there is a week for those plates to be stolen, and money counterfeiting would get one hell of a lot easier," Millie finished.

"This is a golden opportunity for any and everyone in the counterfeiting world."

"Wait, what is all this about a storm?" Liv asked, confused.

"We spoke about this," Maddie sighed, "wind and rain, thunder and lightning, happening soon."

"Did we?"

"Yes, you absolute moron," she sighed.

The next morning gave Maddie memories of when she and Liv were much younger, as she sat at the kitchen table watching Liv and Trent argue about Liv actually going to school when there was G.U.A.R.D. work to be done.

In the end she relented and took the car to school. It was mid-way through her history lesson when the storm started to hit Willowdale. It rained sideways, and night seemed to come in mid-afternoon with dark clouds enveloping them.

There was nothing more calming to Liv than the sound of the wind and the rain hammering against the windows.

"You look calmer than I think I have ever seen you," Alexa said to her, as she watched Liv sat with her eyes closed, contently listening to the rain.

"I love the rain, the wind, the sound of thunder, the flash of lightning. It is so cathartic."

"How can you love this weather?"

"What's not to love? The sound of that, a piping hot cup

of tea, a massive oversized hoodie," she said, flapping the sleeves of Trent's hoodie that she was wearing over her school shirt.

"Nah," Mikey said, looking at her. "Shorts and t-shirt all day every day, sun shining, long evenings. Perfect."

"Exactly," Alexa added.

"You're both wrong, what do you do in summer when it is too hot? You die. What do you do when you get cold? You put on layers, you warm yourself up, only so much clothing you can remove when it is warm."

They continued the disagreement until the end of school, before using the assignment Mrs. Noah had just given her as an umbrella, Liv ran to the car and drove home. As much as Liv loved the rain, she hated driving in it and she knew that on patrol that night they were going to get wet through.

"Any news?" she asked, as soon as she entered the house.

"No, and - wait, are you in my hoodie?"

"Yes, I am and, well, we were hardly expecting anyone to attempt to steal it in the day, if it happens it'll be tonight or tomorrow most likely."

"See, there was no reason to miss school," he smirked.

"Whatever," Liv said, rolling her eyes.

She and Millie sat in Liv's room, as Liv attempted to unwind and relax before they then went out into the storm on patrol.

Within seconds of being on patrol they were soaked to the bone; despite the nature of the tactical gear, it didn't stop their goggles from gathering water and weighing them down.

Due to the nature of what could potential go down, they carried all of their weapons as if it were a special operation, as opposed to their vigilante work.

"Now, we can't do anything to do with the bank until we have been given the go ahead by G.U.A.R.D. HQ, until then we just do Maddie and Liv's vigilante work," Trent reiterated.

"We know," Millie groaned, having heard Trent say the same thing for the past three hours.

It was an hour and a half later when they were given the go by G.U.A.R.D. headquarters. Having been notified that something was happening at the bank, they ordered the Willowdale police department to stand down and not go near the scene of the Willowdale Central Bank.

When they got closer to the bank, they saw what looked like a small army outside the bank with more men going inside. Reports that the seventeen guards inside were still alive but were hostages, they ran towards the bank and saw the perimeter was completely surrounded. On Trent's instruction, Liv and Millie got onto the roof of the bank to see if there was a way in undetected by the heavily armed militia stood outside.

There was, but the fire door was most certainly going to be alarmed, if opened. So, they took a different approach. With the sound of the pounding rain and the occasional rumble of thunder, Millie and Liv took out some of their preferred G.U.A.R.D. equipment, axes and Bo Staffs, and readied themselves.

They used the axes to cut a rough hole in the door big enough for them to slip into. They then notified the others and waited for further instructions.

Trent told them to wait for Pete to join them before heading in, whilst he and Maddie got a full count of people outside.

When Pete joined them, they headed down through the fire door and into the bank. Maddie and Liv had only been in the bank a few times and generally used it as a vantage point, but they knew they had at least six floors to cover without being detected.

Whether it was the weather or it was intentional, there was no power inside the bank; no lights, none of the computers and no electronic locks.

"Trent," Pete whispered over the comms, "they're either stealing the entire vault or they are about to bring in drilling equipment."

"Understood. Our objective is to get the hostages out safe and sound and, if we can, the plates. I want to avoid a war."

The viciousness of the storm against the bank windows ensured an acceptable amount of cover for their footsteps as they cleared the offices on the upper floors, and ensured their guns had silences on them. However, they shortly discovered it was not just them who was doing a sweep of the upper floors. They needed to keep the element of surprise for as long as possible, so they knew that taking out those doing a sweep silently and swiftly was of paramount importance.

"Trent, we have hostiles incoming."

"Engage but do not shoot, Maddie and I are on the second floor now. We need to get the hostages out."

"How?"

"The roof, how you came in. We entered through a window. First things first.

Close and lock the front doors; nobody in, everybody out."

"Understood."

As the footsteps approached, Liv, Maddie and Pete all slipped into different offices and waited to see if they would check the offices.

They did.

Pete disarmed the man as fast as he could, taking his weapon and ammunition.

They got to a position where they could see the main entrance to the bank. The door was being held open, to stop the doors, which was were on a mechanised hanger, from slamming shut.

"All we need to do is shoot the coil which is preventing the doors from slamming shut," Pete whispered.

"I'll take the shot, Trent and Maddie go around and down to see if you can see any of the hostages. The slamming of the door may make this place go haywire."

Millie went back up two floors in order to get the best vantage point, she only had one shot at the mechanism to cause the doors to slam.

It took two shots.

The first ricocheted off the mechanism, the second caused the door to slam and lock mechanically. Gun fire sounded and flashes of barrels came from all over the first floor and the ground floor.

"What the fuck was that?" they heard someone shout, as they ran towards the door.

"The winch must have broken," another shouted.

"Find us an exit out of the fucking bank."

"Teams of six, sweep every level of this place and find us an exit out of here."

"That's all the info we need," Liv said.

"Stay sharp. You're faster than death, stronger than a mountain," Millie said to Liv as they passed each other, preparing themselves for a fight.

Maddie was positioned on the first floor, Trent on the second, Pete on the third, Millie on the fourth and Liv was on the fifth floor. They watched as six well-organised teams went up the stairs from the ground floor.

Thunder rumbled and lightning forked. Those on the lower floors knew they would have to wait for a team to reach Liv's floor before engaging. When Liv engaged, the others engaged.

Liv grabbed one of them and simply launched him off the balcony. She loved buildings like this. As he fell to the lobby of the bank, she hurled throwing knives as she darted into one of the offices. The floors below would have seen and heard him; they now knew they were not alone in the bank.

Trent heard him plummet and knew he needed to engage swiftly. However, as the best marksman in the group he made swift work, eight shots and six men hit the floor.

Pete was almost as successful; it took him twelve shots to take down his team of six. With them down, he moved to the floor above to help his sister as Trent went down to the first.

Millie had taken down two of the men but was pinned down when Trent arrived. Maddie had disarmed three and injured one.

Liv took cover as she went to reload, as she found, she was out of ammunition.

"I'm out of ammo," she said over the communication system, launching the empty magazine at one of the three left standing.

"Join us on first once you're done," Trent said.

Pete went down to first, and Millie joined Liv on her floor as back up firepower.

Finally, with Millie providing Liv with additional ammunition, they met the rest of the group on the first floor and they each went to one of the four sides of the building, looking down at the lobby.

They waited to see who would make the first move, as they waited the rain hammered against the windows.

"You out there," somebody shouted over the rain and the wind. "Surrender or the hostages die."

"Let the hostages go and take us instead," Trent said. As he did so, he signalled to Pete that now was the time to call in the police and anyone else to take out the rest of the militia that were waiting outside, unable to enter the bank.

"Why would I want you?"

"We were tipped off to what was going to happen by a mole. We will tell you who gave us the tip," Trent lied.

"The door is on a timer, it cannot be opened till later in the morning, having the hostages up there with you would do you no good," the man in the vault shouted.

"Would make us feel a lot safer about them knowing they were not hostages," Trent responded calmly.

"Millie, Liv, start acting like spider monkeys and see if you can get down without anyone seeing you," Pete whispered over the coms.

Liv thanked the rain as it muffled her landing on the lobby. She saw three people with guns pointed at the stairs leading to the first floor, where the other Juliets were.

They were the only people, it seemed, in the lobby. The rest appeared to be down in the passage to the vault, on the left of Liv and on the right of Millie.

They nodded to each other and took out the three men.

"Down in the vault passage. Let the hostages out," Trent shouted, having just seen what happened.

"I can wait it out till morning, then my men outside can just walk in and end you. I have thirty men outside with fifty on standby to call."

"Actually, at this point it is more like three men outside, and call them anyway," Trent said, as with a swift hand signal to Pete, he ordered a signal jammer to be activated.

Millie and Liv heard someone curse in the hallway, potentially noticing the activation. Unfortunately, with them still unable to see round corners or through walls, they did not know exactly what was happening.

"In case you didn't hear that gunfire, that is three more down and out for the count. You either leave alive, or you attempt to kill the hostages. We hear gunfire, storm the vault and you all leave dead," Trent said, presenting a final ultimatum.

"Or you let me leave with the plates and I don't kill hostages."

"Do you have the plates?"

"No... not yet."

Liv didn't hear Trent's response as she had a brilliant idea, signalling for Millie to cover herself under one of the desks, she pointed her gun up and fired into the skylight.

Heavy rain and glass showered down upon the lobby, the rain that had been beating down on them for hours was now quickly making the lobby floor very slippery, however it also provided Liv with an opportunity to attempt to see what was happening, using the reflective glass on the skylight in an attempt to see round corners and into the vault.

Millie, seeing what Liv was attempting to do, started to do the same. As lightning forked across where the skylight used to be it provided the opportunity for the corridor to be illuminated.

From what they could see, there were three people there; hostage or hostage-taker, they did not know.

Millie shuffled across the floor towards the corridor, at the bottom she faintly saw lights and glow sticks next to a drill. They were clearly about to start drilling when the Juliets interrupted them. She also saw the hostages sitting down against the vault door with guns pointed at them.

Millie pointed her pistol at the shoe of the person she believed was having a shouting match with Trent. She fired, and turned around quickly as he let out an agonising scream of pain.

Using the skylight, they saw other people coming to help the fallen man and Millie and Liv did the same thing again, turning and shooting the others in the foot.

With four people now on the floor clutching their feet, Liv and Millie waited to see if more people would come.

They signalled for Trent, Maddie and Pete to come join them in the lobby.

"Now, we would like to continue the negotiations," Trent called.

He only got profanities back in a response.

Pete lit a flare and threw it into the corridor, illuminating everything.

They moved, Trent and Liv disarming those that had just shot. Whilst the others moved on the hostages, they secured the drill and the vault and led the hostages out of the vault, through the lobby, which was now slippery from the rain, up onto the roof and down the fire exit to safety.

Trent then contacted G.U.A.R.D. to get additional manpower inside the vault corridor and some non-special forces around the bank.

"Liv, they would like to speak to you."

"Ooooh you're fucked," Pete said.

Liv stuck up her middle fingers before taking the phone. "Hello...Yes...Yes...Well yes...No... No...Go fuck yourself."

She handed the phone back to Trent, who groaned at Liv swearing at them.

"How did that go?" Millie asked her.

"Trying to have a go at me for shooting out the skylight," Liv shrugged. "We would still be there if I didn't."

"Trent," Millie yawned, tugging his arm and looking up at him. "Can we deal with this in the morning? Can we please go home, have a drink, get into some warm pyjamas and pick this up tomorrow?"

"We do all look like drowned rats," Trent admitted.

When they eventually arrived home, they changed out of their tactical gear in the kitchen, to avoid trailing water through the house as Maddie gave out towels.

They were all bruised and bloodied, whether it was tiny shards of glass or just the result of fist fighting.

The gym had been somewhat disassembled to make a suitable bedroom for Pete, with Trent sleeping in the living room and Millie sharing with Liv. They went off to bed for a well-deserved rest.

With the rain, wind, thunder and lightning along with the condition Liv was in, the Juliets deemed it best that she stay home from school that day. She needed to recuperate and Trent privately did not trust Liv to drive in these conditions.

So to compensate, they lit the fire in the living room and curled up to watched films. Millie introduced the group to what Pete called 'her cat tendencies' when she curled up in a ball right next to the fire, stealing all of the heat and using Liv's thigh as a pillow whenever Liv sat on the floor.

The storm only worsened over the next two days, which meant that Liv got the best night's sleep she had ever had, due to the sound of the rain and the wind. It also meant she would not be in school, which suited everyone and meant Maddie was suitably distracted from having to think about her recent break-up with Deanne.

Not leaving the house for a few days did wonders for everyone in terms of health and just general happiness. However, as the storm was dying, Liv was contacted by G.U.A.R.D. who said she would need to be in school the next day.

She groaned and attempted to get ready for school without waking Millie. When Liv crept downstairs it was to find Trent in the kitchen with a recently boiled kettle and a cup of tea waiting for her, as well as a hot water bottle, as he sat with a stack of paperwork which needed completing.

"You are the most precious thing in the world," Liv said gratefully, taking the cup and looking at him.

"Me or the tea?" Trent asked.

Liv didn't give a response but sat drinking her tea, savouring the taste and the warmth before stepping out into the wind and the rain.

As Liv sat in the seniors only area enjoying the sound of the rain and the wind, she was joined by Alexa and Mikey. Despite Liv's attempts, the conversation turned to the news.

"Did you see what happened in the Willowdale Central Bank in the midst of the storm?"

"Yeah," Mikey said.

"There were so many people keeping guard outside whilst they tried to rob the bank, how they failed I will never know," Alexa added.

"I heard it was the remnants of the BoK making one last attempt at a big heist," Mikey said, nodding.

"Not possible, every higher member of the BoK were taken down and arrested, the only ones who managed to escape prison were too low down and too stupid to organise something as sophisticated and strategic as that," Liv said, not looking up from her cup of tea.

"You seem to know an awful lot about it," someone said from behind her.

Looking around, Liv saw it was one of Robyn's friends, whose name she didn't know.

"The mayor gave us a debriefing on the situation the night the BoK were brought down after my father resigned, she explained everything before they went on their vacation," Liv said to her casually.

"You know the mayor?" They all asked quizzically.

"Not 'invite her round for a drink', but well enough for her to check in on us every now and then."

"Must be nice not having your parents there, free house. Just you and your sister!" Alexa laughed.

"It has its benefits, speaking of which, you should come over on Friday, we are throwing a party."

"Sounds good!" Alexa said brightly.

"It does," Mikey said nervously, before asking Liv for a word in private.

Liv, who needed to make a cup of tea, took Mikey to the kitchen so she could listen to him.

"So, me and Nattie have been dating for a couple of weeks."

"You have?! That's... I am happy for you. Is it a secret?" Liv asked.

"No, everyone knows."

"Why the pulling me aside?"

"Because, she is one of Robyn's friends and I want you to be okay with her occasionally hanging around with us, and also would kinda want her to come to the party if that's okay?"

"Yeah, I have no issues with her coming... do you need me to clear the air with Robyn?"

"Please."

Later that day, Liv rolled up her sleeves and went to find Robyn, who was sat chatting to Nattie and the others.

"Hey," she said awkwardly, to get them to turn around. "You're all cool, I have no issues with any of you. Stay tight."

"Is this you clearing the air?" Robyn laughed.

"Is that a real tattoo?" Nattie asked.

"Yes, and yes," Liv said, answering Robyn and Nattie's questions.

Robyn stood up and directed Liv away so they could

actually talk, as opposed to Liv standing awkwardly.

"You look like shit, Liv," Robyn said.

"I thought we were clearing the air?" Liv said, rolling her eyes.

"Well, it needed to be said. I did your make-up for months. I can see everything through your make-up. You look rough."

"Yeah, well you know. Been busy," Liv shrugged. "I am sorry for everything, you know."

"Yeah, stopping bank robberies," she smirked. "I overreacted as well, and I apologise for that. I should have supported you through thick and thin."

"Well, getting stabbed can freak people out. Besides you've still kept my secret and I'm thankful for that."

They stood awkwardly before hugging for a moment, then Robyn went to join her friends.

Chapter Ten:

When Liv returned home, she found Maddie with a new haircut and a more vibrant shade of blue, in the kitchen discussing the arrangements for Friday with Millie.

"Amazing undercut, Mads," Liv smiled, as she threw her bag down.

"Yeah, I needed a change and the hairdresser, Lizzie, suggested an undercut and here we are," Maddie yawned.

They readied themselves for Trent's delicious cooking, as Liv and Millie spoke idly about Liv's monotonous day at school, before Millie continued with Liv's rudimentary Japanese lessons.

Once they had eaten as much as they could, they retired for the evening, Pete declared that 'he wasn't going to be at the party because he couldn't think of anything worse than being at a party with a bunch of Maddie's friends and a few of Liv's as well'.

Thankfully, Friday night came around fast. Trent and Maddie ensured the house was fully stocked with party drinks, whilst locking the finer whiskeys and other spirits away. Millie and Liv ensured most of their weapons, special ops gear and vigilante gear was locked safely in the gym so that they could not be found by any wandering party goers.

Soon everyone began to arrive. Trent and Millie were introduced to the others and they all began to drink and enjoy the music. However, there was a very uneasy elephant in the room which seemingly needed to be discussed; the fact that they were all meeting since Deanne broke up with Maddie.

Jessica said that university had changed Deanne and not for the better, saying that they hadn't spoken since Deanne first got settled.

Once they had discussed Deanne the air of awkwardness was lifted, and they could just enjoy their night with no distractions.

"They're actually a really cute couple," Liv said to Alexa, as they watched Mikey and Nattie play beer pong against Trent and Millie.

"Yeah, I know."

"The whole 'you're the missing piece in my jigsaw' aspect is a big gross though," Liv laughed.

"Incidentally, what is that you're drinking?"

"Horny Hangover."

"A what now? Excuse me?"

"Horny Hangover. Shot of bourbon, shot of black sambuca, shot of Jäger, shot of spiced rum, shot of peach schnapps and shot of amaretto all mixed and topped up with lemonade."

"Jesus, sweet Jesus," Alexa laughed.

"So, how come you and Mikey never dated? You two were flirting like crazy."

"Oblivious bisexual," Alexa sighed. "We were never flirting with each other."

"Yes, you were."

"No, we weren't. He was flirting with you and he isn't my type."

"What is your type then, because you were flirting?"

Alexa rolled her eyes before going to get another drink.

"You need to learn how to flirt," Millie whispered to Liv.

Liv elbowed her hard and went to join Trent in a game of beer pong. However, before they could begin the doorbell rang.

"I thought this was everyone you invited?" Millie asked.

"It is," Liv said suspiciously, going to the door.

When Liv opened it, she squealed with excitement to see Pete there.

He pulled Liv outside and began speaking in a hurried tone. "We don't have much time. Millie is going to need to fake too much alcohol and need to be rushed to hospital. Whilst that is being done, get everyone's special ops gear and every single weapon we have, there are more waiting for us at the hangar, but we need to go. Go."

Liv ran back inside, grabbed Millie and took her upstairs and out of the way. She then turned off the music and in a scared voice explained to everyone what was going on and that they had to leave.

This was not a popular decision amongst the guests but Liv and Trent ushered everyone out.

Alexa was particularly disgruntled to be leaving and kept asking questions, but there was no time.

"What the fuck is all this about?" Maddie asked.

"We've been called up for a mission," Pete said, now entering the house as Millie began bringing down all their gear.

With everything packed, they all squeezed into the one car. Pete was driving as he was the only one who legally could. He began handing out fast food and cups of tea to sober the others up.

When they arrived at the airstrip, that they were now

becoming increasingly familiar with, Pete had already packed a lot of weaponry and ammunition onto the plane, so all he had to do was get the rest of the Juliets onto the plane.

When they were on the plane, they continued eating and sobering up as Pete began explaining what was going on.

"This," he said, showing them a picture, "is Øistein Dahle. He is a former Norwegian diplomat and politician, tipped to become their next Prime Minister. Unfortunately, his policies have annoyed a group called the Yesteryear National White Alliance or Y.N.W.A. They are recruiting at an alarming rate and being backed financially by an unknown source. Someone on the far right, who is clearly not a fan of Dahle."

"They are planning an assassination?" Millie asked.

"Yes, we have moved him to a compound, and it is our job to protect him from dying."

"Norwegian terrorists are a new one to me," Liv laughed.

"Y.N.W.A. are a Norwegian group but the coup is being influenced by a foreign power. They are a bunch of men's rights activists and far right extremists. They aren't trained enough for an assignation of this level, so they have help.

That means that someone has employed a private army

for this job. G.U.A.R.D. are working to disable to Y.N.W.A.'s finances but we are to take out the army and the far right MRAs who are part of this assassination pack."

After the initial brief they attempted to sleep on the plane in order to be fully refreshed.

Turbulence awoke them with only half the flight gone, so Liv reached into her travel bag and pulled out a battered book and began to read.

"You should attempt to sleep," Pete said to her, looking up from his phone.

"She is reading, you'd have better luck pulling her tooth out," Maddie said, before going back to sleep.

They were all sober, awake and refreshed when the plane touched down in Norwegian airspace. They dropped their things off at a safehouse and began getting into tactical gear.

They sat round the table as Trent began discussing their plans. He had a blueprint and pictures of the compound that Øistein Dahle was in and he began instructing them.

There were two points of attack for the Y.N.W.A., with the house having a river on one side, a fjord on the other.

"So, they can either just walk up to the front door of the

compound via the drive or the woods, or via boat?" Millie summarised.

"Essentially yes, now listen for your positions. We camp, then move in for attack."

"This is a stealth mission," Pete said, looking at all the girls. "Keep the explosions to a minimum."

"Shame we can't shoot a skylight and get some rain involved," Liv laughed.

They gathered supplies and carried as much ammunition as possible. Liv and Millie also made sure their concealed battle-axes, seax and other knives, which had been so affective in Japan and in the bank heist, were fully sharpened before they set off.

Camouflaged and ready, they spread out where Trent had positioned them. They sat in the long grass and waited.

G.U.A.R.D. had trained them to ignore the elements. They sat and waited for any sign of impending trouble.

"I don't like this, it is almost TOO quiet," Millie muttered.

"I don't like staying still," Liv said, through gritted teeth.

"We know, Liv, stakeouts suck, and you should just run head first into all of them and take them down,"

Trent said, rolling his eyes, despite none of them being

able to see him do it.

"I'm glad you think so!" Liv said, a little brighter.

"Sarcasm. Stay put."

They sat there for three more hours before there was finally movement.

"We have movement," Pete said. "Twenty coming down the drive."

"Thirty coming from the woods," Liv added, using her night vision scope.

"They're spreading out into teams of ten," Trent said, taking the safety off his weapon.

"What is the plan of attack?"

"I could sneak around and start picking them off from behind?" Liv suggested.

"I think I have some explosives," Millie said.

"Covert. Fucking. Stealth. Mission," Trent said. "Liv, go. Millie, stay put and do your job."

"Liv may be the distraction that we need. When Liv engages with her ten, we lay down the firepower."

Liv knew she would have to act quickly.

As one of them was bringing up the rear she knew what needed to be done. A simple rear naked choke, a personal favourite of Tula's and one that they had used countless times to render an enemy unconscious.

She did this to two more people, before Trent began the more traditional approach. Maddie, Millie and Pete followed his lead.

The members of the Y.N.W.A., and whichever hired army were working for them could not hear the gunshots, but it lit up the night sky.

Trent was more strategic with his shots as the men scattered and dropped to the ground. Maddie and Millie spotted someone in the distance and fired at whatever they saw.

Liv's job of picking them off one by one was made more difficult by this but nonetheless, with her battle axe in one hand and a sidearm in the other, she successfully stopped her ten.

However, Millie called for aid as she was pinned down. Liv ran in her direction to help out.

"Trent, did you call for backup?" Millie screamed, as Liv joined her and attempted to even the odds.

"Nope. Did you, Pete?"

"Fallback fifteen feet," Trent screamed, as Pete was pinned down.

They fell back, but they were spread too thin on the ground. They retreated again but after a while ammunition was running low. Trent, being the expert marksman, was the only one who kept the playing field even but even his ammunition was running low.

"We've got more incoming!" Pete shouted.

"Fuck off!" Maddie replied.

"I think we have another fifty, by the looks of it."

"Fuck off!" everyone screamed.

They moved closer to the front of the compound and became closer as a group.

However, Millie's use of explosives proved useful, but they were running low on ammunition.

The sound of explosions and screams were joined by the sound of a helicopter which flew over the fjord and bullets flying over their head towards the enclosing Y.N.W.A. members.

"What the fuck is that?" Maddie asked.

"I thought you didn't call for back-up?" Pete screamed to Trent.

"Is the helicopter playing music?" Millie asked.

"Oh, fuck off, oh fuck off, oh fuck off. It is playing 'Flower of Scotland'," Trent said, still shooting.

The unknown people in the helicopter had taken out every member of the Y.N.W.A. However, as the helicopter was landing, Pete ran over to Trent and began to disarm him of every firearm he was carrying.

"Why are you doing that?" Millie asked.

"Canadians," Pete said.

"What?"

"Q-Squadron, Quebec. Now follow my lead."

Pete then positioned Millie and Liv in front of Trent, with Maddie and him on either side of Trent. They stood and watched three people walk towards them from the helicopter.

They stepped closer, the one in the front was the tallest, about five foot eight inches, and by the way their long blonde hair was billowing it was a woman. When they saw her, she was dressed all in leather, her leather jacket had two-inch metal spikes on both of her shoulders.

Next to her was a man smaller than all of them, barely over five foot. On her other side was a man with square shoulders and a lot of muscles.

"Shock, horror, I am saving your life again, Trent," she said to him in a thick Scottish accent, Pete moving everyone inwards, blocking Trent off.

"And yet, anytime I'm close to you it feels like death," he responded.

"Pete didn't tell you this was a two-squadron job... evidently."

"No, he didn't, otherwise I would have shot myself," Trent grunted. "Juliets, this is Sjöfn MacMhoirein."

"I was shot earlier!" Liv shouted, sensing the tension. "Can we leave please?"

"WHAT?!" All eight of them shouted.

Trent glared at Sjöfn and the rest of the Q-Squadron before he ordered the Juliets back to the safe house.

"Wait, is she called Sjöfn, from Norse mythology?" Liv asked, still clutching her thigh but ignoring their cries.

"What? The name is from mythology?" Millie asked.

"Yeah, the goddess of love. She was focused on turning the minds of people, both men and women, to love. When Christianity was forced upon the Scandinavian area, they found the goddess to be so beautiful and held in such high regard that they erased her from history.

Same with Friday the thirteenth," Liv said, knowledgably, "They also just fucking hated the concept of Goddesses hence the lack of stories about Eir, Vor and Lofn."

"Friday the thirteenth?" Millie asked her, attempting to keep her mind off the pain in her thigh.

"Friday the thirteenth was a day of love, good luck and sex, but Christianity butchered thousands because you couldn't have extramarital sex or love so due to the murders it became unlucky," Liv said.

"Back to you being FUCKING shot, AGAIN?" Trent said, dropping to his knee to take a look at her thigh. "It's not a deep graze, I can patch it up when we get back."

"I said it wasn't a big deal. I just wanted the attention on me. So, who was the attractive woman and the dude and the man?" Liv asked.

"Sjöfn MacMhoirein, TJ Porter and Archie Hart are G.U.A.R.D. special ops. Same as us. Q-Squadron. I was also in the Army Special Forces with Sjöfn and Archie. TJ is the fucking man," Trent said through gritted teeth. "Sjöfn and I were together. We were on a mission in Budapest. Mission went sideways. Archie blamed me. There was a mole in the intelligence committee that was leaking information. There was no evidence it was me, and Sjöfn believed Archie."

"So you left?" Millie asked.

"G.U.A.R.D. had been trying to headhunt me for a while, so I accepted their offer and then, yeah, was given you lot."

"Still puzzles me why she chose to believe him," Pete said in a bored voice, having heard the story before.

They returned to the safe house and got changed out of their tactical gear. Trent then made Liv sit on the kitchen table as he began to stitch her leg.

Liv cracked the seal on a bottle of whiskey which was in her travel bag and poured it directly into her mouth.

Mid-way through Trent's stitching, the door to the safehouse opened causing Liv to throw her battle axe towards the door in alarm.

It was Sjöfn, TJ and Archie. Alarmed, they walked further into the house.

"Can G.U.A.R.D. not afford two safe houses?" Millie asked the room loudly.

"No they can't, it was short notice that it was to become a two-team operation," Sjöfn said, "so we are sharing a safehouse."

She handed Liv her battle axe and looked at the bloody mess that was her thigh and Trent's fingers.

"How is your thigh?" she asked Liv.

"Well, a bullet flew through an inch of skin and I've lost a shit load of blood. So, you know, had you turned up on time to help us and out take on an army ..."

Trent snorted and Millie choked on Liv's whiskey.

"Excuse me?" Sjöfn muttered incredulously.

"Well, you know, we had taken out a hell of a lot of people before you decided to turn up in a helicopter. That would have been mighty helpful from the start," Liv retorted through gritted teeth.

Sjöfn looked at Trent, shocked, but he kept his eyes firmly on Liv's wound.

"We didn't turn up late," Archie shouted.

"We arrived as soon as we could," TJ shrugged. "G.U.A.R.D. only decided last minute that we would need more people and a helicopter for firepower."

"Clearly not soon enough," Millie said, a small knife twirling through her fingers.

"Where were you carrying that?" Maddie whispered. "You're in pyjama bottoms and a crop top."

"You don't get to talk to us like that, you would all be dead if we had not turned up," Archie snarled.

It was the first time most of them had seen him speak. His

hooked nose and nasally voice made Maddie's skin crawl.

"And hearing you speak, I wish I were dead," Maddie said.

"Trent, control your team," Sjöfn said, taking objection to the way they were speaking to her team.

"I can't. I am stitching up a member of my team," he said, not looking up. "Maddie, don't kill yourself yet, you've not heard him chat shit yet."

Trent's phone saved him from having to respond to Sjöfn. He cleaned his hands and picked up the phone, ordering Liv to wait and not attempt to finish off her leg.

There was an uneasy air of silence whilst Trent was stood outside, other than when a whiskey glass needed a refill.

"That was G.U.A.R.D. wanting a debrief," he said, washing his hands again.

"How is it that we finish off the mission, save you and yet they call you to debrief?" Sjöfn asked him.

"Because I am the grown-up, probably."

"Also, hard to give the details if you don't actually do much on the mission," Liv said from the table.

"Watch your mouth, you ungrateful shit!" Archie snapped, getting up and walking to Sjöfn's side.

This was a mistake.

Liv knocked Trent's hands off her thigh and limped over to Archie.

She towered over him and growled, "Isn't it past your bedtime? Best run along before you get hurt."

"I am older than you," he sneered.

"Act like It!" Liv said, looking down on him.

Liv grabbed him under the arms and threw him back to where he was stood before.

"Trent, want to call off your attack dogs?" Sjöfn said, as Millie also readied herself for a fight against Archie.

Pete and TJ were the calmest of the group, but with Millie readying herself for a fight it meant Pete was as well.

"If I wanted to do that, Liv wouldn't be ready to snap Archie and Millie would have put her two knives away."

"You're in pyjamas, where are you keeping knives?" Sjöfn asked Millie distractedly.

"Archie, don't let your ego write a cheque that your body cannot cash," Maddie said, as Archie got himself back up and walked towards Liv.

"Cute pop culture reference, you blue-haired dyke, but

the grown-ups are -" Archie began, but 'what the grown-ups were doing', the room never heard.

Liv had grabbed Sjöfn, thrown her back into the table and dived at Archie. She grabbed his throat with one hand and began punching him repeatedly in the face with the other. TJ sprang to his feet, as did Pete. Millie leapt in front of Sjöfn to stop her from getting involved.

After a few minutes of pandemonium, order was restored. Millie and Trent helped Liv back onto the table, as she had ruptured the stitches Trent was putting in her leg and widened the gash. He then proceeded to physically throw Archie out of the door before locking it.

"Keep your pack in check," Sjöfn growled.

"Sweetheart, shall I spell it out for you," Liv said, hobbling back to the table. "What that was? That was L O Y A L T Y." Liv's voice was so sickly sweet it was dangerous.

Trent was seething with Archie and took a while for Millie and Pete to calm him down. Sjöfn was also annoyed with Archie but more annoyed with Trent. Her blood was at boiling point and Trent was very happy to see this.

TJ sat with Pete, a look of disgust on his face at Archie's actions. "I don't even like Archie," he muttered.

Sjöfn and Trent argued in the kitchen. Millie took over from Trent stitching up Liv's leg, which was worse than when she was initially grazed by the bullet.

"Okay, SO, I have been PLANNING our next squad tattoo," Liv said from the table, her voice pitch changing due to the pain in her leg.

"Excellent priorities," Maddie said from the sofa, swilling her whiskey glass.

"How are you so calm with Liv getting ANOTHER bullet wound?" Trent asked from the other side of the room.

"You say that like I am always getting shot or flesh wounded by a bullet," Liv said from the table.

"You are wearing a mangled bullet around your neck which went into your shoulder, another grazed your arm and now you are having your leg stitched up. That is three too many," Trent said sternly.

"Well I wouldn't have been shot, if these Canadians had turned up on time."

"Go fuck yourself!" Sjöfn spat.

"I would, but I'm going to need to buy a walking stick now as I can't walk properly."

Everything was just calming down; Pete was asleep, Millie was sleeping using Liv's good thigh as a pillow, Maddie and Trent were talking when they heard the lock begin to click open.

Liv opened her battle axe and readied herself, however it was Archie trying to sneak back in after Trent had thrown him out of the house.

"Get. The. Fuck. Out!" Liv said to him.

"I am not sleeping on the street," Archie growled.

"Yes, you are," Trent said, "most people are asleep. I want to keep it that way."

"Fuck off, you! Traitorous mole!" Archie spat at Trent.

This was a mistake. Millie, who was woken up by Liv talking, launched a knife at him. It missed, however, due to Sjöfn punching him in the stomach.

"He was never a traitor, so find a hotel," Sjöfn said to him, before shutting him out of the house.

"Go with him, Tinkerbell. You believed him then, might as well believe him now," Trent said. His voice was calm but Millie noticed his hands were beginning to shake, so she took his arm gently.

"Is that what you believe? What you've always believed?" Sjöfn looked visibly shocked.

Maddie, Pete and TJ were awake by now, watching this happen.

"It was the mission before Budapest," she said.

"What the piss does Vietnam have to do with this?" he asked.

"G.U.A.R.D. were headhunting you, then we landed in Vietnam. I was sick that morning, and the morning after. We were almost shot on that mission."

"As we were on every mission," he shrugged.

"Yes, but when I was sick, I thought it was morning sickness, then we were shot at. We were together and I was scared, we were sloppy on missions. Love was blinding us."

"This is where she drops a child on you," Maddie whispered.

"No, it was just the Vietnamese pork, but by the time I had taken a pregnancy test, I was pushing you towards G.U.A.R.D. and you were being accused. I didn't stand up for you and by the time I knew I should, you had accepted G.U.A.R.D.'s offer and we had broken up."

"You never stood up for me. Everything Archie said out of infatuation of you, and you never stood up for me.

Then bring him to G.U.A.R.D. as well and not once do you try to reach out? I'm calling bullshit," Trent said, his shaking a little more pronounced despite Millie calming.

"Didn't they call us children, and yet they can't communicate like adults?" Millie whispered.

"So… you were saying about tattoo design?" TJ said to Liv, attempting to break the horrible silence.

"Yeah, narrowed it down to two designs," Liv said. "But we should all probably sleep."

Trent suggested that Sjöfn and TJ took the rooms, with the others sleeping where they could.

Chapter Eleven:

Trent's phone awoke them a few hours later, as G.U.A.R.D. headquarters rang him to say that the compound was now cleared of the members of the Y.N.W.A. and the militia.

They also informed Trent that the cyber division had financially destroy the Y.N.W.A. and were working on where their money had come from. They also said that it meant that Øistein Dahle was safe to go about his duties without fear of being murdered.

"So, he is safe?" Pete asked him.

"Well, he is still going to get hate speech online but nothing more than that," he chuckled, before they got ready and he ordered them out of the house.

Their first stop was indeed to buy a walking stick to aid Liv, as charging at Archie and Sjöfn last night did far more damage than the bullet that nicked her thigh.

With less pressure on her thigh she was able to direct them to a tattoo parlour. Once there she explained her two ideas, the first one was a simple vegvisir, the other was a simple Mjolnir design with the protection rune in the middle of the hammer. Liv then intricately put the runes for love, strength, safe travels, grace, courage, energy, health and good luck in a circle around the Mjolnir.

She showed them all the designs and they got it inked on the inside of their upper left arm. With the tattooing complete they had a few hours to spare and explore before they headed to the airstrip to take the plane back home.

When they met back up, Pete was very suspicious of Trent and the way he was acting.

"You've been doing something stupid."

"Is that a question or a statement?" Trent responded, cocking an eyebrow.

"Statement," Pete muttered, before turning to the girls. "He has been to some coffee shop for a drink with Sjöfn."

"We talked over G.U.A.R.D. leader things and she attempted to rebuild some bridges," he shrugged.

"How do you repair a burnt bridge?" Liv asked.

"That is what I was wondering, hence why I went along." He didn't continue with this as they heard noise outside.

They were not thrilled to see Q-Squadron join them on the plane, which was the cause of the sound outside. TJ threw a jar of ointment to Liv to help with the pain in her leg, and sat next to Pete.

Sjöfn sat uncomfortably across from Trent with Archie, who everyone was still furious with, sat at the back of the plane. Sjöfn informed them that Archie had been severely reprimanded by G.U.A.R.D. headquarters for his actions and that he had been taken off special operations, like Tanith had been after she interfered with Maddie and Liv.

After the plane took off Liv asked Trent a question that she had been pondering for a while. "How many relatives am I having die for these missions? What are G.U.A.R.D. telling my school?"

"She is still of school age?" Sjöfn asked.

"We are struggling with that," he sighed, ignoring Sjöfn. "We either keep coming up with excuses, tell the headmaster the truth or replace the headmaster with a G.U.A.R.D. agent who lets everything slide."

"Wait, how old are your team?" Sjöfn gawked.

"OOOOOOH option three please, and old enough to beat your team," Liv smirked.

TJ sniggered, Sjöfn looked annoyed and thankfully for all involved Archie didn't say anything.

"G.U.A.R.D. should do the third option," Sjöfn reasoned, she seemed to indicate to Trent that they would need to talk in private away from the very interested ears of Maddie, Millie and Liv.

What this resulted in was the jovial family atmosphere

that they normally had was gone and with an uneasy silence they used it to drift off to sleep.

Trent and Sjöfn were the only ones left to awake. She watched him as he plugged Millie's second earphone into her ear, and removed the book from Liv's hands and put a blanket over her.

"You really are a father to them all," Sjöfn said, smiling as she watched him doing this.

"If you don't care about each other then it is hard to work together, trust each other."

Sjöfn smiled but didn't say anything as he fussed over them before he took his seat opposite her. They both sighed deeply before eventually continuing to talk, they only stopped when the plane began its descent and the others began to awake.

As they were all making their way off the plane, Sjöfn's way was blocked by Liv's walking stick. Turning, Sjöfn saw Liv, Maddie and Millie all scowling at her.

"Do we need to actually threaten you or are you just going to take this as the threat?" Maddie said.

"I note your concerns for Trent, and I also know that you are not going to believe me when I say that I am truly sorry for what happened with me and Trent, and I want to repair the damages the best I can."

They said nothing more, but Liv put down her walking stick allowing Sjöfn to leave. Moments later they followed her off the plane.

Maddie and Liv bid farewell to the rest of the Juliets before they made their way home. Exhausted and restless they slumped in the living room, not bothered to clean the aftermath from the party they held on Friday night.

Eventually Liv announced she would soak her leg in a bath before turning in for a night's sleep, Maddie agreed that sleep was the best option for them at this point.

Liv's sleep was interrupted by her alarm. She swore and grumbled her way through her shower and getting ready for school.

As Liv got ready, she thought about the excuse she would need for her walking stick.

Millie needing her stomach pumped was a great excuse for leaving the party, however as Liv looked like she had just fought off a right-wing army to stop them

from murdering a politician, and had a bullet scrape a chunk of flesh out of her thigh which she then ripped further by attacking someone who made a homophobic slur against her sister, which she had to admit to herself was something most seventeen years olds didn't look like.

After testing her thigh by walking unaided, Liv made the

Decision that for the next few days at least she would need to walk with a walking stick and drive the car to school as opposed to her beloved Harley Davidson

As she drove, she thought about excuses to use for her leg. When she arrived at school, she had come upon the rather poor excuse that when getting Millie into the ambulance after her party Liv had caught her thigh on a metal instrument, tearing her skin in the ambulance and that this was the reason for the walking stick. It was a poor excuse but the best she had

Whether anyone believed her story or not she didn't really care. Liv sat in her class and moaned with relief as she stretched out her leg. Mrs. Noah however, who didn't see Liv do this, tripped over her walking stick and spent the first ten minutes of the lesson reprimanding Liv for leaving it lying around.

When Liv returned home it was to find Maddie working on the engine of the run-down car she had bought.

Maddie was restless and wanted to go on patrol that night, despite Liv being in no condition to do so.

"We've never really done solo patrols before," Maddie said, "but I need to, I am restless and jumpy and just need a good patrol."

"Think we are skilled enough to go by ourselves," Liv reasoned. "I am in no state to go. I am gonna sit here and finish the upholstery on this bike seat before starting work on polishing and cleaning up the speedometer."

"You don't mind me going alone?"

"As long as you don't die!"

"Deal."

Chapter Twelve:

That night, Maddie left the house alone. In the back of her mind she had a vision of when Liv left the house alone and got shot. However, she couldn't think like that. They were better trained than they were back then, and she was ready for anything that was thrown at her; not that she was expecting an eventful night.

As Maddie patrolled the city, she checked for any signs of unusual activity. In Willowdale City there were shiatzu parlours and gyms that were open all day and night, and in nightclubs the mayor's husband worked freelance for gangs and anyone involved in crime, patching up wounds.

Maddie never noticed a dentist's office that was twenty-four hours, yet as she ran along the rooftops, she noticed what looked like torch lights flickering past the window and there was a lorry parked outside. Whilst she watched the dentist office, she checked her phone.

Thanks to Pete's upgrades she could see whether the office was alarmed, it did but it had been disabled. A disabled alarm was enough to draw Maddie's suspicions.

She went to investigate. From her experience, the power being cut to a building from the fuse box was sophisticated work. She entered the building and quickly made her way up the staircase. Slipping into an office she waited, trying to assess the situation.

Unfortunately, someone entered the room she was hiding in. Reacting instinctively, she threw an elbow into him and then a fist. She disarmed the man, knocked him unconscious and dragged him further inside the office. Slipping out, she closed the door behind her.

Seeing someone else on the landing she charged at him, knocking him down. Throwing punches, he let out a yell that alerted everyone downstairs. Reacting impulsively, she judo-threw the man over her shoulder before throwing him down the stairs onto the people below.

Maddie ran down the stairs, and like a bowling ball to pins she toppled four people and then did her best to keep all six people down on the ground.

Police interrupted the scene, with Maddie needing to make her escape through a window so she wasn't arrested with them.

As odd as robbing a dentist's office was, Maddie didn't think much of it as she continued her patrol. Willowdale was a changing city after all.

"Who robs a dentist's office?" Liv asked Maddie the next morning.

"That's what I thought," Maddie said, spooning sugar into her tea. It took Maddie a while to notice that Liv was not in her school uniform, instead was in her favourite pair of ripped jeans tucked into her boots, her leather jacket, beanie hat and her favourite long-sleeved top.

"Bunking school?"

"Non-uniform day," Liv yawned.

"So naturally you wear one of the leather jackets you've decorated."

"We were born in your world... But you will die in ours," Liv said, turning around so Maddie could see the words Liv had emblazoned on the jacket.

"Cute, but I think you should go for your denim 'She's beauty, she's grace, she'll punch you in the face'. I like that jacket."

"I was gonna, but that goes well with my fishnet shirt and a crop top. But it is cold and it is raining."

"Winter is upon us," she sighed.

"I know, it's amazing," Liv said, as she just listened to the sound of the rain.

"Well get to school and I'll see you soon."

Liv waved, her thigh bandaged and her walking stick a precaution under her arm as she left the house for school.

"You look ... different," Alexa laughed. "Not in a bad way,

just you dress differently."

"I walked past three boys wearing the same thing!" Liv said exasperatedly.

"You look like someone made a mood board for an angsty, rock and roll feminist," Mikey said, walking over.

"You look like every generic straight boy, in trainers, light blue jeans and an overpriced t-shirt from a brand nobody has heard of."

"Rude."

"You do dress in a way which can only be described as generic," Nattie said, joining them.

"And that. That is from your girlfriend," Liv laughed.

"Like, look," Liv said, pointing to three seniors she never bothered to learn the names of, "those three are dressed the exact same!"

As Liv and Alexa set off for their lessons, they all made arrangements to go for drinks after school, something that gave Liv a reason to put up with the rest of the day.

When she sat down in her first lesson however, she began researching not only the Irish Rebellion under the Tudors, as per the instructions of Mr. Powers, but also the other uses for all equipment found in a dentist office, curious as to why of all the places to rob, they chose there.

Based on some of the alternative uses for all of the equipment, Liv texted Maddie and asked her to see if there had been any other dentisits that had been broken into recently, and waited for her response as she moved to her next class.

Liv groaned as she saw Maddie confirm that five had been broken into in the past fourth months. Before that, there hadn't been a recorded one in over four years.

"Can you apologise to Mrs. Noah, I'm going to be late," Liv asked Alexa.

She then rang Maddie.

"We need to let G.U.A.R.D. know about the break ins."

"Why?"

"It was bugging me, why a dentist office? So I was researching and all dentists have X-ray equipment. X-ray equipment can be used to make diry bombs."

"Well. FUCK!" Maddie sighed. "Leave it with me."

Liv disconnected the call and went in to face her inevitable telling off from Mrs. Noah for being late.

She knew that Maddie would keep her up to date with any developments, so she went about her day in school the best she could before they headed into town.

With Liv, Alexa, Mikey and Nattie all having the last lesson of the day a free period was a godsend, so they left early and headed into town. Liv being the most knowledgeable, directed them to the *Terrible Dragonfruit* and was pleased to see Shayna behind the bar.

Alexa, Nattie and Mikey all bought their drinks but when Liv went to buy her own drink, Shayna told that her Miss Lynch's Bexploding Drink Of Fire had been paid for.

"By who?"

"That girl over there," Shayna said, nodding to a corner. "Seems you have a stalker, or a crazy ex."

"Well, I'm single and no exes so definitely a stalker," Liv smirked

"Not a bad looking girl to be stalked by," Shayna reasoned, nodding to the corner.

Liv looked over and was shocked to see Sjöfn sat there. When they saw each other, Sjöfn raised her glass as if she was toasting Liv.

"I wish it was you buying me the drink," Liv sighed to Shayna. "I'll join you guys in a minute," she told the others.

Taking her drink from the bar, she went over to see Sjöfn.

"What are you doing here?" Liv asked her, sitting down

opposite her.

"It's nice to see you too," Sjöfn smiled, not taken aback by the hostility of Liv's tone.

"Seriously, Sjöfn, what are you doing here? This isn't a coincidental meeting."

"No ... no I suppose it isn't," she said slowly.

"So, what brings you here?"

"You do. As you've seen, Q-Squadron are a shamble. Even before Archie's antics, we weren't bonding well and we were in need of more recruits."

"So, you want me to recommend some people from school?"

"No, I want you to join. Your talents suit a smaller team, higher promotion prospects. It would be a different dynamic; you would thrive in Q-Squadron. Drop out of school now, move out. Special operations full time."

"Thanks, however, I'm a Juliet. You want to talk to me about my job, you go through Trent," Liv said, tapping her tattoo before getting up a joining her friends again.

"Who was that?" Nattie asked her.

"Friend from work," Liv shrugged.

"Work?" they asked her.

"Work. Maddie's work, I just know her," Liv said, shifting uncomfortably.

She quickly moved the conversation along and attempted to distract them, when she turned back around Sjöfn had gone, and Liv was very happy about it.

They only had two drinks before they all had to be back home. When Liv got home, she changed into shorts and a white t-shirt and joined Maddie, who had been in the garage for most of the day.

Maddie and Liv chatted merrily as they worked. Liv sat on the floor polishing and removing the rust and cleaning the dial on the fuel gauge as Maddie worked on the exhaust of the car.

As they walked, they barely noticed two people approach the garage and stand there waiting for them to realise that they were waiting for them.

"Thank God we aren't intruders," Sjöfn said, after serval minutes, causing Liv to drop warm water everywhere, and Maddie to sit up so fast she hit her head on the bumper.

"Sjöfn, Colonel Rathe. What are you doing here?" Maddie said, rubbing her head and smudging oil onto her forehead.

"Well. Dirty bombs tend to make me anxious," he said,

cocking an eyebrow.

"Come through to the kitchen," Maddie said, directing him and looking suspiciously at Sjöfn.

They all sat in the kitchen. When Liv had made them cups of tea they waited for an explanation.

When one didn't come, Maddie spoke, "So, the rest of the Juliets are on their way back down, but why is she here?"

"Because there is a possibility of a dirty bomb being made in Willowdale. You've discovered something much larger than some thugs robbing a place."

"No, we know that," Liv smirked. "Was more about why specifically Sjöfn is here? Last time G.U.A.R.D. sent someone into Willowdale it was Tanith and well, look how that turned out."

Col. Rathe sighed deeply before saying, "Emily is one of the best bomb disposal experts in G.U.A.R.D., so that is why she is here. J-Squadron will continue your patrols around the city looking for the dirty bombs, and then back-up G.U.A.R.D. agents will be standing by ready to jump in should then need to."

"Emily?" Liv asked

"Wait, dirty bombs? Plural?" Maddie questioned.

"Yes. Dirty bombs. I'll explain later," Sjöfn said.

"We are going to import undercover G.U.A.R.D. agents into Willowdale."

"They will follow our command. Or at least the command of Trent and J-Squadron. The others are arriving later tonight," Maddie said sternly.

"No, this is above your paygrade, this is a delicate game of chess, it needs to be paid strategically. Something you two are not."

"Fuck chess," Maddie said. "In chess you make sacrifices, you let the opposition take pawns. Not in our city."

Col. Rathe didn't say anything, but just looked at Maddie as if attempting to see through her.

"So, explain how this has gone from us being paranoid, believing that nobody in their right mind would rob a dentist's office so there must be a different motive, to actually having something to worry about, like dirty bombs all over the city?" Liv asked, slightly confused.

"Your last mission."

"The Y.N.W.A?"

"Yes."

"What about them?"

"One of their biggest financial backers is behind this. The

cyber-division has found who is behind this. You've tangled with the backer before."

"We have?" Liv questioned.

"The serial killer that G.U.A.R.D. and yourselves apprehended."

"The religious nut?" Maddie said, her eyes widening.

"He had been indoctrinated into a Christian cult. The leader of the cult was a financial backer of the Yesteryear National White Alliance," Col. Rathe said to them. "We believe they are co-ordinating a collection of the dirty bombs in Willowdale before moving them nationwide for co-ordinated attacks."

"There was, or is, a plan in the pipeline to send a few agents undercover into the cult compound as couples seeking God. This was established as soon as the serial killer was caught and we found out his religion. The cyber division have been talking to the church online for months."

"If you tell me that me and Trent are to be married, I will cut you," Maddie laughed, before looking at Sjöfn.

Col. Rathe looked confused, before Sjöfn whispered, "Lesbian," causing a look of comprehension on his face.

"Was, or is, in the pipeline?" Liv said.

"Would have taken place after Christmas. So, onto the bomb at hand," Col. Rathe said sternly. "We will be dropping off some equipment for you to search the city for radiation exposure. At night then you will be clear to engage, secure the scene and the bomb will be defused. During the day, G.U.A.R.D. agents will do the same thing but with stealth, then you can engage."

"What are we meant to do during the day?"

"Well, you will be in school?" Col. Rathe said simply.

"Fuck off?!" Liv said, stunned. "There are multiple bombs across the city, and you expect me to be in school?"

"What part of special-operations unit are you forgetting?" Sjöfn said.

"Probably the bit where it could cost people's lives," Maddie said.

"I don't know if you know, *Sjöfn,* but people dying is what we in Willowdale call an Oopsie-No-No," Liv said, smirking.

Col. Rathe sighed deeply as Sjöfn didn't know whether to laugh or throw her mug of tea at Liv.

"If bombs are being smuggled or hidden, we know people we can get information from."

"You have criminal informants?" Col. Rathe asked,

impressed.

"No? we just know people to punch really hard," Liv nodded enthusiastically.

That night they left a door unlocked for the rest of the Juliets and headed into the city centre to find one person. His friends and associates called him Shiraz, a club owner and a fence. You could take him anything from stolen art to a kidney and he could sell it for you, as they discovered tracking a painting that had been stolen months ago.

Unfortunately, despite delivering the proof that he had the painting, the police decided not to raid Shiraz and his building and the painting soon vanished.

Maddie and Liv watched him leave the club he was in through the side door. As he attempted to light his cigarette, they moved closer to him.

Maddie, using her height and strength advantage, simply lifted him up, clamped one hand over his mouth to stop him from yelling, carried him to an alleyway three streets over and deposited him on the floor.

Liv, gave him back his cigarette as, after all, they weren't unreasonable.

"Oh fuck. Not you guys again," he said, accepting a light off her nonetheless.

"Hey, you should be flattered. Not many people get to say *again* to us. So be thankful," Liv said to him.

"Can you please provide us with some information?"

"Probably not as I am a nightclub owner."

"Don't make us extract the information, Shiraz."

"X-Ray equipment has gone missing throughout Willowdale and is being imported from cities into Willowdale. Any information?"

"I do not know anything. I am a nightclub owner."

Maddie stepped on his knee until he relented.

"I heard rumours. That's it," he moaned.

"Do, tell what these rumours are," Maddie implored.

"Priest McCulley. I heard the talk. One of the rooms that was usually used for Sunday school was being hired out because a large donation was made to the church. Some people in the club were bragging that the old boy had no idea what it all meant. That's it. I don't know if is related, it could be anything."

"Any idea on which church?"

"No, can I please get back to my establishment?"

"I suppose."

When Shiraz was out of earshot, Liv let out a short whistle. "So we have to search every church in Willowdale."

"Who is this Priest McCulley?" Maddie asked.

"He is the head of the religious association," Liv said knowledgably.

"So, every church, including the one run by Deanne's father, every mosque, every synagogue, Buddhist temple. The leaders of them all meet up in a council. He chairs the council."

"So, our search has been narrowed down from citywide to citywide."

"Essentially, yes."

Liv's mood was as foul as the weather when she awoke later that morning, as she dressed for school. She wasn't sure if it was sleet, rain, snow or hail outside but a storm was brewing and despite her loving this weather, this was one of the few occasions in which she wished she was not out in it. Even Trent, who had arrived a few minutes after they got in from patrol, insisted on driving Liv to school, not fully trusting her to drive in these conditions. Although it didn't improve her mood, Liv was thankful for this as it meant she could keep her eyes closed for a few minutes longer in the car.

"I think the Juliets should just relocate to Willowdale, you're spending so much time here," Liv said, behind a wide yawn.

"Probably will at this point," he chuckled, "We could always use more vigilantes to help us clean up this city. Like, I even ran into some trash in a bar! A bar, Trent! In the daytime."

"Did this trash look like she was sculpted by the Gods, voice of the scots, sit down and use their incredible beauty in an attempt to lure you away from the Juliets?"

"A name lost from the history books. Did she tell you?" Liv asked.

"Yeah," he paused for a moment. "Said I had some truly loyal people around me and it made her think a lot about her life previously."

"You believe her?" Liv tried her best to keep the scepticism out of her voice, but thus far Sjöfn hadn't painted the best image of someone to trust.

Liv getting dropped off at school by Trent didn't go unnoticed by Nattie's eagle-eyes and Liv had to endure teasing about who her new boyfriend was for most of the morning. They agreed, despite the weather, to go for drinks again after school. Winter was approaching and warm alcoholic beverages were sounding like a godsend midway through Mrs. Noah's class.

"Find the chapter boring, Olivia?" Mrs. Noah said to her, as she noticed Liv's eyes slide out of focus.

"Yes. In all honesty, all of the old crime books or any book involving murder are awful. They are useless at it."

"So, you, a schoolgirl, think you know better than some of the literary greats," she scoffed.

"If it is a premeditated murder, like most are, you take a fresh aftershave or perfume. One not commonly worn so any odour left at the scene on the body or clothing is not one that is associated with you. Furthermore, wear shoes larger than your normal for any footprints left at the scene, if you can you weight the shoes down. Leather gloves, a hat or hairnet. Decrease room temperature and fill a bathtub full of ice or kitty litter. Both have the same affect in altering the time of death should the body be discovered. Also, there is no harm in setting off a major incident in the city, so smaller crimes aren't investigated."

There was a stunned silence in the class, with Alexa and Robyn looking non-plussed and everyone alarmed at this seemingly serial killer level of pre-planning just off the top of her head.

"Hypothetically," Liv added innocently.

As they left the class Robyn, on her tiptoes, reached up and whispered, "Smooth way to not tell anyone you know how to solve crime and commit murder."

"Eh, you read enough books and you learn to plan a murder subconsciously."

Alexa was still half impressed, and half rather worried. As, they walked through the downpouring of hell, Liv noticed there were G.U.A.R.D. agents everywhere in town, they nodded at her and she nodded back. She didn't know how many members of G.U.A.R.D. were in town but she hoped it would be enough.

None of the others noticed anything as they entered what was becoming their usual hangout, but then again, they weren't trained to. Liv made an excuse when the light began to fade, to leave them all and she headed home.

Pete and Millie had turned up during the day and she was glad to see them all, as she changed out of her soaked through clothes and changed into soon to be soaked through tactical gear.

"We will split up, cover every religious site in the city. Millie and Liv -" Maddie began to explain.

"Team Awesome," Millie said, cutting her off.

"Pete and myself -" Maddie continued.

"Team Loser," Millie said again, cutting her off.

"Trent will be teaming up with Sjöfn -"

Team Loser and Team Sexy With The Beard," Millie said,

cutting Maddie off again.

"If anyone detects high level of radiation or anything like that, we contact the group and converge."

"Sjöfn is the best bomb disposal expert there is. So, keep the communication chat clean, we are working it out, so just be a bit nicer," Trent said, imploring but smiling at Millie, who was still chuckling to herself about the group names, pretending not to take notice.

Chapter Thirteen:

They left the house and began to patrol. The mess that was coming down from the sky had changed. The rain element had gone, instead it was just snow and sleet being whipped around them by a ferocious wind.

"There is something rather dodgy about sneaking about religious places," Millie said over the coms.

"Makes a good brooding place though," Liv said, beckoning Millie over.

Liv then posed on the roof of the church, her hair billowing everywhere in the wind, covered in snow. She looked out across the city as she made Millie take her photo.

"Anyone find anything yet?" Sjöfn asked.

"Yeah, about half an hour ago. Just decided to wait till now," Millie laughed.

Millie could imagine Trent groan in his head but luckily Sjöfn didn't retort.

"My fingers are gonna fall off in a minute," Pete grunted. "Can someone find this pissing bomb."

"Yeah, 'cause that is the downside of a bomb in this weather, your fingers," Millie snapped again, the cold clearly getting too her.

It was at this point that Liv pulled Millie into an alley for a few minutes break and protection from the wind. She kept Millie close and they regained their thoughts before they continued.

"Bingo," Maddie said to them all. "Converge on Saint Lawrence's. It's here."

"Are you certain?" Trent asked.

"It is the only church we have come across where there are heavily-armed guards outside as well as radiation levels."

"Understood."

They converged. When they were on a roof across from the church, Liv took control.

"Sjöfn, how do we do this without triggering any of the shit inside?"

"We need to take down as many of those outside without alerting people, but we need to enter the church and do what we can," she said.

"Understood," Liv sighed, "Trent, Pete and Maddie. You three take down all of the guards outside, whilst we slip in and deal with everything inside."

"NO," Trent said firmly.

"Trent, you're the firearms expert and that is where we are putting you. It is our city and the three of us are better inside the church, close combat fighting," Liv snapped, slapping her snow-covered palm on his chest.

"Secure the perimeter and let's get this resolved," Trent agreed.

"Everyone should leave," Sjöfn said.

"FUCKING DO WHAT WE SAY!" Liv commanded.

They did as she said. Maddie, Liv and Sjöfn slipped inside of the church and began looking around.

"Holy shit!" Maddie breathed.

"This. Is. Fucked. Up," Liv said, her words barely making a sound as she watched people patrol inside the church, machinery and equipment placed on the altar with tools, and men running between the altar and one of the back offices.

"I'm following you in. Millie and Pete have the perimeter," Trent said.

Liv growled, but didn't say a word about this.

They engaged inside, Mille and Pete had the perimeter secured through stealth and bullets whilst the others converged on the altar.

Maddie, Liv and Trent beat every armed person inside the church until they reached the altar. They were outnumbered but then again, they had tricks up their sleeve.

"Listen up, twats," Sjöfn said to them all, "we have twenty people engaging and bombs to disarm."

Sjöfn disengaged the latest member of the religious group closest to the altar, as Millie, Liv and Trent controlled rest of the church.

Finally, they all converged on the altar.

"One disabled. Get rid of this one," Pete ran forward, taking the X-ray equipment, and Millie taking the explosive element. They ran from the church to the outside.

"Second one disabled," Sjöfn said, her hands starting to tremble. Liv and Maddie removed this bomb and placed them far outside a potential blast radius.

When Pete and Millie had removed the third bomb, they stood on the altar awaiting Sjöfn's instructions.

"Trent, baby, remember when we were in the capital of Somalia," Sjöfn said, trembling slightly.

"Command bollocked me because you gave me a hickey on the plane to Mogadishu... why?"

"I was thinking more the 'evacuate everyone and if the gods bless us then we meet'," Sjöfn stammered, her voice panicked.

"Disable the bomb, Sjöfn, we can reminisce when we are drinking whiskey," Maddie insisted, looking at the wires.

"I'm not sure this one can, it has three different fail-safes and what looks like a tamper switch," Sjöfn said rapidly.

"Counteract the explosion?" Liv asked, not understanding everything. "It doesn't matter about the explosion, but can we disengage and remove the irradiated equipment from it?"

"Maybe. Trent, baby. Get the girls out of here, get them to a safe distance, then we can remove the irradiated x-ray equipment."

"I'll take the x-ray equipment," Liv said, stepping forward.

"No, we only have one shot at this, and we have done this before," Sjöfn said, her hands shaking violently now.

Pete grabbed Millie around the chest and forced her towards the doors. Liv and Maddie didn't move as Sjöfn began working. She started by simply and gently moving wires around and seeing where they led.

"Liv, Mads, this is the point you leave," Sjöfn said.

They didn't move until Trent looked at them; his gaze was

so penetrating that they knew to back down.

They cautiously started stepping backwards, awaiting any signal to either engage or run.

"Baby take this," they heard Sjöfn say.

Liv shivered, the tone of Sjöfn's voice tonight was one they had never heard before. The confidence, finesse attitude, her personification of beauty was gone from her voice. She was a scared twenty-five-year-old attempting to defuse a dirty bomb.

When Trent had the equipment in his hands, they all began running towards the door. Trent hating himself, stayed as close to the altar until Sjöfn instructed him to run.

They ran towards the exit. Maddie made it through first with Liv forcing her through the door and out through the botanical gardens which, thanks to Millie and Pete, were littered with incapacitated bodies through securing the perimeter.

Liv turned around to see Maddie with the X-ray equipment in front of her and Trent behind her and Sjöfn seconds behind Trent.

Her eyesight was blinded and every sound she heard was obliterated by the sight of a red and orange explosion; the velocity of the explosion sent Liv, Maddie, Trent and

Sjöfn flying forward, debris following them and landing on and all around them.

Liv's ears were ringing so loud she doubted if she would ever hear again but using sign language she commanded to Pete and Millie to ring an ambulance. Blood trickled from her hairline over her eyes, her mouth mask and into the pristine and crisp white of the snow now settling on the ground around them.

However, G.U.A.R.D. had trained them for non-verbal communication. Liv, her eyesight wobbly, staggered towards Trent as Pete ran towards Maddie.

Liv had never heard a pitch higher in her life, yet she directed the best she could. Sjöfn was put in the ambulance with Trent riding with her.

They spoke mostly in sign language. Liv said to Pete that he needed to re-check the perimeter again, and that she would deal with the police.

It wasn't long before Maddie and Millie were taken away in ambulances, Millie had a severe concussion and was Millie, was seemingly communicating in a hybrid of all the languages that she knew. However, as none of the others knew Japanese, Spanish, Arabic, Mandarin, or French they made little progress explaining to the doctors what had happened

Liv then screamed down her coms to all G.U.A.R.D. in

Willowdale to converge on the church, before the Willowdale city police department arrived.

Pete secured the radioactive x-ray equipment, and co-ordinated with the local residents, who had seen and heard the explosion.

Liv ran around commanding G.U.A.R.D. agents, on crowd control, securing the people who were guarding the church as well as dealing with Willowdale police department, who were attempting to run into the smouldering ruin of the church as well as arrest G.U.A.R.D. agents who had jurisdiction and authority over them.

Pete began leading G.U.A.R.D. agents into the rubble of church, to ensure it was safe and there were no other bombs that hadn't been detonated or triggered in the initial explosion.

Liv spotted Chief Kyle. "Chief Kyle, this was a gas leak," she said, before turning away when she saw a much more pressing matter walking towards her.

Col. Rathe was walking with determination and Liv was in no mood to piss him off. She left Chief Kyle and removed the tactical gear so Col. Rathe could see her face.

"Explain what happened, Olivia?"

"Well, we have good news and bad news. Bad news is the

bomb went off, causing a massive explosion and fire. Good news is, we aren't going to die from radiation, and this was the only bomb that went off."

"I want a full debrief."

"You'll get one, but unless you're here to help, please piss off as you're not helping."

"Excuse me?" he said, a fury in his voice.

"Sjöfn and Trent are at the hospital. Millie and Maddie are on their way to the hospital, as she definitely has a concussion, God knows the condition of the rest of us. So, you poncing down here isn't fucking helping. So, you'll get a debrief soon, but either help of fuck off!"

Col. Rathe walked away from Liv towards Chief Kyle, and Liv was grateful that he was actually going to do something productive. Relief teams of G.U.A.R.D. agents secured the scene, meaning that Liv and Maddie were ordered to the hospital by Col. Rathe.

For the first time ever, Liv was not the one who was badly injured, so she ignored Col. Rathe and stayed behind to continue co-ordinating the clean-up of the bomb sight. Maddie was ordered by Liv to join the others and get checked up in the hospital but also to give an update on Trent and Sjöfn who were in a worse way.

Maddie had attempted to go into the hospital room to

see Trent, who refused to leave Sjöfn's side, despite him being in physical pain. Neither were in a life-threatening condition, according to the nurses.

"Listen, you let me in or I will snap you," Maddie growled at the nurse.

"Visiting time is closed, and due to the nature of the injuries they are to be interviewed by Willowdale Police Department before anyone is allowed in," the nurse said.

"We outrank the police, now let me in before you lose your medical licence."

"Maddie, calm down," Col. Rathe said, stepping out of the elevator.

"Then tell this fucker to let me in," she snapped.

Maddie was finally allowed in to see Trent and Sjöfn. Trent's beard was singed, his wrist had a minor break, but it was the force of explosion that caused most of the injuries that both Sjöfn and Trent had.

Liv gently wrapped Trent in a hug as he sat by Sjöfn's bed, holding her hand.

"How is she doing?" Maddie whispered.

"Not life-threating, but they're keeping her in for the next few days," Trent said, his voice cracking.

"Pete has been cleared. I can sit here whilst you shower and change, he is bringing you some clothes in."

"Thank you."

Pete arrived shortly after with clothes for all of them. Millie, who was still rather dazed, was happy to be wrapped up in one of Trent's hoodies, much larger than her size.

The silence in the hospital room was broken when Col. Rathe walked in demanding an update. "Where is Olivia? She was meant to debrief me on the situation."

"She is still at the bomb site," Pete said, wrapping a scarf around Maddie to ensure she was warm enough.

"I ordered her to get herself checked out."

"For the first time ever, she is the one who probably doesn't require medical attention," Maddie said.

"Also, you said you wanted a debrief. I couldn't do that if I fucked off, could I?" Liv said from behind them. She was covered in snow, it was stuck in her eyelashes, hair and to every part of her tactical gear.

"You look like you're frozen solid," Pete said, looking at her. "Here, you need to change into these," he finished, forcing a scarf, a jumper, two pairs of leggings, a hat which Maddie had knitted, Liv's favourite t-shirt and a hooded top of Trent's.

Liv returned a few minutes later wrapped up tight and feeling unbelievably content in the clothing Pete had brought for her. He truly knew how to make everyone feel better. Liv let out a low moan as she stepped into the hospital room.

Once they were all in Sjöfn's room, Col. Rathe ordered them all home. Trent threatened to snap him over his knee, so the colonel allowed him to stay.

They received a lift home and all went to bed. The snow ferociously whipped around the house from the moment they put their heads down until a disgruntled Liv got up at the sound of her alarm and got changed.

Not waking anyone, she went to the hospital. When she arrived, it was to see Trent still where they left him.

"Listen up, dickhead, you need some proper sleep and to rest, I will let you know if her condition changes or if she wakes up."

Trent attempted to protest, but Liv kicked him in the shins and handed him her car keys. Liv, removing three of her layers, sat in the seat she had forced Trent to vacate and put on some music for Sjöfn, in the hope to bring her round to consciousness.

Her selfless and dangerous acts yesterday had changed their perceptions of Sjöfn and made them all realise that they should probably trust in her and Trent a bit more, despite what happened in in the past and in Norway.

Liv sat there for five hours before Sjöfn began to regain consciousness.

"Trent," she groaned, not strong enough to lift her head from the pillow.

Liv lifted the bed controls the best she could, so Sjöfn could see.

"Liv?" she asked, shocked to see her sat there.

"Yeah, I sent Trent home. He hadn't slept in a day and a bit and stank the hospital out," Liv smiled.

"How long have I been out for?"

"Not long. How are you feeling?"

"Fucking shit," she groaned.

"Well, rest up. You're all staying in Willowdale for a while, and over Christmas and New Year, Pete has booked you and Trent a hotel room."

"That sounds nice, don't think I'll be moving for a while."

"No shit, that's why I said rest up," Liv chuckled.

This made Sjöfn laugh, which was a mistake given pain she was still in.

A nurse came in to give Sjöfn morphine and scowled when Liv asked for some as well, which again caused Sjöfn to laugh. Liv let the others know Sjöfn's condition but made them swear not to allow Trent to come back until he had slept thoroughly. Sjöfn's incoherent babbling kept Liv amused, as she savoured the sound of the wind and the joy of not being in school. It was the last week before they broke up, but anytime that she was not in school was an added bonus. Liv dozed off in the chair before she was finally kicked out by the hospital staff.

Sjöfn was released two days later, and she and Trent came around for Maddie to make them all dinner.

It was a good atmosphere, completely different to when they first sat around a table in Norway. There was something about defusing multiple bombs and almost getting killed by a bomb that brought people together.

"So, the local news bought that it was a gas explosion?" Sjöfn asked.

"Yeah, they're not too bright," Maddie admitted.

"They haven't picked up on vigilantes running around the city," Millie pointed out.

Chapter Fourteen:

The snow did not relent over the coming days, which unfortunately meant that when it came to Christmas shopping it was not an enjoyable affair.

Millie pointed a shaking gloved hand at a tea shop, and they ran inside to escape from the cold.

"Remind me why we didn't just do all of our shopping online?" Millie shivered, as she clutched her cup in both hands, allowing the steam to rise into her face.

"Because everyone would know what everyone got everyone," Maddie reasoned.

"We're shopping together," Sjöfn reasoned. "Now, do you know where in Willowdale I can get presents for Trent?"

"There are a few places, although, I'm reluctant to go back out in this," Liv said. "We would be fucked without Maddie's hand-knitted delights."

There was a murmur of agreement around the table. They finished their hot-chocolates and cups of tea before venturing back out into the city.

The following days were spent preparing for Christmas. Trent and Maddie went out to do all of the Christmas food shopping, Pete and Liv stocked up on the alcohol they would need, with Millie and Sjöfn, being the ones most excited about Christmas, left to do the decorations.

The house was festive, and Trent had been cooking the Christmas pudding using his great-grandma's recipe, meaning the house smelled delightful as they relaxed and recuperated around the fire.

Millie, who was seemingly always cold, was in a turf war with Sjöfn over who could get closest to the fire without being burnt by it.

Trent watched them squabble with a grin on his face, as it was a sure-fire sign that Sjöfn was getting back to full strength, since she went shopping and could now fight with Millie over being closest to the fireplace.

"Stop it, Trent, you're making me feel ill," Liv said, appearing at his side.

"I do not know what you're on about."

"You looking at Sjöfn with that adoration and love."

"Such a cynic, you'll find love soon enough."

Liv mimed vomiting into her drink at this response, causing Trent to roll his eyes and the others to look around.

"What are you vomiting at?" Sjöfn said suspiciously.

"Don't worry about it," Liv muttered innocently.

Sjöfn glared at her suspiciously, before insisting they all gather round the fire for board games and a nice drink.

"Do we have to play board games?" Pete grumbled, as Millie dragged him to the centre of the room.

"It is Christmas Eve. Yes," Sjöfn said, glaring at him with such intensity that he sat down quietly on a beanbag, after dethroning his sister from it.

The games went on well into the night and it was only when Millie fell asleep, knocking her drink over, that they decided to go to bed.

With the constant snowstorms, it was tough to know when it was day and when it was night, which was made more difficult by how early Sjöfn and Millie woke the house.

In pyjamas and bleary-eyed, they sat around the tree with Christmas music playing and began handing out presents. It was as picturesque a Christmas as it could be for a group of special operative vigilantes.

Trent was overjoyed with his gifts of beard oil, a travel personal grooming kit so 'they wouldn't have to listen to him complain he didn't have his other personal grooming kit' as Liv put it, some non-stick pans and cooking utensils and whittling book for when he was bored.

Pete was overcome with emotion when he received a

new set of watercolours from Liv, computer components from his sister, an ornamental hand-crafted bong, and a digital tablet designed for drawing.

Liv received what was essentially a make-your-own wardrobe kit, sewing machine and materials included and a set of Damascus knuckledusters with a retractable knife, so that she could carry them for emotional support whenever she was not on a mission or on patrol.

Maddie was delighted with seventeen balls of yarn in different colours, a complete new set of bath bombs and a brand-new toolbox to help with her car repairs.

Millie was delighted when she received a mountain of sweets and chocolate for her sweet-tooth cravings. She also received an XL hoodie from Trent so that she would 'STOP STEALING ALL OF HIS CLOTHES' and, much to everyone's dismay, a child's joke set.

With none of them knowing Sjöfn as well as Trent, he was key in all of them getting her presents. Liv and Millie thought their presents were hilarious. Liv got Sjöfn a book called *'how to defuse bombs'* with Millie getting her a book entitled *'Trust and relationships'*. Sjöfn found it funny once she knew it didn't come from a place of malice. Maddie got her a perfume from a celebrity she had never heard of and Pete's name was on a present that Millie had bought for her, which was a make-up palette she had wanted for a while.

Trent and Maddie were in and out of the room as they began preparing for Christmas dinner.

"Why are you starting the dinner now?" Sjöfn groaned, as Trent detached his arm from around her.

"We have a lot to cook, including an extra turkey."

"Why in God's name are you doing an entire extra turkey?" she asked, utterly bewildered.

Trent didn't say anything but pointed at Millie, who was just taking a bite into a humungous slab of chocolate.

"What?!" she said, attempting to swallow it in one.

Sjöfn looked at her sceptically, and then looked at Pete.

"I wish it was an exaggeration; I've never seen anyone who eats as much. Giant appetite and even bigger metabolism."

"Last time she was here, Mils ate us out of house and home," Liv laughed, not looking up from her pad of paper in which she was writing down slogans for new clothes.

"Oh, this is going brilliant to watch," Sjöfn chuckled.

"What do we do after dinner? What's the tradition?" Millie asked.

"We normally watch God awful B movies or classics or

both. But just contentness and drinks with film and family."

"Contentness isn't a word," Millie said.

"Fine, have two. Fuck off," Liv yawned.

Sjöfn was rather taken aback by Liv's use of the word family but didn't say anything, instead just took a sip of her drink.

They waited impatiently for Trent to finally order them to the table for their Christmas lunch. The table groaned under the weight of it all. For all of their safety they let Millie load her plate up with food before they all got theirs. None of them spoke much through three helpings of food and Trent's great grandma's scrumptious Christmas pudding.

None of them spoke much after eating either, they slumped in the living room and watched from Maddie and Liv's collection of terrible B movies until they all began to doze into a food-induced sleep.

Boxing day was spent in such of the same way, the few leftovers that Millie left were put in sandwiches.

"Liv, have you ever heard of the sixteenth century word Cacoethes?" Sjöfn said, not looking up from what she was reading.

"No, why?" she said, puzzled.

"It means an irresistible urge to do something inadvisable."

"Why are you telling me this?"

"Just thought it would make for a title of your autobiography or a tattoo or something."

"Rude."

"Accurate as fuck," Millie nodded, walking into the room.

"What is this bullshit?!" Liv said, looking up. "What are you reading?"

"Your G.U.A.R.D. file."

"Why are you reading it?"

"To update it on any injuries you got in Willowdale due to the bomb."

"It is your file that needs updating," Liv retorted.

"Stop bickering, children," Trent said, lifting Millie up off the sofa so he could sit next Sjöfn.

"Liv, what is the New Year plan?"

"Not a big fan of New Year, so we don't really have one," she sighed.

"We could just get drunk?" Pete said, from the depths of

a beanbag with a sketch book on his lap.

Getting drunk was exactly how they spent their New Year's Eve, the drinks flowed smoothly and the atmosphere was good.

A few days after New Year, Trent, came into the kitchen following a trip into town with supplies and with news.

"Maddie, this is for you," he said, handing her a box.

"Hair dye?" she said instinctively, reaching up to her flicked blue hair as if Trent had insulted her firstborn.

"Yeah. You're dying your hair."

"Why?"

"Because you and Pete are going to be a couple. The married couple will be going undercover with myself and Sjöfn on a mission."

Liv and Millie sniggered at the look of complete disgust on Maddie's face as he said this.

"What's the assignment?" Liv asked.

"What are we meant to do?" Millie said, following up from Liv's question.

"The serial killer that Liv and Maddie caught, the Y.N.W.A.'s financial backer and the bomb in the

Willowdale church all link back to the same church. The same cult. We are going undercover at the church."

"What does the serial killer, the Y.N.W.A. and these bombings have in common?" Millie asked.

"Your serial killer was radicalised by this church, the Y.N.W.A. were finically backed by this church and the bombs we believe organised by the leader of this church." Sjöfn explained to Millie who had not being in Willowdale when Col. Rathe and Sjöfn debriefed Maddie and Liv.

"We are going undercover as recently converted church members to see what happens on church grounds. We believe that those who are converted are radicalised and made to kill by the leader," Trent continued.

"We are going in to join his inner circle, learn his ways, gather evidence. Physical evidence that he not only financed the Y.N.W.A. but also that he actively teaches his church members to kill when they leave the compound. Once we have this information, we will then bring him to justice and escape the cult," Sjöfn added.

"What denomination is this?"

"The leader is called Elias Olorephy; he is a populist, who believes he had God speak to him. He uses the Old Testament and the New Testament but also the Book of Olorephy, a book that God told him to write for the modern age."

"Are we going to have to read it?" Pete groaned.

"No, it isn't released to the public," Sjöfn explained. "The book is so holy it can only be read in church or at the compound. The release of the holy books is what has led to the demise of religion and the cause of evil."

"Oh, fuck, make it stop please, this is making feel ill," Liv said, as she mimed vomiting.

"Yet another reason why you weren't picked for this mission, Liv," Trent laughed.

"Liv losing her faith is almost as good as her coming out story," Maddie smirked.

"I need to hear both," Sjöfn said, looking at her quizzically.

"All in due time," Liv winked. "Trent, what are Millie and myself meant to be doing whilst you're undercover in the murder cult?"

"Patrol Willowdale, go to school, kiss boys, kiss girls, destroy the patriarchy. Whatever you normally do," he shrugged. "You're on standby for us to give the go ahead to storm Elias's compound and extract him and us."

"Anyone else noticed a flaw in this plan?" Millie said, looking around the kitchen at them. "I doubt a highly religious murder cult ran by a populist moron who believes God spoke to him will allow you to just text the outside world."

"I can make a computer out of essentially nothing, they could have nothing but scrap metal and old circuits and yet I could still get you a message. We will have trackers and distress signals built into wedding rings. Worst comes to worst we will just break into somewhere on the compound."

"Still can't believe we have to pretend to be married," Maddie grumbled.

"Well you're not my type either," Pete said.

"I'm the correct gender, though."

"Enough, we can bicker about this in a bit, we have work to do," Trent commanded. "G.U.A.R.D. have been working on this case for months, working with the church and being converted online. We need to learn these months of communications."

"False identities and pseudonyms?" Maddie asked.

"No. Pete will be married to Maddie, and Trent will be married to Emily," Trent explained.

"Emily?" Millie, Maddie and Liv said together.

"You didn't think I was christened Sjöfn, did you?"

"Kind of, yeah," Millie said.

"Nobody told us it wasn't your name," Maddie said.

"Who the fuck has that knowledge of Norse mythology to call you that?" Liv asked.

Sjöfn smiled lovingly at Trent, who was looking pleased at the gobsmacked look on Liv's face at Trent's secret love of history and mythology.

"Now, we need to learn and read all of the conversations between G.U.A.R.D. and the church for when we go undercover," Trent said.

"I best get a tax expense rebate for the paper and the ink," Maddie said, as Trent began sending documents to the printer.

"That sounds shit," Millie scoffed. "Fancy going into town, Liv?"

"Sure," she said sweetly, to add salt to the wound of them being free from work.

It was a different story when they weren't with the rest of the Juliets and Sjöfn from Q-Squadron.

Both Liv and Maddie were furious at the fact they were to be excluded from a mission for something as frivolous as their age, as much as they couldn't bitch about being seventeen because they were sat in a café with two alcoholic hot chocolates.

When they returned home, neither Millie or Liv could be described as being in a good mood. In order to de-stress, Liv went to the garage, sat on the floor and began working on her motorcycle. It was nearing the final stages, with just the exhaust to weld, before it could be certified safe for road use. She couldn't concentrate for very long before she launched the welding goggles at the wall, narrowly missing Sjöfn who was stood in doorway.

"What did those welding goggles ever do to you?" she asked, picking them up and handing them back to her.

"They're covered in blood so they're barely usable," Liv said aggressively.

"Why are they covered in blood?"

"I used to pull them down to make myself more intimidating. then had a balaclava over my nose and mouth, to complete the look."

"Why?"

"How did you see?" Sjöfn questioned.

"I struggled."

"Okay, I'll ask another question. How are you still alive?"

"Well, it took being stabbed before we got some shoddy body armour, but we used to just wear hoodies, leggings and boots, which worked well enough, I suppose."

"Oh Jesus. Anyway, let me help you."

As Liv sat on the floor next to her bike, Sjöfn took off her fluffy jumper and embraced Liv in a hug. Liv thought privately that Sjöfn gave incredible hugs, as she rested her shoulder in the embrace. When they finally broke apart, Sjöfn was very complimentary of the work Liv had already done. She complimented the leather, the dashboard and the handles. But Sjöfn was a brilliant welder and sped up the process of the exhaust.

As Liv and Sjöfn worked on the front and back bumpers respectively, Liv asked a question she had been curious about for a while. "How did you get the nickname Sjöfn?"

Sjöfn laughed before saying, "I'll tell if you tell me either the story of how you lost your faith or your coming out story."

"Fine. But you first, *Emily!*" she winked.

"Okay," Sjöfn said, getting comfortable with a glint of pure adulation in her eyes. "Our first date, I was in a dress, Trent was in a t-shirt and jeans. Naturally the heavens opened on us the second we left the place we were having coffee, and we were absolutely drenched.

We made a run for it into an independent bookshop. As we burst through the door, dripping water onto the carpet, we interrupted a class of six-year-olds learning about the Vikings. Whilst we were there, there was a presentation about Gods from Norse mythology who we have no stories about. Sjöfn was one of them and Trent then called me it."

"That is fucking adorable," Liv said, beaming at the look of the reminiscing happiness Sjöfn was displaying.

"It stuck after that, got to the extent that Emily sounded odd."

"What did Choovio call you?" Liv asked, cocking an eyebrow.

"Emily for the first week and Sjöfn after that. He is just the sweetest!"

"Are we discussing the same fucker?!"

"Your turn to tell the story," Sjöfn prompted.

"What would you like?"

"Coming out story, obviously."

"Oh God, it does not paint me in a good light. It was a normal day in school, hating life as you do. So, I am in school and we were in a biology lesson discussing how in the animal kingdom homosexuality is common; as most

animals don't care what they shag as long as it is a shag. Then one of the dickheads in the class made some kinda slut-shaming joke about how that was like most of the girls in the class. So although I sat in the corner I decided to blurt out, 'Given the fact that everyone in the room, based on gender, is fuckable to me, you would be the bottom of the list, based on your personality, face, and the fact you look like you have a tiny shrivelled penis, you emasculated twat!'," Liv finished.

Sjöfn burst out laughing at the end of the story.

"I then proceeded to kick him in the balls. I then proceeded to do the same to everyone who then made jokes about me being bi. Now, the language I used and the fact I booted him in the balls meant I landed in detention. But yeah in order to put this guy down I revealed to the class that I was bi and then I started kicking everyone in my year."

"Smooth," Sjöfn said, still laughing.

"That spread round the school like wildfire, so for the rest of the school year I had to listen to comments about being greedy, and attention seeking and being offered threesomes," Liv said, unfazed.

"Did you make them stop?"

"Well I just kicked them in the groin and they stopped themselves."

"Was this before or after you two became vigilantes?"

"Oh, a few weeks before, might have been the end of the

previous school year. I can't really remember."

As Liv and Sjöfn chatted and worked on the bike, they didn't notice that behind them Trent was stood in the doorway, looking upon them with nothing but pure adulation in his eyes, at the scene of the love of his life finally getting on with his team and his friends.

When they finally did notice him, he sat down with them.

Trent could sense the frustration in Liv, so decided to use some positive reinforcement and compliment to the work Liv had done on the motorcycle, given her relative lack of practical experience.

Liv smiled at the praise so they moved the conversation on to the welding goggles that Liv had almost hit Sjöfn with.

"I do like these, minus the blood on them. Very steampunk."

"Yeah I enjoyed wearing them, leaping across rooftops in hoodies and leggings, a pair of boots, it was fun," Liv reminisced.

"How on earth did you make it alive long enough to join G.U.A.R.D.?" Sjöfn laughed.

"Well I was stabbed and shot and we are both majorly cut up," Liv admitted.

"Was the adrenaline rush good?"

"Oh, it was incredible. You should come with us for one!"

"Why not have a girl's patrol tonight?" Trent suggested. "Get some anger out of your system?"

"Sounds fun, but I'm not sure I am fit enough for that yet," Sjöfn said, but indicated that Millie, Maddie and Liv should still go out.

It was a few hours later and Millie, Maddie and Liv had set out in their tactical gear on a night's patrol. Maddie was already bored of reading the drivel supplied to her by G.U.A.R.D. and was excited to be out of the house.

They ran across the rooftops at lightning speed but it was a quiet night; a quiet night that put Maddie and Liv on edge.

Two hours into patrol they leapt onto a rooftop to realise that they had interrupted something, as they were not alone on the rooftop.

The girl on the rooftop leapt back in horror at the three people who now joined her.

"Who are you?" her voice said, trembling almost as much as the rest of her.

"Sorry, we were just passing through this rooftop," Maddie said gently, looking at the girl. No older that sixteen and her skin that wasn't bruised was as white as the snow around her.

"Who are you, why are you dressed like that?"

"Just your friendly Willowdale vigilantes, we mean no harm," Maddie said softly, making an effort to ensure that all of the weapons were hidden and that she posed no threat.

"You're real?" she asked, shaking even more violently, her feet moving back ever so slightly.

"Yeah, we can tell you all about it," Liv said, in a voice so soft it took the other two by surprise. "But just to stop me shaking, can you take a step away from the ledge?"

Liv put her arm out to show the girl that she was indeed shaking almost as much as her. The girl didn't move.

"What's your name?" Millie asked, sitting down on the rooftop, the other two following her lead.

The girl didn't answer, but shook violently near the edge.

"Please leave," she begged.

"We would and will. But you're just a little too close to that edge," Maddie said.

Liv kept her arm outstretched.

"I can't do anything other than this. Please leave."

"Why can't you?" Liv said gently, removing her googles and revealing her face to the girl.

"They're drinking again… my dad and my uncle. I can't handle them when they drink," she sobbed.

"What's your name?" Liv asked again.

"Tianna," she trembled.

"Beautiful name. They're drinking, but why does that bring you to this snowy rooftop, Tianna?"

Tianna didn't answer.

"Tianna, would I be able to join you on the ledge?" Liv said.

Again, Tianna didn't say anything, so Liv slowly took steps forward, the crunch of the boot on snow caused Tianna to flinch.

"Nobody is going to hurt you."

"You don't know me," she said.

"I know. If we did then we would ensure that you would not be on a snowy rooftop in January."

"I can't believe you're real," Tianna said, shaking her head. "I have hoped you are real for so long."

"Why, Tianna, do you need our help?"

She nodded, before looking tentatively at the edge of the roof. "They're monsters."

"Well, what's say we get some food. Move away from the edge and we will help you," Maddie said from behind.

Tianna did not move.

Liv removed her glove and offered Tianna a hand; she took it but they didn't move. The stood there for a while, both shaking. After a while they walked towards the middle of the roof where Maddie and Millie were sat.

"Do you have any diet requirements?"

Tianna shook her head.

"When did you last eat?"

"A...A few days ago," Tianna trembled.

Maddie text Trent to whip up a broth in a flask, some food and a thick blanket as well as some warm clothes and deliver it to the bottom of the building; he did not ask why but said he would.

They sat in silence for a bit, Tianna still shaking violently.

"Delivery is here," Maddie said, as she indicated for Millie to go down and get it.

When she returned, she wrapped Tianna in the blanket and0 gave her the backpack full of food and the broth.

Tianna wrapped herself tightly in the blanket and began to sip the broth.

"That'll warm you up," Millie said, as she watched the steam rise into Tianna's terrified face.

"So why did you want us to be real?" Maddie asked. "If we can help, we will."

"I live with my dad and my uncle," she said.

"And you wish you didn't?"

Tianna nodded, shaking violently at the mention of her family members.

"What is your last name?" Millie asked.

"Lloyd," she stammered.

"Tianna, we can give you an escape if you would like?"

Liv and Maddie stayed silent, watching Millie curiously.

"We work for an organisation called G.U.A.R.D. They could help you escape Willowdale, set you up in a new city. Even give you a job within G.U.A.R.D." Tianna looked up from the broth with the faintest glimpse of hope in her eyes. "We can also pay a visit to your family. But your safety and wellbeing are our priority."

"You could get me out of Willowdale?"

"Yes, set you up in a new city and even put you through school and then get you a job in our organisation or get you set up anywhere else."

"You... you could?"

"Absolutely. Want me to make the call?"

Tianna nodded ever so slightly.

"Call Tanith," Liv said, handing her phone with the number on to Millie.

"Do you need anything from your home to join you at G.U.A.R.D.?" Liv asked her, Millie walking out of earshot as she spoke to Tanith.

"My Boo-Boo, a teddy bear of a polar bear. I didn't want Boo-Boo to see what I was going to do."

"Well we can get your Boo-Boo," Maddie said reassuringly.

Tianna nodded, relieved by this.

Tianna asked Maddie and Liv a few questions about their vigilantism, in a bid to feel more comfortable in their company.

"Tanith will be here in an hour to take you somewhere safe and better explain your options to you in a warmer environment," Millie said softly.

"Who is Tanith?" Tianna said fearfully.

"She works in G.U.A.R.D." Millie said.

"She's attractive," Liv added.

Tianna laughed ever so slightly. "Will one of you come with me?"

"I will," Millie said sweetly.

"Take these with you," Liv said, handing her one of her knuckle dusters and one of the knives from her ankle. "Nobody can hurt you anymore."

Tianna took the knuckle duster but was hesitant in picking up the knife, but she eventually took it.

"What's say we wait on the ground?" Millie asked, holding out her hand to Tianna.

Soon the four of them were safely on the ground, and as much as they didn't mind the rooftops under normal situations, they were thankful on this occasion.

When a car pulled up and they saw Tanith was the driver, they opened the door for Tianna and Millie got in the other side.

Liv and Tanith exchanged a look that Liv couldn't quite understand, but before anything could be said she pulled off to drive Tianna to safety.

Maddie gave a sigh of relief as they watched the car turn around the corner.

"Did you get the location of Tianna's father and uncle?" Maddie asked.

"Yes," Liv said, her voice turning sour.

"Where?"

"A bar fifteen minutes from here. I got her house number as well, so we can collect Boo-Boo."

"Let's collect Boo-Boo first," Maddie said.

Liv's hands were shaking violently. The anger inside of her was close overwhelming her.

Neither Liv nor Maddie said what was on their mind, but they didn't need to. Tianna looked malnourished on the

rooftop, she looked beaten, bruised and had burn marks on her.

When they got to the house, they moved round to the back of the house. Maddie gave Liv a lift up and she managed to unlock the window and slide in. From inside, Maddie and Liv found Boo-Boo with relative ease, as

Tianna had told Liv it was in a box under her bed, but they should destroy the contents of the box after they had removed Boo-Boo from it. With Boo-Boo and the box secure, they waited until they heard the sound of two drunks enter through the front door. They looked at each other and moved downstairs to where Tianna's father and uncle were.

"I wish I could say I didn't enjoy that," Liv said bitterly, as they arrived home a short while later.

"Bedroom window locked, left through the front door. They won't have a clue," Maddie said, anger still coursing through her veins.

"Get some sleep, Mads. You have stuff to learn tomorrow."

"What are you gonna do?"

"Deliver Boo-Boo."

Chapter Fifteen:

Liv changed into some comfy clothing, as opposed to tactical gear and drove to the G.U.A.R.D. base located a few hours away from Willowdale.

It was morning when she arrived. She found Millie, Col. Rathe, Tanith and Tianna in the food court eating breakfast.

"Olivia. Fancy seeing you here!" the colonel said brightly upon seeing her.

"Here to drop something off, eat and then pick someone up," she smiled.

She handed Boo-Boo to Tianna, who took the bear gratefully, but still looked terrified. Liv grabbed some food and joined them at the table, and they began eating. The conversation at the table was mostly Col. Rathe explaining some things about G.U.A.R.D. to Tianna but her, Millie and Liv were eating as much as they could. She mostly nodded when she understood things but kept her eyes averted.

"The most important thing," Millie said, swallowing a fried egg whole, "Is you're out of that environment. So, until you decided the next stage you can remain here and G.U.A.R.D. can help."

"What stages are there?" she asked tentatively.

"Well. Two basic options; you could join G.U.A.R.D. or we can move you to a different city and help get you set up in a job." Col. Rathe explained before pausing, "This is after we put you through G.U.A.R.D. schooling."

"Now, G.U.A.R.D. isn't all special operations, like Millie and Liv here," Tanith said. "We have office workers, data analysts, nurses, doctors, office workers, tech specialists, builders, designers."

There was a glint of hope in Tianna's eyes at Tanith's words.

Tianna embraced Liv, Millie ad Boo-Boo in a tight hug when they had finally eaten as much breakfast as possible, and they each exchanged a tear and emotions that words simply could not do justice.

"Want me to drive back?" Millie offered, as they got to the car.

"Please," Liv yawned.

Before they could go, however, Col. Rathe stopped the car. Millie rolled down the window so he could speak to them.

"I'm very proud of everything you did last night. It won't be an easy road for her."

"It won't, keep an eye on her and make sure she is safe," Liv instructed.

"Make sure she feels safe as well," Millie added. "She felt comfortable in the car last night, so maybe keep Tanith close."

"Understood. Well done girls."

"Wow. Praise from Colonel Rathe," Millie chuckled.

"I know, the times they are changing."

When Millie and Liv returned home, they collapsed into bed and slept for most of the day, allowing no distractions for the others to learn about their online conversations.

***

Millie and Liv spent the next few days away from the others for their own sake. It was mind-numbingly boring for them to just read conversations between people pretending to be them and religious fanatics.

"I am sick of reading fucking bible passages," Sjöfn said, storming into the kitchen.

"That bad?" Millie asked, not looking up from her book.

"But, er, Judah's firstborn was wicked in the LORD's sight; so, the LORD put him to death. Genesis. I don't care. I just want to get into this compound and then beat up a cult leader," Pete groaned, quoting the bible literature from the paper in front of him.

"When do you go into the cult?" Liv asked.

"Once we've finished learning everything here. I'm going on patrol with you lot tonight," Sjöfn said in a matter of fact tone.

"Excellent, gives me something to look forward to before school tomorrow."

"Well, if you're going out, just remember if anyone schemes and kills someone deliberately, that person is to be taken from my altar and put to death," Trent said from the doorway to the kitchen, a pen hanging from his beard.

"Don't," Sjöfn whispered, softly removing the pen from his beard and kissing him softly, only stopping when Liv, who was miming vomiting into her cup, starting coughing and Millie had to slap her hard on the back.

Millie, Liv and Sjöfn set off that night and were battered from all sides by the early January weather. They didn't see anything until four o'clock in the morning.

"Ooh we have a break in," Liv said, checking her phone.

"Where? Electronics shop. Seven minutes away," Liv said, reading from her phone screen.

They set off at full place towards the electronics shop.

"What is the strategy?" Sjöfn said.

Millie began laughing and rolled her eyes. "Follow Liv's lead."

"Sjöfn, slash the tyres on the cars parked outside. Millie and me will head inside. Join us once they're slashed," Liv instructed.

They followed her instructions. There were two cars parked outside with ten people inside the shop.

"They have crowbars and knives," Millie whispered over the coms system.

Liv snuck inside and made her way towards the back of the shop, Bo Staff at the ready.

Liv and Millie then started to pick the robbers off one by one; the element of surprise was key when they were so outnumbered.

They lost the element of surprise when Liv applied a choke hold with her staff across one of the would-be robbers' throat and the man dropped the crowbar, making a noise which reverberated throughout the shop.

A seven on three situation was not ideal, but it was the situation they were in.

However, without the element of surprise, they could be frenzied, which was exactly how Liv and Millie liked to fight.

Liv ran towards one of the men and jumped, her knee connecting with the jaw of one of the men. He hit the floor instantly and for good measure she punched him, ensuring he stayed down.

Mille was in the other corner. Being smaller than the other two, she had the momentum of the attackers to her advantage. Ducking and weaving, she threw punches into their throats before grabbing them behind the head, and with all of her strength forced them head first onto the shop floor.

Sjöfn took a measured approach, precise punches and kicks. She ended by grabbing one guy by the jaw and smashing him against the cabinet he was attempting to rob from.

One of the men had his wits about him to just run. He grabbed one of the bags they were filling with goods and made a ran towards the door.

Liv followed him and hit a tackle through the glass window he was attempting to leave from. They both landed hard. Liv landed on top of the man and threw a punch.

As she was getting up, one of the few men followed her through the window and, using a shard of glass, slashed at Liv's side causing the snow outside the shop to turn crimson.

She let out a scream of pain. Turning around, she smashed him with her Bo Staff repeatedly until the glass-wielding assailant was crumpled. However, Sjöfn was there in a flash to join the beating.

"Are they all down?" Liv asked, clutching her side.

"Yes," Millie said.

"Are you alright?" Sjöfn asked.

"Call the police, let them know about this," Liv said.

"Done. Let's get you home," Millie said.

Sjöfn and Millie supported her as they made their way home.

They clattered through the front door and into the kitchen, removing tactical gear to see the damage the glass shard had done to Liv's side.

"Millie, get the cling film out. I can stitch this up but you're gonna be benched whilst this heals. It's on your side so this can rip easily if you do anything strenuous. Like fighting."

"But that's like my favourite thing?!" Liv said, laughing. "In my defence, who smashes the glass to get into a shop these days?!"

"Stop laughing, it's making more blood come out," Sjöfn

said, slapping Liv round the back of the head.

Millie went up to bed, as Sjöfn stitched Liv's side up and wrapped her stomach and side in cling film.

"Sleep. You've got school in a few hours," Sjöfn said, when she was finally done.

"I'll follow you up," Liv said.

Liv did not follow Sjöfn upstairs to bed, she poured herself a whiskey on the rocks. After a while she lay down on the kitchen table, and using a tea towel as a pillow, she slept there.

It felt like a second later that Liv was being woken up by Maddie shouting at her.

"Huh?" Liv said, sitting up and wiping the drool off her chin.

"You're disgusting. Go shower and get ready for school."

"Fine," Liv growled.

"How are you not even fazed at the fact she is wrapped in cling film and is cut up?" Sjöfn said.

"Nature of the job."

Sjöfn looked stunned at Maddie's reaction.

"If glass can get through, it just shows we need to

improve our tactical gear," Liv said, leaving the kitchen.

"They're made to stop bullets, not glass shards," Sjöfn reasoned.

Sjöfn re-wrapped Liv in cling film and put the roll in her bag, before Liv left for school. Due to the nature of the injury, she took the car instead of her motorbike.

Liv's mood was not a good one as she returned to school. The noise and the bustle of people seemed to put her on edge. She kept her earphones in, although no music played, just to deafen the sounds of school life, her Bo Staff on her thigh as always.

Liv, Alexa, Mikey and Nattie sat together in the seniors only area after her second lesson and caught up over presents and how they spent the Christmas period. As Liv stood up to make another cup of tea she got knocked back into the table by a passing student.

"Fucking watch it," Liv said, turning around to see one of boys she never bothered to learn the name of walking past. He turned around to stare at Liv, he was shorter than her but significantly heavier.

Liv clutched her side and wheezed as he looked at her. He had an arrogance about him that Liv could not fathom where it came from.

"You watch it," he replied.

"I'll watch you cry when I plant you if you do that again.

Little bitch," Liv growled, shoving past him as she went to make a cup of tea.

"Who the fuck do you think you're talking to?" he asked her.

"I don't know, some tubby fucker with a daft face who's name I don't know," Liv snarled, almost daring him to continue the row.

"Liv. Play nice," Alexa said nervously.

"Yeah, Liv. That is Chad Clarke. He is royalty. He captains a *sports team,*" Nattie smirked.

"OH. MY. GOD," Liv said, putting on a sarcastic shocked voice, "I guess I should forgive him for being a dick if he captains a *sports team.*"

Neither Chad nor his friends found this amusing but Liv didn't care. She was tired, she was cut up and she was still bitter about the fact she could not go on the mission to the compound.

"Watch who you're speaking to, you freak."

"You knocked into me. You. Daft. Fuck," Liv said, readying herself for a fight, Sjöfn's words about not fighting in the back of her mind.

Out of the corner of her eye, Liv saw Robyn come over and whisper something to Nattie. But Liv could see

Chad's brain working to attempt to figure out what to do in this situation; he did not want to look weak in front of his sports friends but didn't seem like he was ready for a fight.

"I believe you were about to apologise to me?" Liv said, stepping forward and looking down at him. Liv altered her stance from how she normally stood to protect her right side.

"For what?"

"Knocking me, and then your ego assuming I knew who you are."

"Fuck you."

"Oh, you want to, everyone does, but if you don't apologise, I'm gonna rip one of your teeth out."

"Liv," Robyn, Nattie, Alexa said together, cautiously.

Liv didn't need their words of caution as she grabbed his wrist, twisted it round so he was tapping on his own shoulder blade. She grabbed his fingers with her other hand, and as if they were a wishbone, pulled them apart until he squealed an apology.

She released his arm, as one of Chad's friends rushed

towards him to check if he was okay. He elbowed Liv's side and she let out a howl like a wounded animal. She instinctively launched a kick connecting with his jaw, sending him to the ground.

They all looked around at her as blood began seeping through the cling film and through her shirt. Everyone who was in the vicinity recoiled in horror as Liv's shirt started to become crimson.

"Oh, fuck sake!" She said exasperatedly, not looking at any of the others.

She walked past all of them towards the toilets.

As Liv walked into the toilets, she unbuttoned her shirt, and taking out her knife she cut the cling film off to reveal that her stitching had become undone. Liv moaned as she took a spare shirt and the cling film out of her bag and began to dab at her side with toilet roll and paper towels. She was joined momentarily by Nattie, Robyn and Alexa in the bathroom. All of them worried about the fact a simple knock on the side had caused blood to come through her shirt.

"Jesus fucking Christ!" Nattie and Alexa said, looking at the knife on the side, the bloody shirt and bloody clingfilm Nattie and Alexa both looked at Robyn, who wasn't overly shocked at this.

When Liv was finished with her rush job, she cleaned it,

wrapped it in cling film and put on a new shirt. However, when she turned around they saw the cuts, bullet wound and stab wound on Liv's stomach, chest and back.

"Jesus, Liv," Nattie said, pity rather than horror in her voice.

"We got a cat," Liv shrugged, laughing.

Nobody believed her.

"Robyn. Fancy helping me explain everything?"

"I don't know all of it."

"You know most of it," Liv reasoned.

Robyn began to explain most of Liv's out of school activity, from when Liv and Robyn met; Robyn's partial involvement, Robyn's non-involvement and the vigilante experience. Liv sat awkwardly as Robyn told the story as she knew it.

"The cat's out of the bag," Liv sighed.

"Explains a lot to be fair," Nattie said. "I thought you were either a drug dealer or a user."

"Painkillers only," Liv laughed

"Alas, now is the time where I give the obligatory threat," Liv sighed. "Keep my secret or I will have you killed."

"We swear," Alexa and Nattie said together.

"Excellent," Liv said happily.

When she arrived home, she got Trent to redo her stitches. As Trent was stitching Liv's side, Pete kept a digital record of Nattie, Alexa and Robyn should G.U.A.R.D. need to intervene or they spill her secret.

Chapter Sixteen:

It was two weeks later when Sjöfn, Trent, Maddie and Pete got the orders that they were going into the cult.

"So, they leave tomorrow," Millie said to Liv, as they were in the gym.

"Yeah," Liv said, a knot tightening in her stomach.

Liv didn't say anything more, her arms began to shake too heavily.

"It's not gonna be easy being away from all of them," Millie said.

"Yeah," Liv said again, her legs giving way as she slumped onto the floor violently shaking.

"Liv?" Millie said, dropping down next to her.

"I ... I've never been away from Maddie for this long," Liv said, rocking slightly, the knot in her stomach making her feel physically sick. "Like, she isn't going to be here. She isn't going to be a text away."

Liv shook even more violently as the realisation that she was going to be separated from her big sister was setting in. Millie, who had never seen Liv have anything that resembled an anxiety attack before, sat next to her friend in shock.

"You're not gonna be alone, we will have a live feed of the compound and you've got me here. You're never truly alone," Millie said.

After that they sat in silence for a while, Millie with her arm around Liv as she shook and gasped for air.

They went downstairs after a while, Liv feeling a bit more secure thanks to Millie's reassuring words.

Maddie's hair was no longer blue, which was hilarious and made Liv feel slightly better.

"Emily, do you have the wedding rings?" Trent asked, as they sat around the kitchen table.

"Yeah," Emily said, getting the boxes out of her bag.

"Still weird calling you Emily," Maddie said, as she took the ring.

"It's weird hearing it," she nodded.

"So, these rings contain recording equipment?" Liv said, looking at them.

"Yeah," Pete said proudly.

"The diamond looks so real," Emily laughed.

"They are real," Pete said, rolling his eyes. "If we get to keep these rings, I don't want to lose them by them doing a simple diamond test."

"What time tomorrow?" Millie asked, her eyes still cautiously on Liv.

"We are meeting some people from the church at six o'clock," Emily said, also now looking at Liv, who was scratching her hand subconsciously.

"Then you just pretend to be very religious until he attempts to convince you to murder?"

"Essentially yeah," Maddie said, glaring at her reflection and the lack of blue hair.

They all went to bed early that night, with Millie and Liv getting up to see of the others as they left the house. Maddie and Liv had a long embrace before they left, a few tears escaping. They all stood on the doorstep and had a group hug before the group left, and Liv and Millie turned back into the house and went into the kitchen.

Maddie, Pete, Trent and Emily walked across Willowdale together. They knew what they needed to do; they knew how to do it but they knew it was not going to be easy.

They arrived in a car park and there was a minibus parked there, with someone in long cape-like ensemble waiting for them.

"Looks like this is us," Trent said cautiously.

They approached the minibus and the man in his cape.

"Welcome, my children. This is the first day of the rest of your lives. Blessed be the Lord who will love you all."

"Thank you. I am Trent, this is my beautiful wife, Emily. Pete and his wife, Maddie. We are excited for our new lives to begin."

"I am a Child of Elias, and I am so glad you all are ready to become Children of Elias." He opened the door to the minibus. "This is the start of your new lives," he said, dramatically inviting them into the minibus.

Holding hands, they all boarded.

As they drove, the Child of Elias began quoting scripture and explaining how only through Elias Olorephy they can be saved, like so many others before them had been saved.

Trent and Emily did most of the talking, with Pete being more of an introvert and Maddie despising mornings, it was easier that way. They sounded eager and desperate for a new change and a chance of redemption.

"So, when we were talking with the Children of Elias online, they said that some people lose their name when they come to the church and other people keep the names from their previous life. Is that correct, can you perhaps elaborate for us?"

"Some choose that their previous birth names are a reflection of their previous sins. Others believe that when they join the church, they give themselves a new name, it depends on the sins the new children believe their old names have. Some will introduce themselves to you as simply a Child of Elias, others with their name."

"It's remarkable how the church can offer so many different options to so many different types of people," Emily said in a proud voice.

"I haven't seen any of your conversations from the children who deal with the interweb. What is it you're looking for in the church?"

"A new outlook on life," Maddie said, knowing this was the time for her to chime in. "I spoke in detail about how I previously worked for different charities in the hope of combatting evil in this world. The church said combatting evil is something that God spoke to Elias heavily about, especially in the modern age."

"That is how we met, years ago," Pete said. "We all worked for the same charity, attempting to combat evil in the world and strive towards something better."

"Which is hard to do without the Church of Elias in your heart," he said, looking at them in the rear-view mirror. "I believe you will find the learnings of the church most beneficial but also find healing of the body and mind in the different things the church offers."

They drove through a set of gates and down the long drive to the church. There was a large church in the centre of the compound. Surrounding the church were different buildings including one that looked like a gym, swimming pool and spa.

There were different log-styled cabins on the outskirts of the church. They could see people coming and going from them as they seemingly pleased. Everyone was dressed the same, in cream tracksuit bottoms, a white t-shirt and a cream zipped hooded top.

The minibus stopped and they got out, looking around at the compound.

As they walked people came over and greeted them, welcomed them to the compound. They were led to two of the log cabins where there were clothes for them to change into. They got changed and joined the Child of Elias who drove them to the compound, for a full tour of the facilities. There was a large food hall where they would have their meals, classroom-like buildings with chairs, beanbags and sofas in them and then obviously the church. As well as the gym, spa and swimming pool they saw on the drive, there were also clay pottery, painting and other forms of expressionist tools.

They were taken to one of the rooms in the church to sign in and register as members of the church, following their registration as official members of the Church of Elias Olorephy.

"And now, new children, I will leave you here, as you are now to meet some other members of the church who will talk to you from here," the Child of Elias said before bowing and leaving.

"Welcome, children. I am Neal Adams," a man said to them. He was a short, plump man with a walrus like moustache and a scar over his right eye. As he approached them, he indicated the taller slimmer gentleman he was with. "This is Dennis O'Neil. We have been at this church since it was founded. We are here to explain some things to you and then introduce you to the man who has spoken to God; Elias Olorephy."

"Thank you, Neal," Trent said, extending a hand for him to shake.

"This way," Neal said, leading them to another room in the church.

"We would like you to tell us a bit about your relationships," Dennis said, dabbing sweat off his bald spot.

"Our relationships?" Trent asked, a little surprised.

"Indeed," Dennis said, taking a seat on one of the armchairs as Neal sat behind a desk. "Make yourselves comfortable."

Trent and Emily opted for beanbags. Maddie and Pete

went for the sofa; in order to ensure they looked like a couple, Pete put his arm round Maddie and she held his hand as Emily began.

"I was working at this charity event one evening, it was a charity dinner."

"And auction," Trent added. "She always forgets the auction part of this story."

"How silly of me," she tittered. "So, I walked in, very stressed as this was my first event of this size and I wasn't looking where I was going and I bumped into Trent here, who was ensuring things to go to auction were given lot numbers. He was just back from an expedition and we got talking. as I had no idea he was working for this charity, his passion for the charity work and the good he wished to do was just so inspiring. We fell in love from there."

"It was through our love and the charity work we met Pete and Maddie," Trent said, looking at them.

"Thanks to Trent, it is how we fell in love," Maddie said, kissing the hand she was holding. "So, I was a naïve sixteen-year-old, thought I could do some good in the world and started working with this charity. They were about to send me on this expedition, and they wanted to send a blogger with us to attempt to get our message out further. I didn't think anything of it."

"I then turned up at the airport ready to fly off and that's how we met. It was Trent who put me in touch with the charity, who allowed me to blog and therefore meet my wife," Pete said, ending it with a kiss to her head.

"How did that lead you to this church?" Dennis asked them.

"War, famine, droughts, natural and man-made disasters. We raised money and just did not see it put to use in the way it should. We began as a group to attempt to find the correct way to fight evil, we then turned to religion to see how we could combat the evil," Emily said.

"None of the texts explained how to do so in the modern era," Maddie sighed.

"Until we began speaking to some Children of Elias online. Now we sit in front of you," Trent finished.

"I see," Neal said, nodding slowly. He reached into one of the desk compartments and took out four small boxes.

"Before you are introduced to the church we like to know where the love of our members comes from, to ensure the marriage should continue into the rebirth," Neal said. "We believe yours can and to symbolise that you will remove the bands of your old life for these of your new."

He handed them each a wedding ring that was just a plain ring. They removed their old rings and put on the new ones, Dennis O'Neil collecting the old ones from them.

"Now it is time for us all to go to the main hall to introduce you to the Children of Elias and formerly induct you into the church," Neal said, guiding them.

He made them wait at the side of the stage where the lectern was front and centre. He approached the lectern as hundreds of people filled the church pews.

"Welcome, Children of Elias," he said.

"Welcome, Child of Elias," they repeated back to him.

"Before our lunchtime service, we introduce four people, two young couples to the church today. Trent and his wife Emily, Pete and his wife Maddie. They are here to leave their old lives behind today."

He extended his arm and they walked onto the stage.

"Now, to complete their entry into the church today and to lead the morning service, Our Father Elias."

Elias Olorephy walked onto the stage and towards the four of them and the lectern. He looked the part of a charismatic cult leader. He walked in a long sweeping cape of emerald green with a high collar.

His facial hair was dark, a moustache that came down like a horseshoe to hang three centimetres off his chin. The sides of his hair were white, but the top of his hair was black.

"Welcome, children, young and old," he said. Enunciating every word perfectly, he spoke slowly so they hung on every word. "Today, we welcome new people to the rest of their lives. Step forward, my new child, Trent."

Trent walked over to him humbly.

"Repeat after me, my child. Today is the day."

"Today is the day."

"That I give my life to God."

"That I give my life to God."

"The evil in this world, can no longer be saved."

"The evil in this world, can no longer be saved."

"Only to learn how to combat the evil through the teachings of Elias Olorephy."

"Only to learn how to combat the evil through the teachings of Elias Olorephy."

"Can I hope to save myself, my loved ones and the wider world?"

"Can I hope to save myself, my loved ones and the wider world?"

"Now step forward, my child, shake my hand and take a seat."

Trent did as Elias had instructed and then watched as Emily, Pete and Maddie went through the same process. Once they were all sat down, Elias began his afternoon sermon.

"My children. As today has proven the evil in the world becomes too much for some, they seek better ways to deal and combat the evil in the world. When God spoke to me, he told me many things. God himself once explained that there is evil in the world. The words of the Holy Scripture has not had a positive effect on this world. The world changed from Deuteronomy 13:9 to what those who claim to speak for me say now. However, the only way to combat evil is together. Together with the church, together with loved ones, channel the church. Your church shall be the vessel in which I should act. The three parts of the Father, the Son and the Holy Spirit are not enough. You need to split God through your teaching, so the three parts are thousand folds." Elias finished his speech with a shudder, looking to the heavens dramatically.

Trent and Emily were subtly communicating through hand squeezes as they listened to their first scripture from Elias. When it was over, Dennis O'Neil came back over to

them and led them out of the church.

"Your first few weeks in the church may be a little disorientated and a little strange, given how much of a change from your previous life it may be. To counteract this, your first few weeks will be scheduled a little more than those longer members of the church."

"Whatever helps us," Pete implored.

"From six till eight you can use the gym, spa and swimming pool. Exercise and relaxation are key. Eight till nine: the food hall for breakfast before your morning sermon. After the morning sermon it will be either myself, Neal or Father Elias himself who will teach you from the Book of Elias. Twelve till one: the food hall before afternoon sermon. After the afternoon sermon it is back in the classroom for a discussion and teachings. Three till four you will have gender expressionist time, where the girls can walk with each other, alone or with other female Children of Elias and the men can do the same. Five till six: dinner before evening sermon, evening lecture then from eight till nine a final hour of pure relaxation before you can retire to your cabins."

"That sounds wonderful. Thank you," Trent said earnestly.

"Come, it is time for your first teaching. You'll be joining some people who are relatively new to the church."

When they arrived in one of the rooms, they each opted for beanbags as a couple in their forties had already taken two of the comfy-looking armchairs.

"Hello," Maddie said brightly, to one of the Children of Elias who was already in the classroom.

"Oh, hello young one. Welcome to the Church of Elias. It is so nice to be joined in these lessons so we can learn with someone new."

"You joined the church a few months ago, is that correct?" Maddie asked, positioning her beanbag close to the woman's chair.

"Yes, they were providing such a positive influence on us online. We made the decision to completely renounce our old lives. We sold the house. Left our immoral jobs of old. Emptied the bank so Father Elias could put the money to good use and then we came here."

"We are so much happier now we are Children of Elias," her husband said.

"Your story is inspiring," Emily said sweetly, hiding the sorrow she was feeling for the couple whose life savings and house was unbeknown to them being used to fund far right organisations across the globe similar to the Y.N.W.A. and enable serial killers such as the one Maddie and Liv caught in Willowdale so many months ago.

Chapter Seventeen:

As with many cult leaders they preyed on the vulnerable, but they were seeing it within hours of arriving within the church compound. It was harrowing for Emily to see just how many vulnerable people were having their life savings going towards funding hate groups and terrorism. Had they not received specialist training about how to deal with these types of missions then the constant reassurance about how special they were and how much potential they have would have made them believe in the lies they were being told by the church.

Potential was, in fact, what that lesson was about. Dennis explained how those whose minds were being controlled and engulfed by the forces of evil had their potential limited, but through the teachings of Elias they could unlock their truest potential.

"Evil cannot prosper when a vessel of God knows their truest potential," Dennis said to them to end their teaching.

"Maddie, Emily, would the two of you join me on the walk?" the woman asked them as they left the room.

"We would be honoured. Thank you, Child of Elias," Emily said.

"It would make us feel most welcome," Maddie added.

Her husband offered the same thing to Pete and Trent, and as they vacated the room they left in separate directions.

This was an opportunity for them just to exercise, talk to other members of the church and discuss in Dennis' words, "Womanly or manly things should they wish to do so."

However, for the Juliets it was the perfect time for them to gather information on the church's inner workings, and the more lessons they were taught the longer they were with the church. Maddie and Emily had to turn their sorrow for the other into a sense of pride when they heard stories of all the personal sacrifices that people had made in order to join the church.

They spoke to a Child of Elias who had left her children on the doorstep of their father before she joined the church. They also met a woman who was on her very last gender expressionist time, as she was leaving the compound the next morning.

When they were reunited with the others, they went into the food hall. Trent was particularly tense about this part of the stay at the compound; partially for his palate but also as there was no way of knowing if they laced the food with drugs in order to make them more susceptible to the teachings of Elias.

Luckily, Emily was prepared for this. They watched as she

dipped her finger in her water, waited to see the colour of her fingernail and with it wet did the same thing with everything on her plate. After examining her fingernail to see there was no change to the black nail polish, she began eating and the others followed her. Trent and Pete were thoroughly confused by this and Maddie had to try her best to explain that if her nail varnish changed colour then it meant it was drugged.

It wasn't bad food, they thought as they chatted to the other children who, as they were perhaps instructed to when anyone new enters the compound, showered them in congratulations and affection in order to make them feel as welcome as possible.

Love was seemingly the ultimate way to combat evil; although what evil was hadn't been explained to them. They spoke about this to two divorcees who found each other and had gotten married on the compound.

The man, who gave his name as Gary, spoke in length about how he believed the evil in the world outside of the compound stemmed from liberalism and a freedom of movement between the countries leading to the watering down of traditional values, and how it was fantastic that Elias was restoring him and more importantly the world.

None of them had the right to point out that this was essentially the view of right-wing populists, but praised him for his views and how he was now finally doing something about it and learning from Elias, and hoped they would get the knowledge he had quickly.

Neal Adams took the evening sermon, but the teachings they had after the evening sermon were their first teachings by Elias himself.

Despite knowing what terrors he financed using church donations they could not deny that he, as so many leaders were, was a fantastic story teller and orator. His tales about his conversations with God were creative to say the least.

"Maddie, my child, may I ask you a question?" he asked her suddenly.

"Of course, my Father, I just hope I will be able to answer."

"Why do you think evil mutates?"

Maddie paused before giving what she hoped would be a good answer. "I suppose that it is like a virus. If it is not medicated properly then it grows stronger and mutates, and the old cures like antibiotics are not effective anymore."

"Fascinating analogy, my child. When God spoke to me, he said, 'Elias, my voice vessel, evil has transcended. The evil of four thousand years ago is unrecognisable from the evil today. The evil today is so much worse. The floods and plagues God sent in the times of the Old Testament cannot resolve the evil of today. People ignoring God breeds resentment. Sadly, the word of God gets ignored.' So, the God above said that only we can counteract the evil that has transcended above him in this new modern era."

They nodded understandably, absorbing the words but still, despite the talk of evil there was no definition provided by Elias as to what evil was.

The spa was enjoyable after an anxious day. But until Pete could ascertain that there were not listening devices in the cabins and in the spa, they could not break from their role. Instead they spelt out letters on each other's wrists under the covers, which made Maddie feel uncomfortable.

They didn't sleep well before they were awoken at six o'clock for their early morning leisure time. Pete and Trent went to the gym with Maddie and Emily chose to go to the swimming pool before they re-joined in one of the jacuzzis, in which they talked about their first full day inside of the compound.

The morning sermon focused heavily on the ways evil can manipulate the minds of those in the world, the news outlets that spread the evil and do not give the facts, the politicians who create hateful laws that water down the values of God, the other religions with prophets who preach from a time period that is not modern and thus cannot accurately depict the modern world.

Pete let out a faint groan as they left the sermon. In order to stop independent thinking, Elias was bombarding them with information and analogies, and it was giving him a headache.

The cold winter air meant that they huddled together when Neal provided them with their morning teachings. Neal explained to them how the church helps and what it now meant to be a part of something more. Neal spoke about the people the church had brought in over the years and how they had been saved.

"It's a lot to take in and absorb," Maddie said, rubbing her temple with both hands as they left the classroom.

"It is, but once we learn of all the evils in this world then through love and the other methods Elias will teach, we will be saved," Trent said.

"Precisely, Trent," Neal said from behind them, "the vulnerable get scared by evil. Combatting evil is the only way to overcome the fear; once you are no longer scared of evil you will find what exactly it is."

Emily spelt out the word *riddles* with her thumb on his hand.

During their gender expressionist walk, Maddie and Emily spoke in hushed voices about how to proceed, however they needed to seem properly indoctrinated which meant they needed to be patient; neither of their strong points.

"Given how vulnerable we were portrayed online, and everything we had experienced so far it was absolutely what we were taught to expected from a cult. We now just need to play the game," Emily said reassuringly.

They couldn't continue their discussion as three Children of Elias came over to them.

"Father told us you are feeling a little overwhelmed with all the information about your new life," one of the girls said.

"I suppose that is an accurate statement," Maddie laughed.

"To comprehend evil was to succumb to evil and to tolerate it. See that it is evil and act accordingly."

"Is that one of Father's teachings?" Emily asked.

"Indeed. He told that to me when I was new and it has been at the forefront of my mind since, I hope it does the same for you."

The afternoon sermon was soon upon them. Elias stood at the lectern ready to talk.

"The deceit of the innocent brings the rapture upon us all," he yelled suddenly, causing them all to jump.

During this sermon he spoke with urgency about the ever-encroaching evil, using both natural disasters and the acts of humans to prove his point. His urgency seemed to energize the entire church as if it were a concert.

With everyone energised, those whose were scheduled to have their meals at the same time as the Juliets were louder than they had ever heard them before. The energy in the room was palpable.

When Maddie turned the bubbles on in the jacuzzi and listened to them, she thought of the patience it was going to take to deal with being in a cult.

Once they had gotten into the routine it became slightly easier. They did not think for themselves over the next two weeks, they just went along with what they were told, listening to Elias say such things like, "You cannot morally rise up against the immoral. Only through vanquishing the immoral and the moral remaining can God succeed."

Despite themselves, they ended up repeating his message. Maddie received a shock when, in his sleep, she heard Pete say, "The only innocent loves are the young and those that belong to God. Both can be corrupted. Stay in the light of God." Something Elias had told them that morning.

"Liv would have liked Elias' words from this morning," Emily whispered.

"Which ones?"

"Your blood should not be spilt for the flesh of the living, only for God. If it is your blood do not spill it. Act cautiously and avoid the acts of blood. Only unworthy blood should be spilt."

Maddie laughed. "God knows what they're doing."

Chapter Eighteen:

Over the past two weeks since the others left, Millie and Liv still had to abide by the days of the week, and for Liv, much to her dismay she had to remain in school. G.U.A.R.D. happened to be keeping Millie busy whilst Liv was at school, and the nights patrolling and stopping crime in Willowdale kept them both busy and allowed them to get some aggression out of their systems.

Liv arrived home exhausted to see Millie stress-plaiting her hair, something she had not seen her do before.

"What's got you stressed?" she asked, bringing the kettle to boil so she could make them both a cup of tea.

"Transcripts from a criminal organisation have been intercepted. Willowdale was flagged in it, but it is confusing, it is Japanese, Spanish, and both hieroglyphics and runes."

Liv threw her stuff down and sat next to her, reading the transcripts. They sat drinking their tea, attempting to make sense of the gibberish in front of them.

"These are Younger Futhark runes; used during the Viking age. The same rune sign is used for voiceless and voiced consonants. See here the rune úr could stand for u, o, y, au. However, all they have done here is written English in Norse runes," Liv said, pointing to various points.

"Right ..." Millie said, looking at her, confused.

"Icelandic is the closest to the old runes in which we can translate, someone who is fluent in Icelandic can translate accurately written Norse runes, however with this all we need is a simple rune to ABC," Liv said, getting the laptop and puling it towards her.

"Can you speak rune?" Mille asked.

"You cannot translate anything into runes. Runes are not a language, they are signs devised to represent the sounds of a language, in the same way as letters," Liv said.

"That helps massively," Millie said.

Liv sat with her feet up and watched Millie work. Using both of their laptops and a pad of paper she worked well into the night, with Liv making some food for them both as Millie worked.

"Willowdale Museum," Millie said after a while.

"It's a start. I'll arrange a meet," Liv said.

As Liv rang the police chief, Millie cursed whoever wrote the transcripts. It was a riddle in two languages, Norse runes and Egyptian hieroglyphics.

Millie was still cursing when Liv came back.

"We are meeting the curator of Willowdale Museum at

two thirty this morning," Liv said.

"Good," Millie replied.

"Bring that with you, just in case," Liv said, indicating Millie's work.

The Willowdale museum was modelled on the Parthenon, with pillars along the outside of the museum and a courtyard in the middle separating the two buildings.

They saw the curator step out of the shadows into the courtyard that morning. He was nervous as he looked around for them.

They approached him and he looked petrified.

"Don't worry. No need to be nervous," Liv said.

"I get a call from the police chief to meet with vigilantes that I didn't know actually existed."

"Yeah, I can see as to why that would potentially make you nervous. Our apologies."

"What's going on?" he asked, shaking.

"Do you have a new exhibit starting soon? Any shipments or deliveries?" Millie asked.

"Y-Yes. Tomorrow night, we have a cargo plane landing at a private airport."

"What is on that plane?"

"Two new exhibits. A paleontological exhibit containing five dinosaur skulls and another exhibit called The Possession of Love, featuring art pieces and jewellery."

"Makes sense. A dinosaur skull makes me intoxicated in love and a bit raunchy," Liv said sarcastically. "What is the content of the plane worth?"

"Upwards of twenty million for the art and jewellery. The skulls can't really be priced."

"What do you make of this?" Millie said, showing him the transcript. "It was intercepted. Hieroglyphics, Norse runes, Japanese and Spanish all making a riddle."

"We have someone who works here," he said slowly. "Caden Flores. Slimy, greasy man. Very bitter and angry at the world. Works in one of the back offices. He creates some of the puzzles and activities for the kids to do. He knows Spanish and has a good knowledge of Hieroglyphics."

"Would he know about the exhibits?"

"Yes. It is set to have a huge opening night once we announce it to the public."

"Would he have a gripe against anyone at the museum?"

"Annabella Florence is the one running the Possession of

Love exhibit. She turned him down on a date recently?"

"We will need everything about the plane. Landing time, size, proposed route for the lorry or lorries picking it. Everything."

"One moment. I will head to my office. The exhibit was due to open the day after tomorrow," he grumbled.

When he returned, he gave them all the information he had and they spent some time reassuring him that they would not let anything happen to either exhibition.

"Thank you," he said gratefully, as he left.

They spent some time scouting every inch of the museum and the roads around it.

They returned home and began looking at every possible route from the airport to see where it could potentially be hijacked.

"I can't work in tactical gear," Millie scowled, before running up to get changed.

Liv followed suit and they arrived back in the kitchen before the kettle had finished boiling.

"We are gonna need to bring G.U.A.R.D. in on this, maybe a relief team to follow," Liv said, talking fast. "I can use my restored motorbike to follow the lorries, you'll need a car though."

"Liv, did you cut that top into a crop top?" Millie asked, with her phone to her ear.

"Yeah, I realised I never had a long-sleeved crop top, so I made one."

"Why?"

"Nobody told me I shouldn't. Maddie is like ninety percent of my impulse control. Why are you not helping here?"

"I am on the phone with G.U.A.R.D., some dick has me on hold," Mille spat.

"I am not a dick," came Tanith's voice down the phone.

"Hey, Tanith," Liv said.

"What can G.U.A.R.D. do for you at this ungodly hour?"

"We need a car, a relief team, a helicopter on standby," Millie said, scribbling furiously.

"We may also need essential roadworks to be done on some on of the roads into Willowdale," Liv added.

"Christ, what the hell is going on there?" she asked.

"A heist worth twenty million and a lot of priceless dinosaur skulls," Mille said.

"Fuck!" Tanith said, before getting Col. Rathe in on the

call.

Millie explained the situation as Liv paced furiously, adding comments when it was necessary.

"Do you have a plan?" he said after a while.

"Yes," Liv said quickly. "I'll be at the airport when the plane lands, see if they attempt to steal it directly off the plane, if not then the lorries which we will put trackers on will be followed from behind. We will cut off several roads for essential maintenance work, streamlining the route the lorries have to take."

"It is a two-hour drive, so there's a lot of places it can go wrong. Hence the need for a relief team. I will be parked midway through the journey to continue the tracking of the lorry, to engage if necessary," Millie said.

"If it gets dicey our priority is to take out the hostiles, get into the driver's seat and drive the lorries to the museum," Liv finished.

"That... is actually a decent plan," Tanith said, a surprised tone in her voice.

"No need for that tone," Liv spat, forgetting Tanith could not see her, so she just scowled at the phone.

"We will be round in the morning with a car and to finalise everything," Col. Rathe yawned.

With as much planning as they could do that night, Liv and Millie went to bed.

Neither Liv nor Millie had a good night's sleep. They awoke restless and as if they hadn't slept at all.

"With the rest of the Juliets on a mission, it was only fitting that we get a mission of our own." Millie yawned as Liv poured her a cup of tea.

The doorbell rang before Liv could respond as Tanith, TJ - formerly of Sjöfn's team, and Col. Rathe stood there expectantly.

"Cavalry has arrived," Millie shouted.

"An old horse, a benched horse and a TJ horse," Liv replied, as they walked into the kitchen.

"It is too early for your cheek," Col. Rathe grumbled, accepting the cup of tea from Liv.

"Is this the outcome of that transcript we intercepted?" Tanith asked Millie, looking in bewilderment at Liv's long-sleeved crop top with loose threads from where she cut it.

"Jesus, you have no impulse control," she sighed.

"Liv will be at the airport most of the day. She will be keeping an eye on the comings and goings. With it being a private airport, any people lingering will draw suspicion and she can investigate," Millie explained.

"There are two lorries that will be at the airport, correct?" TJ said, reading Millie's notes.

"Correct."

"But the intel was only about the paintings and jewellery?"

"If they are robbing the plane, they will steal all of it," Liv said from behind her mug.

"Why, do you think?" Col. Rathe and TJ said together.

"The jewellery and the paintings are worth upwards of twenty million, you don't sit on that kind of money. If you're stealing that, then you have a buyer. A buyer will most likely want something as priceless as a dino skull," Liv said. "Furthermore, if that plane is carrying a triceratops' skull then that'll be stolen as well. There is a huge black market for them because of the skull and horns. But all dino bones sell highly."

"Also, the plane crew loading the boxes will have no idea what is in the boxes or what goes in which lorry. They load and the drivers drive. They will need to rob both to ensure they get everything," Millie added, confident in her knowledge.

"Liv, let's see this map of yours. What roads are we

closing?"

Liv laid the map across the table to show them the exact route they needed the lorries to take. She also indicated the most likely points that a convoy could easily wait to intercept the lorries.

"Okay. We will have G.U.A.R.D. agents at the museum. We will have three teams of three positioned along the route," Col. Rathe said, looking at their plans.

"Helicopter on standby here, should we need to follow the lorries," Tanith said. "I will lead one team of three, TJ another, Millie the other."

Liv reached into a kitchen drawer to pull out a wakizashi blade. She placed it on the table and grabbed her mug, draining it. "Let's fucking do this," she said, as she slammed the mug.

As she went to get ready, she heard Col. Rathe ask why she kept a blade in the kitchen and heard Millie's laugh as a response.

They joined her in the garage as she put her wakizashi in her side holster, Pete's expertly designed weapons on her back and thighs, and a gun on her ankle. She packed a bag with a flask of tea, binoculars with night vision capabilities, a map and rope with a grapple just in case.

It was all fine until they saw her walk towards the motorbike, she had spent the last few months rebuilding.

"Wait, you're taking that?" Millie asked, looking at the repaired bike with some scepticism.

"Well yeah, I'm not taking Penelope," Liv said, as if this was the most obvious thing in the world. "Jessika will hold up fine. Don't be mean to her, it took a lot of work to get her to this stage."

"It doesn't look the most stable thing," Tanith said.

"The welds will hold. It works. I've test driven it," Liv said defensively.

TJ looked between the Harley Davidson, Liv's pride and joy and the battered, beaten, welded and reconditioned motorbike next to it and laughed.

Liv took the bike she had christened Jessika out of the garage and began the drive to the airport. The welding was awkward and the bike did not sound quite right. However, it got her to the airport just fine.

"I fucking hate a stakeout," she grumbled to herself as she parked up, took the flask out of her bag with the binoculars and sat waiting. She also pulled out the flight manifest. She waited and observed. As mind numbingly boring as it was, Liv was glad she was not sat in the church compound listening to an old man read to them from a book he had written, like her sister and the rest of the Juliets were.

Once Liv's flask of tea ran out, her impatience grew exponentially. Finally, the dark encroached all around her as the final plane of the night was approaching its landing. This was the plane she was expecting and she watched it land with no hiccups.

As it landed, Liv watched as two lorries drove, one by one, onto the runway. She observed as heavy wooden crates were unloaded off the cargo plane and into the lorries. Liv sat up stiff as a board and sat on the seat of her bike. IF there was going to be a heist this would be the time to do it. But no, the lorries were loaded securely and they began to drive.

Liv followed at a safe distance; she drove with the front light on her bike off so they didn't see her following.

They drove for about thirty minutes in the correct direction. Liv was now within range to get a secure line open to talk to the others and she gave them constant updates over the sound of the wind as she drove.

All of a sudden, the lorries indicated to go right. This was not on the planned route and it suddenly clicked. The lorries weren't going to be hijacked, they had already been hijacked.

"THE DRIVERS OF THE LORRIES ARE IN ON THE HEIST!" Liv screamed. As she turned to follow, she sped up, the bike making an ominous sound.

She was soon joined by the three cars; one driven by Tanith, the other by TJ and the last by Millie.

"Attempt to box the lorries in," Tanith said.

The lorries were limited to sixty miles per hour, which was good as Liv didn't think the bike could do more than sixty-five. Liv drove the best she could, as Tanith overtook the two lorries before slowly braking in front of them. Millie positioned herself in the lane next to the lorries, preventing them from pulling out, with TJ on the rear of the lorry. Liv drove the best she could along the inside, approaching the lorry. As she drove, she saw a glint of silver out of a window and saw the flash of gunfire.

"Well, they're shooting at us," Liv said, not sure anyone could hear her as she sped up, the exhaust vibrating violently as Liv pushed the bike to her limits.

Approaching the door of the lorry, she saw the passenger who had shot at her taking aim and Liv took instinctive action. She reached onto her thigh and unsheathed her wakizashi; using it she swung it towards the hand that was holding the gun. She swung the perfectly balanced sword with one hand repeatedly until she heard a shriek of pain and she saw the gun drop.

Liv drove alongside the lorry and reached up to swing open the door. As the lorry swerved with the door open, Liv knew what she had to do and she hated herself for it.

"I'm sorry. I love you," she said. Using the bike as a springboard, she jumped at the cab of the lorry, knocking the passenger and causing her bike to spin out of control.

As Liv jumped into the cab, the wakizashi swung wildly. Liv scrambled into an almost standing position to get sure footing, punches and a wakizashi flying. Liv chopped the wakizashi, once, twice, three times at the passenger seatbelt snapping it clean, all whilst the driver and the passenger attempted to throw her from the vehicle. Liv took multiple punches to the face from the driver as he swerved the wheel with his other hand. Liv grabbed the passenger and threw him outwards. Slamming the passenger door, Liv and the driver exchanged punches.

He swerved and Millie had to avoid the lorry smashing into her car. The wakizashi cut the seatbelt and into the driver's thigh. Liv managed to force him out of the driver's door. She got into the driver's seat and took off her motorbike helmet.

"I am driving the lorry," she said.

"We guessed by the swerving and chaos," Millie said.

"We still got a lorry to take over," Liv ordered.

Tanith braked and pulled alongside the second lorry with Millie on the other side. Millie and Tanith both simultaneously copied Liv and commandeered the lorries.

They pulled off at the nearest exit and began to drive back to Willowdale.

"Package secure," Tanith said, "let's get these to the museum."

"We aren't out of the woods yet," Liv reminded them. "Stay sharp, we don't know if anyone is coming."

Liv was not handling the lorry well but was it was still going in the right direction. "I think I'm getting the hang of this," she said, shredding the gearbox as she changed down. "TJ. Pull up alongside me," she ordered.

"Well, you're gonna need to. We have company," TJ said.

The three cars kept the lorries as guarded as possible, and three other cars attempted to ram the lorries and the G.U.A.R.D. convoy off the road.

"TJ, shoot the shit out of the cars, would you?" Liv said, as she swerved onto the pavement, narrowly missing a car but almost hitting a lamppost in her attempt to lose one of the cars attempting to re-steal the goods inside the lorry.

Liv also reached for the gun on her ankle and fired at the bonnet of one of the cars, before throwing it onto the seat next to her to attempt to build some speed, but her lack of experience with a heavy goods vehicle was holding her back.

The sound of tyres squealing were soon drowned out by the rotating blades of the helicopter, which had just arrived shining a light on the situation. A further G.U.A.R.D. relief vehicle turned onto the road, to shoot the tyres out on the pursuing cars.

"Now we are in the clear!" Millie shouted, the helicopter near, ensuring that the convoy would not experience any other issues.

An hour or so later they finally arrived outside the museum. They were met by the curator, Col. Rathe and fifteen G.U.A.R.D. agents.

"Jesus, Liv, you wrecked the gearbox. I could hear you coming," Col. Rathe said to her as she jumped out of the cab and walked to the back of the lorry to help the G.U.A.R.D. agents unload the goods.

"Oh my," the curator said as he saw Liv.

"What?" she asked before realising her fists, face, and the wakizashi on her thigh were dropping blood onto the pavement.

"Oh yeah, it was a little complicated getting the lorry back."

"I am so grateful," he implored.

"As am I," a woman said, joining him at his side. "I am Annabella Florence. It was my exhibit they were attempting to steal. As well as three priceless triceratops skulls."

"AH-HA!" Liv exclaimed. "I told you they were triceratops skulls; the horn and skulls and the underrated awesomeness makes them valuable."

"In order to thank you, may you both attend the black tie opening of the exhibits tomorrow night?"

"We would be honoured to," Millie said.

She handed Millie the tickets so that Liv did not get blood on them, but they stayed around to ensure the crates in the lorries were undamaged and taken inside.

"I'm getting sick of Willowdale," Col. Rathe said gruffly, turning to go back to his car.

"Hopefully we won't see you for a while," Liv said mid-yawn.

"Oh, Liv. Don't forget you have school in the morning," he reminded her.

"Bastard," she muttered.

They returned home exhausted, and in Liv's case more

than Millie's, bloody.

Liv begrudgingly arrived at school with the alibi of food poisoning. She joined Nattie, Alexa and Mikey as she drank as much caffeine as possible before her first lesson with Mrs. Noah. However, Mrs. Noah walked into the seniors only area to make an announcement.

"ATTENTION!" she bellowed over the sounds of the chattering teenagers, music and Liv cracking her second energy drink and pouring some of it into her cup of tea, much to the disgust of her friends. "All seniors have been given an invitation to the Willowdale museum for the opening of the two new exhibits including the newest one, which all English students will be doing a piece on, the Possession Of Love. School uniform will be worn and we will all meet promptly at seven o'clock outside the museum," she finished, looking around at them all.

Liv awkwardly walked over to her and Mr. Powers.

"No exceptions, Olivia," Mrs. Noah snapped, before Liv could even speak.

"Why don't you wait till I open my mouth," Liv snarled at her, before turning to Mr. Powers. "Mr. Powers, Annabella Florence, who is the one who is running the Possession of Love exhibit, has invited us to the V.I.P. area of the exhibition. Black tie gala. My uniform does not count. It also starts an hour earlier than the general opening at seven."

"What part of no exceptions did you not hear, Olivia?"

"The part of the black tie, V.I.P. tickets before your totalitarian dictatorship told me I was going!" she snapped.

"Mrs. Noah is the one who organised everything and given you will have to do a project on it then it is what she says," Mr. Powers said to Liv.

Liv mouthed *traitor* to him, before walking to the classroom where Mrs. Noah would no doubt make her life hell. As she walked, she texted Millie to inform her of the plan and told her to go and buy a dress and shoes as they were dressing to impress.

Millie and Liv dressed to annoy Mrs. Noah. Millie had bought a stunning turquoise dress and matching shoes.

Liv's harshly shaven side was more prominent than ever, as instead of it being swept over, she put it in a ponytail. The red of her hair contrasting with the all black four-piece suit. The jacket, shirt and waistcoat and trousers all black and tailored perfectly.

"I have never seen you this smart. I half expected you to have a crop top suit," Millie said as Liv walked into the kitchen.

"Until Trent and Sjöfn get married, I won't have a reason to get dressed up so there is time to buy one," Liv laughed.

Millie's high heels made her closer to Liv's height, who was in smart shoes as they arrived at the museum.

"Thank you for coming," Annabella said to them. "You're better dressed than the last time I saw you," she winked.

"Well my school are here, and they said I had to wear uniform and I wasn't allowed to accept your invitation. So, I thought I would show them up and truly honour your magnificent exhibition," Liv smiled.

They walked around the exhibition hall and saw why somebody wanted to rob this. The paintings were accompanied by diamonds, emeralds, rubies, sapphires and pearls in all forms, from rings to brooches.

They worked well together, Millie thought, who wasn't overly fond of art but did like-the jewellery on display.

"This has given me a new tattoo idea," Liv said to her, taking two glasses of champagne off a tray from a passing waiter.

"Two G.U.A.R.D. missions on at the same time. So, a triceratops wearing a diamond necklace for our mission and then put a nice halo and angel wings for their mission."

"That sounds awful," Millie laughed.

"Admit it. With Pete's art it would look good!"

Millie conceded it would, as Annabella Florence came over to see them again.

"This is a remarkable exhibition," Millie complimented.

"It is, I look forward to doing a project on it," Liv smirked.

"Well, I will send you everything about the exhibition," Annabella said, pushing her glasses up her nose and smiling at her. "If you wanted to cause heads to turn and piss to boil then you're about to. They've just turned up. I'll have to greet them."

They watched as Mr. Powers, Mrs. Noah, one of the teachers who taught the younger children and the headmaster walked into the exhibition with all of the seniors behind.

Liv and Millie were talking to Police Chief Kyle, who was also in attendance, when Mrs. Noah and the others noticed her.

"You enjoying the well-deserved night off, Chief Kyle?" Liv asked him.

"I am. Thank you, Olivia. I don't think you've met my wife, this is Sharon," he said, introducing the woman he was stood with, who gave them a kind smile.

Before Liv could properly greet Sharon Kyle, an angry

voice shattered the pleasant ambience of the evening.

"Olivia. Winters. How… how dare you!" Mrs. Noah said, her voice shaking with a furious anger.

"How dare I do what exactly?" Liv asked politely, barely concealing her grin.

Mrs. Noah was visibly shaking as Liv waited for her to speak. When it looked like she wasn't going to, Liv turned back to Chief Kyle to tell him to enjoy his evening as they were going to look at other aspects of the exhibit.

"Liv, are these friends of yours?" Millie asked her.

"No, not friends. I don't get why they are here getting angry at me," Liv said sweetly.

"Olivia. You cannot just disregard everything I say," Mrs. Noah hissed.

"I received an invite to something I already said I would go to, before I was told I had to abide the words of a self-centred twat who told me to do what I would previously had done if she had not butted into my life," Liv said, a wide smile cracking on her face.

Liv and Millie started to walk away when Mrs. Noah grabbed Liv's wrist. This was a mistake. Liv grabbed Mrs. Noah's hand and twisted it behind her back, twisting her wrist in the completely opposite direction. Almost instinctively, as if Mrs. Noah's fingers were a wishbone, Liv yanked them in different directions.

"Never. Lay. A. Hand. On. Me," she growled, releasing Mrs. Noah.

"Olivia," Mr. Powers said, shocked.

"Don't inflate your sense of authority, I could murder you and not leave a single trace of evidence, you touch me again and I will snap your arm."

Once they walked away, they were quickly joined by Nattie, who clasped Mikey's arm, and Alexa, who looked radiant and happy to see Liv piss people off.

"Holy fuck. She is not happy with you," Millie smirked.

"I said I wouldn't be turning up in uniform," Liv said reasonably.

This made everyone in the group laugh.

Mr. Powers came back over to the group to apologise for Mrs. Noah's behaviour, but also attempt to reprimand Liv for not obeying Mrs. Noah's instruction.

"We are definitely having the better time," Millie smirked, taking another two glasses of champagne.

Chapter Nineteen:

Emily rested her head on Trent's shoulder as they left their evening lecture, heading towards the spa. A lecture on the purification of the soul had given her a headache. Elias teaching them that only he can save them and teach them the methods to defeat evil was starting to grate on them.

Maddie felt the same way as she sank into the chair next to Emily. They were unable to talk about anything that was not related to the church, so with people around they started to discuss why some people became lethargic about the rapture.

They needed to show that they were model students of Elias, in order to advance to classes where they might learn something about him funding far right groups or inspiring and telling people to murder.

The next morning, they were pulled aside by Dennis who told them that the people who were involved in the discussion in the spa were impressed by their knowledge and thoughts about the rapture yesterday and wanted to continue this further with them.

When they sat together, Elias looked at them all with a penetrating gaze. He looked at them for what felt like an hour before he finally spoke.

"Trent, Child of Elias. How do you make people care about

the rapture?"

"I feel," he said slowly, "that when surrounded by the evil in the world, people become complacent. They think that they do not engage in evil so why should they care about something that they believe is not coming. So, the only way would be to remind them what they stand to lose."

"Interesting theory, my child. It is, however, not a perfect one, can anyone see why?"

"I believe I can, my Father," Maddie said. "Some people may not recognise that what they're doing is a sin. People forget what evil is, also how to properly repent or what the rapture entails."

"So, if people don't know what evil is, is that because they don't want to? Is it because they have been corrupted and blinded from a young age? Evil," he said, tailing off towards the end in dramatic fashion.

A discussion about combatting evil, and what evil is, was a step in the right direction, Maddie mused, although Elias was still not telling them much about what evil was.

They had to wait five weeks to be told what evil was from Elias. "Evil, my dearest family. It is ever encroaching, it surrounds us; it dilutes our values as a society. By diversifying and mutating the nature of society, evil diversifies and mutates along with it. Evil comes in many forms; the first form is leaving God. For as much as my scripture is needed the old scripture is important. The morality of living needs to be readjusted to the old ways."

They nodded earnestly, the Juliets and the rest of the Children of Elias seemed intensely interested in what aspects of morality Elias deemed acceptable but also the aspects of society he deemed evil.

Elias sighed deeply as he looked around at them. "If God remodelled the world in his image and evil corrupted the world, how can vessels of God hope to do what he did without the abilities of God?"

They looked at him, unsure whether this was a rhetorical question or if he was expecting an answer.

"Pete, my child?" he asked, looking at him directly.

"I don't believe a vessel of God can do it, but then again I don't think a vessel of God should," Pete said quietly.

"Elaborate please?"

"Only something as great as God can remodel the world, a vessel of God must attempt to change aspects of the world, by going person to person, family to family using teachings from our Father. The only other alternative would be to get the world in such a state that it is remodelled by the very definition of human's limited understanding of the world."

"Truly fascinating. You have understood my teachings

well," he said, walking over and placing his hands on Pete's head, his thumbs on either side of his temple.

He kept his hands there for a couple of minutes, Maddie sensing how uncomfortable her *'husband'* was feeling, so she subtly took his hand.

He then moved from Pete to Maddie and did the same thing to her. Maddie attempted to look as if she was receiving an honour above anything she could imagine.

Trent and Emily were next, the rest of the class watched them intently, some with curiosity, others with a hint of jealousy.

He said nothing about this and went back to continue with the lecture. When he dismissed them all, they rose from the chairs, sofas and beanbags they were sat on and headed towards the door.

Elias however called them all back.

"My children," he said, his voice shuddering dramatically. "When you arrived at my church you wished to escape the evil of the lives you were currently living in hope of redeeming your souls and finding the true way to live."

"That is correct, my Father," Emily said, not meeting his eyes, bowing slightly.

"I am very proud of you for how far you have come. The next few weeks will be terrifying as they will entail all of the evils in this world. But be strong, I sense you can do great things for this church."

"We would be honoured to do so and with your guidance and love we can overcome fear," Maddie said humbly.

"Such determination in the face of evil. Go rest and enjoy your spa time, my children. You have earned this."

They looked at each other with a happy apprehension as they walked towards the spa. As they worked out in the gym, they noticed that they were being watched intensely by Dennis O'Neil, who was gently running on one of the machines in the corner.

They showered off after quite an intense work out and returned to the cabins, hoping that Elias' words were a foresight into what was to come.

They hadn't been left alone in the church, however they hoped to have a look in any of the offices in the upcoming lectures for some incriminating details about the church.

Pete and Maddie had a conversation that morning about how easy the job would be with some of Pete's equipment and that they weren't likely to be allowed into any offices in the church. Given the fact they were writing what they were saying on the others hand with their finger it was a slow process.

Neal and Dennis took all of their lectures and teachings

over the next four days, so they waited with an anxious trepidation for their next lecture with Elias.

When they finally sat down with Elias, the atmosphere was that of a funeral. His mannerism changed and his voice was slow and sad. He spoke to them in length about the sorrow he felt at what he was about to describe to them.

"My children, you have worked so hard to escape evil through your time at the church but also when you made the decision to reach out to the church online. What I am about to say may take you back to evil, so I warn you. Hold your loved ones and if what I am about to tell you gets too much, it's okay."

There was a long dramatic pause as they waited for Elias to start speaking again. Elias was a master at the dramatics, he kept the silence as long as possible before the mystique of it all was broken.

"Integration of societal cultures causes a weakening of all cultures; each culture blames the other and violence happens. The penguins and the polar bears do not assimilate. The fish stay away from the sharks. Now we must understand that there is nothing wrong with other cultures. Not assimilating is different to actively detesting the cultures. We must live alongside but not collectively with."

As Elias was speaking, Maddie thought back to Sam

Heenan's murder victims one of which was an immigrant from another culture as Elias would have put it, attempting to adapt to the new society they were hoping to be a part of.

"When God spoke to me, He informed me that when the world was young, He had no intention of people experiencing different cultures. This *learning* from other cultures is to prevent knowledge of your own culture and thus a knowledge of evil, the evil amongst us and how to combat evil," he continued, his voice growing to a low fury.

Maddie really wanted to ask how this was to be combated but she knew she could not ask questions. Elias suddenly leapt from his chair towards Maddie. Knowing Maddie's natural instinct would have been to throw a punch, Pete grabbed Maddie's arm as she flinched.

He grasped her temple again and said loudly, "I sense my wisdom inside you. I sense the power of God is giving you a question. What is the question, my child?"

Maddie feigned a terrified voice. "If a lot of evil stems from this integration of societal cultures, how is this something that can be combated? Can… can it be defeated?"

Elias sighed deeply before collapsing to one knee in a dramatic fashion. "Oh, my child, you have seen the difficult questions I seek to answer. These are the questions God needs us to answer."

They waited anxiously but Elias sighed. "God told me how to combat many forms of evil, we need to learn what those are first however, my child. Have faith, my child."

Elias continued his lecture with references to the animal kingdom, which did not make any zoological sense but nonetheless he continued to tell them how the breakdown of every society in history came from sharing ideologies and expansion and amalgamation of societies.

In a bid to overload them with knowledge, making them easier to manipulate, they only had to wait till the next day for the next cause of evil in the world. This time Elias focused on the breakdown of role models within an already weakened society.

These role models came in the form of a traditional Christian idea of marriage. With no accurate knowledge of history, Elias spoke to them in depth about how it was when same sex relationships became more accepted; people from different religions in relationships, people from different social classes in relationships.

The muscle in Maddie's jaw pulsated with rage as Elias spoke about how same sex relationships are the cause of famine, wars, hurricanes and plague. If they were actually brainwashed and vulnerable then it would have been a convincing argument, however what it actually did was make them feel physically sick.

It went on like this for three more weeks. Everyday Elias spoke to them about money lenders, radicals from other religions. He discussed with them how the education policies in school breed hatred and through the misinformation of teaching that responsible leave the door of the mind open to evil to walk through.

Trent had to put a precautionary arm over Emily, and Maddie smirked at what Liv's reaction would have been as Elias began his lecture on abortion rights and where control of the anatomy should lie. They could do nothing but smirk when Elias said each abortion equated to the black plague's decimation of Europe.

From abortion and contraception, Elias went on to speak about how the shift between political leaders from religious leaders was a cause of evil, and politicians having faith is different to it being a religious faith. Like he had done on the previous days, Elias used a selective knowledge of history in order to make this point, but it was effective in proving to the wide-eyed and terrified members of the church.

What these lectures about evil did was provide them the perfect opportunity to learn something about the security on the compound. That night, Maddie snuck out of her and Pete's bed and towards the church. She had a cover story in place for when she was caught, Maddie knew her mission was to time how long it took for her to be discovered in a place she was not meant to be.

She walked across the cold ground and into the church. With the offices branching out from the altar she took a seat in the first row of pews, looking at the locks on the office doors, her hands together in front of her.

She sat there for less than 3 minutes before there were footsteps. She kept her head down until they arrived. Dennis and Neal were both in front of her, with two other Children of Elias that she had only seen a few times.

"Maddie? What are you doing here?" Dennis said sweetly.

"Explain yourself?" Neal said gruffly.

"I am sorry, after today's lecture on evil I felt the need for prayer and to think about Father Elias' words. It was stopping me from sleeping."

Dennis was seemingly taken aback by this and sat down next to her, but Neal stared at her with a deep penetrating gaze, as if he didn't believe her.

"What was it about today's lecture that affected you so?"

"Father told us he would tell us how to combat the fear, but with him teaching us about the fear without combat and with Father not changing the POLITICAL landscape, it worried me so. I apologise if I should not have come here to pray," she put a lot of emphasised hatred on the word political, but sat solemnly after.

"We understand, Child of Elias, you are not the first to venture this way. If you feel this way, we can leave it unlocked for you so it doesn't set off any of the alarms. Run back to your husband's arms, you will find comfort in them."

They left together and they bid her a good night's sleep at her cabin door.

Pete welcomed her back with a hug, but they didn't discuss it till the next morning. They knew the response time but as Dennis said, they could disable the alarm if someone wished to pray at night.

Pete relayed the information to Trent during their gender expressionist time as they sat underneath a birch tree sheltering from the rain. Maddie relayed it to Emily during their walk so they could figure out a plan. A plan that did not come easily to them.

Maddie and Emily were frustrated that even if they got into the offices, they had no way of getting Pete into the offices to transfer information to G.U.A.R.D., with his computer skills being unrivalled.

Pete talked in depth that morning with Dennis and was far more animated than he usually was. He thanked him graciously for being so nice to Maddie the previous night, due to her fear and overwhelming need to pray after the lectures on evil they had the previous day.

Dennis was very understanding, and he and Pete spoke in length about aspects of the Book of Elias which may help in her time of need. Dennis, however, reassured Pete that once Elias explained that they themselves had the power to defeat evil, Maddie's fear would dissolve.

When they arrived at their lecture with Elias, they were nervous that Maddie was to be reprimanded for going to pray, but as Dennis reassured Pete this played perfectly as Elias was sympathetic and a lot more forthcoming with them in that lecture.

Pete was beginning to formulate a plan to let Millie and Liv know they needed to be prepared. When they swam in the pool that evening, Pete took one of the LED lights after kicking it a little too hard on a push off. He explained the situation to one of the Children of Elias who was helping run the spa that night but insisted he make amends for his action and put the new light in himself. He did, placing the old one in his pocket as he left.

Using the switch mechanism from one of the lights in their cabin he rigged up a structure to be able to flash the LED light at any point. He knew where the G.U.A.R.D. cameras were positioned so on their next gender expressionist walk he subtly flashed the LED light three times.

Chapter Twenty:

"Liv, we have received a message from the compound," Millie shouted from downstairs.

Liv sprinted down the stairs, two pairs of scissors in her hands. "What is the message?"

Millie wrestled the scissors out of her hands before saying, "Pete flashed an LED light, presume it means be on standby."

"Oh, well it's something at least," Liv sighed. "I was hoping it was an actual message, like words."

"Same," Millie groaned. "What were you doing with scissors anyway?"

"Was gonna change up my hairstyle. I'm growing out of love with the shaved side and long hair. I was gonna lop off a few inches and have the side shaved with my hair falling towards my jawline."

"Go to a pissing hairdresser, not kitchen scissors. From now on we need to carry our tactical gear and weaponry at all times, in your car and at school. Knowing Pete, his next signal will be a building on fire."

They laughed at the thought of it, wondering how mind-numbing the brainwashing process must be for them.

Emily and Maddie were realising that although the

brainwashing was a deplorable act., They had no concrete undisputable evidence of Elias' wrong doings and extracting the evidence was going to be difficult and dangerous.

Some of the people they walked with had sacrificed everything to come to the church and Elias was their entire world. They spoke to a Child of Elias called Felicity, who was by all accounts a highly sensitive person who believed anything she did could be considered wrong and evil, because she was such an imperfect human and needed criticism in order to learn how to be a better person.

Had they met Felicity outside of a cult there wouldn't have been anything wrong with her. However, because of how willing she was to avoid hurting anyone and how sensitive she was, it was easy to see that Elias had been manipulating her against acts of evil and how necessary it was for her to combat evil. This under the right circumstances could be terrifying

There was no grey in Elias' church. There is God or there is evil. There are the correct teachings of God and there is the teaching of evil. There are the ways to live your life the way God instructs and there are ways to live your life that leads to a prosperity of evil.

Repetition of his rhetoric bored into them as if it were a drill. When Maddie had stayed awake to sneak into the church it had been by design, but now she legitimately could not sleep. She lay there in silence listening to Pete's breathing. Whether he was asleep or awake she could not tell, but Elias' words played in her head like a recording that she could not turn off, until eventually their morning alarms went off and they headed, as they had done for weeks, to the gym and spa.

Before, they would have told Maddie that she 'looked like shit' but they could not express such negativity, so instead they blessed her with a gracious morning and hoped that Father Elias would bless her with wisdom that evening.

Exhaustion setting in, they sat there in a zombie-like state listening to Dennis O'Neil express the same views about how they were now more established members of the church, that their part in the rebirth of the world will now grow exponentially and they could be a beacon of hope to the new Children of Elias joining the church that very day.

They did as they were instructed and welcomed the four new members of the church as they had been welcomed, with the promise of fulfilment and a revolutionary outlook on life. The new members nervously sat with them at lunch, and knowing all eyes were on them they spoke in length about what it was like to be in the presence of Elias Olorephy.

That night Maddie lay there, her eyes stinging with tiredness. Every time she felt like she was about to fall asleep there was a disturbance in the compound or a noise from above keeping her from sleep.

Exhaustion set in and none of them stepped foot in the gym that morning, instead opting to use the spa where they could mercifully just sit in the jacuzzi and let the hot water and bubbles nourish them. They were joined by two of the new Children of Elias from yesterday.

An elderly couple who gave their entire life savings to the church before they joined and were enthusiastic to be in the sanctity of Elias away from the evil in the world, spoke in depth about what they believed the church would offer them and the new life this would present them with.

Trent, who was the one with the most energy, talked earnestly with them about all the church had done for him and Emily as he wrapped his arms around her.

"I am so grateful for what you've told us," the woman said. "Our children and grandchildren, corrupted by hate, were critical of us coming here. They called this wonderland all sorts of despicable names and claimed all sorts of nonsense. The hate and the evil became too much."

"We understand," Maddie said. "Our family were not supportive of the love Pete has given me. We knew the church would teach us how to love and it has done so. You will find your marriage strengthens and you will be more in love with each other than ever before."

This became too much for the man who sat next to his wife, who began to cry silently as she kissed him on the cheek.

Neal Adams' lecture that morning discussed how there is an immobilisation aspect of evil that can sometimes cause someone not to act in the face of evil.

They were getting close to it now, Maddie thought, Elias would teach them how to combat evil.

Elias sat in front of them that evening and looked at them with his penetrating gaze, his eyes boring into their exhaustion-filled faces.

"My children," he said deeply, as he extinguished some of the candles in the room, casting himself into shadow. "The time has come for you to begin down a road that few have walked down. You have studied well, shown bravery in the face of some of the most horrific things this evil-filled world has to offer and yet here you sit. You sit here in front of me and YOU ARE STRONGER." The shout caused them to jump in surprise. "Maddie spoke so passionately about your love today, the new Children of Elias so fearful and so unsure about their future and their faith in me increased, when I have not yet to sit down with them like I am today."

"Thank you, Father," she said humbly. "Trent, for all your physical strength you have showed emotional strength and love for your fellow human in a way many older than you have never managed to accomplish," Elias complimented.

"Thank you, Father," Trent said gratefully.

The way you acted as a father figure for Maddie in a time where the light of God was not there for her," Elias commended. "Inspirational."

"I am honoured, Father," he said, bowing his head slightly.

"Will you all walk down this path with me? Are you willing to combat evil, not just to learn from it and understand how you can save yourselves from it, but become a Child of Elias who will save the world from the evil?"

"I am willing, Father," Trent said, as Elias looked at him.

"I am willing, Father," Emily said, clasping Trent's hand.

"I am willing, Father," Maddie said, looking at him with resolve and passion.

"I am willing, Father," Pete said, puffing his chest out slightly as if he had never said anything with such pride before.

"Sleep well then, my children, your new life will start soon." He bowed.

They did not sleep well. Rather than just lying in silence, Pete lay there with Maddie in a quiet reflection, speaking with their eyes as much was possible.

It was difficult for them to keep their eyes open that morning. Even Maddie, who was the most experienced at running on as little sleep as the human body could handle, couldn't handle the day well. Caffeine deprived and exhausted, they sat expectantly for their lesson with Elias.

When he entered the room, he smiled at them but began in a very gloomy tone. He began to describe a vision he had last night.

The story he told was a dark vision of death, destruction and blood. He spoke for forty-five minutes about the vision before he began to speak about four shining talisman who walked into this darkness; these talismans would light the brightest light known to mankind to counteract the balance of darkness.

"You were those talismans. When you leave the church, you will be shining vessels of light. You, my children, will be brighter than the fiercest sun. You, my children, with the power of God inside of you, will walk towards evil and you will drive it backwards."

"We...We were in one of your visions?" Emily gasped.

"You were. God has shown me your future and it is bright."

"Thank you, Father," Pete said, blinking furiously in an attempt to bring some water to his eyes.

"Now, my children. God has shown me what you are to become but now it is to give you the tools to get you there. The knowledge on how to combat evil."

They waited with bated breath.

"Alas, when confronting evil, you must do it in evil's environment. Under the cover of darkness, you will be able to be the light in the darkest moment in evils playground."

"What are we to do in the precipice of evil?"

"You are to do what you said, show those who are under the veil of evil what would happen if they did not change their ways. As the piercing light in the darkness of evil you know no boundaries, there is nothing earthly that applies to you, so you can go forth into the darkness and be the light in the abyss of darkness," he said to them slowly.

It was on this note he let them leave.

Pete sought out Dennis afterwards to see if he would be allowed access to the church to pray, should he need it that night for a time of reflection. Dennis permitted Pete to do this but reassured him that Elias' teachings were not over and that Pete still had a lot to learn.

When Pete went to the church that night, he sat in the pew looking around the church, noticing there was light shimmering from under a door. Under the excuse of needing guidance, he knocked on the door.

"Come in, Pete," came Elias' voice.

Pete opened the door and walked into an office. Elias was sat at the desk, a computer in front of him and books all around.

"Thank you, Father, I apologise for the lateness."

"Not at all, my child, todays teachings were heavy so I will be here. When your beloved wife came, that is why we rushed because I was not in my office to be of support. Come discuss today's teachings with me."

"The piercing light in the darkness of evil, you know no boundaries," Pete said slowly. "That resonated with me."

"Why?"

"Those who are evil or follow the evil will always teach you that you are nothing and there are certain ways in which we must conform. The laws of the evil. It feels like liberation."

"Good, embrace the liberation as it will only continue tomorrow."

"Thank you, Father," Pete said, bowing. "Now off to sleep, Maddie will be missing you."

Pete returned to the cabin; a plan very much formulated

in his mind.

Pete expressed his plan to Maddie the next morning who then conveyed it to Trent and Emily. With the plan set they waited for Elias to provide them with the last bit of knowledge.

They sat down with him, apprehension running through their veins.

"Today, my children, we take the next step. Beyond the ether, into the unknown, the journey we take today will change the course of history. Now my piercing light of justice, are you ready to step into the beyond?"

"Yes, Father," they all responded together.

"Yesterday we discussed the unlimited potential that you all have as vessels of God. His burning light in the world of darkness. Today we discuss how we channel that potential into the eradication of darkness, so that wherever you step your light irradiates away the darkness," he said slowly, before doing one of his characteristic long pauses. "When you have all of the knowledge I can bestow and you leave this holy place, it will be your duty to spread the light and the knowledge I have given you and to eradicate evil. Evil does not fight fair; evil does not have laws or morality, although you do. You must remember that evil will not relent and will always take advantage of you should you let your guard down. Following me so far?"

"Yes, Father," they responded, Emily and Maddie literally on the edge of their seats.

"Good, as evil, is ever encroaching. We must be ready for evil to engage us at any time. You must be vigilant and ready to engage with the evil should you see it. If you see those engaging in evil. combat the evil. Whatever bounds evil uses you must double it but always in the name of God."

Maddie nodded slowly but looked confused.

Elias seemingly understanding the look of confusion expanded on his ideas. "When I say combat, I mean it more in the biblical sense. The old Books of Samuel said *God trains my hands for battle; my arms can bend a bow of bronze. God armed me with strength for battle; you humbled my adversaries before me.* Combat them in the chamber of words, combat them in the battle place of ideas, combat them online, combat them on the streets, combat them in the buildings they reside in. God will humble them and strengthen you, so that you may never lose. There is no form of combat you would lose in and the laws of evil do not apply to you. But when evil has been vanquished you must leave the word of God on the battlefield so those who see the vanquished evil will know the act was done in the name of God."

Maddie thought back to the bodies of the serial killer they caught who carved bible passages into the skins of his victim as well as bible passages at the scene. She squeezed Pete's hand tightly as Elias continued.

His eyes glazed over, Elias continued his monologue explaining to them exactly how these small combat victories will help the overall war against evil, Elias' story putting them right at the centre of this almighty victory.

When the lecture was over Pete once again sought out Dennis and told him that, like the night before, he may need the church that night.

When they sat in the spa that night, they shook with nerves. Emily and Maddie were particularly on edge, not knowing how the events of the night were going to play out.

Pete sat in the church pretending he was deep in prayer. Blinking furiously, he got up and once again knocked on Elias' door.

"Enter, my child," came Elias' voice.

Pete entered, his eyes watering to look like tears.

"What is it, my child?"

"Your words today, the fulfilment of it all, the process. As scared as I am, I am also proud that God has chosen me for this journey," Pete said, sitting down.

"I am glad you feel the fear as well as the pride, that means the mountainous task is ahead of you," Elias said.

As Elias turned to consult one of the bibles, Pete seized his opportunity and struck Elias hard and repeatedly on the head until he was knocked unconscious.

Pete locked the door, pushed Elias to the side and began using Elias' computer, sending everything to G.U.A.R.D. as well as the distress signal to Millie and Liv.

There was a knock on the door and Pete froze, but when he heard Trent's voice, he unlocked the door to allow Trent, Emily and Maddie in before locking the door again. There was another door leading out of the office which Emily ensured was locked as Pete continued to work, his fingers a blur on the keyboard.

"Done," Pete said.

"Now what?" Emily said.

"Follow this door and hope it goes to the garage?" Pete said. "Millie and Liv have been alerted but hopefully we won't need to wait for them, we get in the minibus or car and just go."

They unlocked the door and followed the corridor, Elias unconscious over Trent's shoulder. However, the passage just led to Elias' private room.

A room with one door in and one door out. They searched the room and found a mobile phone. Pete again messaged Millie.

"They'll be here shortly," he said to them.

"We are, like, four hours from Willowdale," Emily said. "It'll be morning by then and then we will have this whole cult ready to fight us for their leader."

"Liv is driving," Pete replied.

"Okay, they're like two and a half hours away then," Emily conceded.

"Here we go," Trent said, looking on the computer and accessing the security cameras for the entire compound.

Pete took over and uploaded all of the security footage to G.U.A.R.D. for good measure, before they sat watching all of the cameras, waiting for either their escape or their discovery.

"Shit, shit. Fuck. Shit!" Emily said, pointing at Dennis who was walking towards Elias' locked office door.

He knocked on the door but obviously nobody answered. Puzzled, he took out a key, unlocked the door and

stepped inside the office, he looked around before unlocking the door that led to Elias' room.

They turned off all the lights and hid the best they could. When he entered the room, Trent lifted him up, holding him in a chokehold until he stopped struggling and went limp.

"How are we meant to get us and Elias up and out of the compound without being noticed by a riot of pissed off people?" Maddie asked.

"Run like fucking mad?" Pete said.

"I think we should go now," Emily said. "It is almost five, meaning people will be up in an hour. If we are out of the compound by then we have an hour ahead of them."

"I disagree," Pete said, "we wait and make a quick dash to the cars."

"Both. Neal Adams still needs to be taken out. Emily, you take Elias. You and Pete make a run for it, Maddie and I will take him out and join you," Trent instructed.

"Agreed," Maddie said.

Chapter Twenty-One:

Leaving Dennis O'Neil locked in the room, they made their way back through into the office and out into the church. When they left the church, praying they weren't spotted, they split in opposite directions, Emily and Pete sprinting up the hill towards the exit gate, Elias over Emily's shoulder.

"Half an hour till they arrive," Trent said, as he and Maddie slipped into Neal Adams' room. Maddie spooked him, allowing Trent to get around his throat and begin to choke him out. When unconscious, they tied his arms and legs and ran after Emily and Pete.

When out of the compound, they began running. However, as they ran an alarm began to sound from behind them. If they thought escaping the compound unseen and joining up with the Juliets half an hour down the road would be easy, they were mistaken.

"These fucking clothes probably have trackers in them," Pete shouted, as they ran along the country road.

As they ran, they heard the sound of what sounded like hundreds of angry voices charging towards them.

They jumped off the road into the hedges nearby as a number of cars from the compound drove past. From in the bush they could see cars heading down the road in the opposite direction as well.

They waited for ten more minutes, watching as four more cars followed as they hid.

"We are gonna have to continue that way. Let's hope they continue down the road and we miss them," Trent said, picking Elias up.

They ran down the road, to discover that the cars that had passed them had not just driven down the road but had made a roadblock.

"Into the bushes," Emily said.

They dived into the bushes.

"I'll text Millie," Pete said.

They waited in the shrubbery by the road for any sign of G.U.A.R.D.

"HOLY SHIT, THEY'RE HERE!" Emily said, adulation in her voice.

"Is that Liv on the bonnet?" Pete asked, tilting his head to look around a particularly stubborn branch.

"Yes," Maddie sighed, a smile on her face.

Millie now at the wheel, she drove fast before breaking harshly causing Liv to fly off of the bonnet at speed and catapulted herself at the Children of Elias.

She jumped to her feet with her Bo Staff in hand and began taking out some of the Children of Elias who had set up the roadblock. They were no match for her physically, even though they had a number's advantage.

The group advanced towards where Millie was, her SUV smashing through the blockage. Another car joined minutes after, Tanith at the wheel, TJ jumping out to help take out the Children of Elias alongside Liv.

"INTO THE CARS!" Pete shouted, before he and Trent got into Tanith's car, Elias' unconscious body being dumped in the boot.

Emily and Maddie got into the other car.

As they drove, those at the compound threw the wedding rings and clothes out of the window so they could not be traced any further, before speeding off back towards safety and Willowdale City.

"We have them following us," Millie said after ten minutes.

"I got it," Liv said, unsheathing her wakizashi. She opened the window, as Millie slowed the car down.

Liv, her legs in the car and the rest of her hanging out of the window, slashed the wakizashi at the car alongside them. The car was not relenting though, so Liv gave up using the wakizashi and opted for her gun. Four precise shots to the front tyres and two shots into the bonnet of the car, she hoped it would do damage to the engine.

The car tailed off and Millie sped up away from the compound.

Tanith and TJ took Elias to a G.U.A.R.D. base after dropping the others off at Liv and Maddie's house.

When the others were suitably clothed, they joined Liv and Millie in the living room.

Maddie practically ran into Liv's arms as they embraced, tears rolling down Maddie's face. Pete showed more emotion that he ever had before when he embraced Millie in a bone-crushing hug. He wrapped his arms around her and didn't let go for at least twenty minutes.

"How does it feel to be free, Sjöfn?" Liv said brightly.

"A lot better now I hear that," she smiled at her, "it'll take some getting used to but, some normal conversation, alcohol and the ability to fucking swear again will help."

"Here, fucking, here," Pete said, still smothering his sister in a hug.

"Well, when you feel up to doing it, Pete, we have a tattoo design and a story for you," Millie laughed.

"You two had your own mini mission?" Trent asked, beginning to laugh.

"We couldn't let you have all the fun now, could we?" Liv smirked, leaving the room to bring in some glasses and some alcohol.

"To the Juliets reunited," she said, toasting with her glass.

"Here, here," the six of them cheered.

The End....

For now

ABOUT THE AUTHOR

Daniel is a 22-year-old from Manchester, UK. In 2018 he finished his degree in Philosophy and politics with a 2:1, his dissertation focusing on 'how recent media attention on sexual harassment has impacted on female empowerment.' In his spare time when not writing he is usually reading or binging tv shows.

Follow Danny on Twitter
@TiredAuthorDan

Other Books By Daniel

The Adventures Of Maddie And Liv

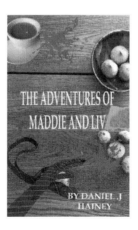

For details of our other books, or to submit your own manuscript please visit

www.green-cat.co

Printed in Poland
by Amazon Fulfillment
Poland Sp. z o.o., Wrocław

53296284R00240